BROKEN

Dove

MARY A. WASOWSKI

Copyright © 2018 by Mary A. Wasowski
Cover Design by Francessca's PR & Design
Editing by Joe Marron
Formatting by JT Formatting

First Edition: November 2018
Library of Congress Cataloging-in-Publication Data

Wasowski, Mary A.
Broken Dove (A Mafia Romance Novel) / 1st ed
ISBN-13: 978-0-9969605-7-1

CHAPTER One

Willow

What's that saying? If I didn't have bad luck, I wouldn't have any luck at all? Today that statement had never been truer. Yes, today would go down as the single worst day of my life. In true disaster fashion, my day began with discovering my ATM card was hacked and my account had been completely drained. I didn't have much, but now my $1,300 savings was in someone's pocket, and I had to fight to get it resolved or else what I had left of my emergency fund would not get me too far.

Thanks to my loving grandmother and the two beautiful words "rent control," I was able to afford to live in New York City. She took care of all the bills, with me depositing a fair amount. My share got deposited every month into her account, and I was eternally grateful for her generosity.

I originally moved to the city with a roommate who bailed after two months to follow her wannabe rock-star boyfriend on a college tour around the US. I couldn't make rent, and I was afraid of starving and winding up in a shelter, or worse, living on the streets. Okay, it didn't get that dire, but I was afraid nonetheless.

Grandma was independently wealthy and made smart choices with her finances after my grandfather passed away. She was only in the city a few months out of the year when she wasn't traveling with friends. At first, I thought I might be in her way, but she said I could stay as long as I liked. It's worked out great so far. My big contribution was $300 a month to cover groceries and whatever I needed. Yes, grandma ruled. My mom believed grandma was accepting it under the guise for bills but really was saving it for me when I was ready to truly get out on my own.

I was grateful for the roof over my head, because days like today would make it really difficult if I didn't have the shelter my grand-mother provided. I didn't think I was ever going to make it in the city, coming from a small shore town in New Jersey. After what happened to me today, I almost missed my small bedroom in my small house in my small town.

After my fleeting moment of feeling sorry for myself, I walked to work. I called my bank and luckily got a very understanding repre-sentative on the phone. A fraud complaint was issued, and hopefully, my funds would be returned within three business days. I did have an emergency credit card, but I better be bleeding out of my eyeballs be-fore I use it. My mother's words, not mine.

I tried to keep my mind busy with work, but it wasn't too great on that end either. I worked for Madeline Waters of MW Designs. She was terrific, a good friend and boss, a little eccentric, but so cool. She made fashion accessories at a cheap price. Basically, she was the queen of knockoffs. She hired me right out of fashion school after seeing a wedding dress I designed for an exhibition which went toward my final grade. I not only designed the dress but the headpiece as well. It caught Madeline's attention, and I was offered a job. It was a beginning, which was all I could hope for, being so young and inexperienced in the industry. I wasn't rolling in the money, but it was a paycheck, and the job allowed me to showcase my own work, which was primarily clothes, handbags, and shoes.

Madeline called me the triple threat of fashion. I usually smiled and kept my thoughts on the many nicknames people around the design floor had given to me. After I delivered the twelve coffees to the multiple staff members who still believed I was a temp, I was finally able to sit behind my design desk and began to run through the end of the week orders for Madeline. Yes, on top of being a fashion triple threat, I was an amazing assistant. I barely took a sip of my coffee when Madeline rushed by my desk and shouted my name in a panicked tone.

"Willow! My office, now!"

She never shouts, I thought to myself. I grabbed my coffee and followed her into the office, closing the door behind me. I asked, "What's wrong? You're practically shaking."

"I have to let you go. I'm sorry, but this is it. I have to close up shop."

Is she serious? This can't be happening right now. Especially after the fucked up morning I just had dealing with some jackass draining my bank account. No, there has to be more to her story than she's letting on. I can't lose this job.

Before my blood pressure could rise any higher, I let out a calming breath and placed the ledger down to talk to Madeline. Her announcement practically stunned me into silence, but I was not just going to allow her to fire me without an explanation. She owed me that much.

"What happened?" I questioned. "I thought we were doing fine with that huge order that came in on Tuesday."

"They canceled it. Zara just called me. I guess someone else's bid was better than ours, and they took it. Of course, Zara dished out all the apologies she could, but it's over. Without that contract, I'm screwed."

"There has to be something we can do. What about the two new dresses I designed? And the wedding dress already in production?"

"All on hold. I'm sorry. Look, kid, you're young, talented, and not bad on the eyes. This city is so fucking jaded, but with everything you have to offer, you will find another job. Sticking with me is just going to make you drown and wallow in regret. Take my advice, and get out while you still can. Thank goodness I own this building, or I'd be on the street in a month."

"Madeline, it's merely a setback and one that I can help you overcome. I didn't only go to school for fashion. I majored in brand marketing too. I can help."

"Yes, I know, but I'm just too tired and way too cynical to keep trying. I want to be able to give my employees something better than a pink slip. If I close my doors now, I can still offer some a severance package."

"But…you'll fire *me*? I'm the one that brought your outdated computer system into the 21st century. I've worked my ass off for you for a year now, and I'm willing to take any scraps offered just to keep a seat at the design table. You promised me more, Madeline. I believed in everything you promised when you brought me on here."

She dropped her head in her hands and then looked up at me. "I'm sorry, Willow. You're right about all of it, but I can't change the fact that my company is facing financial ruin. It's not just a fear. It's very real that I have no choice but to close our doors if I don't land any new accounts soon."

"Madeline, will you give me the rest of the week to brainstorm some ideas?"

"If that's what you need. Why don't you take the rest of the day off and leave me be to drink my failures away?"

After that declaration, it was clear that I was talking to dead air and did as I was told. I began walking through the busy streets of Manhattan when I received an alert on my phone about my compromised bank account.

Just as I was about to read what it said, I was shoved hard from behind, making me lose my balance. I was then knocked to the ground, with my knees taking the full force of the fall. Before I could register what was happening, my bag was ripped from my arm, and my phone was also snatched. As I laid face down on the sidewalk, in shock, all I could see was a blurry pair of sneakers running away with my possessions.

I screamed for someone to stop him, but no one would, and I was left on the ground with two bleeding kneecaps and my fading dignity. I managed to get up on my feet, with the pain already beginning to throb. My clothes were filthy, and my palms were dirty too. *Just great.*

The joke was on the asshole who robbed me. With my ATM card already hacked earlier that morning, I didn't have anything left to steal but an iPhone that was two models too old. My emergency card was safely at home, thank goodness. He only got away with a pre-paid credit card with a balance of $12.50. *Yeah, big score. My lipstick cost more than the contents in that bag, both of which were a freebie from a Victoria Secret semi-annual sale.*

Mom and grandma always taught me to pin my house key on the inside of my clothing. I'd always thought they were being overdramatic, but now I was grateful for the helpful tip. I may not have had my purse but I did have my key and could still go home and be safe.

I'd never been mugged and was still shaking a bit. When I finally composed myself enough, I limped over to an outdoor café to sit down and clean my legs. I sat down to catch my breath, and the owner or manager came outside. He looked at me with disgust and told me to leave, using an unnecessarily obscene hand gesture to go along with it.

"Please, sir, I was just mugged, and I'm hurt. May I use your restroom to clean up?" I pleaded for him to have some compassion, but he wouldn't hear me.

"Yeah, yeah, cry me a river. I have a business to run, and you homeless or working girls are all the same. Move on before I call the police."

Okay, time to bring out my Jersey. I tried to be nice. I stood up and faced him. "What did you just call me? Go right ahead, I hope you do call the cops! I can file a report on my mugging and then press charges against you for behaving like a judgmental asshole prick."

"That's it!" he shouted. A police cruiser was parked down on the corner as he waved him down to assist in removing me.

Unbelievable! What happened to the kindness of strangers? Deciding not to wait around, I sneered at him and limped in the opposite direction, feeling humiliated. I crossed the street and made my way down the block, when the police cruiser pulled up alongside me.

He lowered his window and ordered me to stop, not asking if I was alright, just another asshole assuming the worst. He looked me up and down and offered to take me to a shelter, never asking me one single question. The officer believed whatever the café guy told him and just assumed I was a trouble-making homeless person.

I just stared at the cop while my knees continued to bleed. With his clueless expression, I practically broke down in hysterics. I was already shaky on my feet and so tired when he suddenly grabbed my shoulders and forcibly cuffed my wrists. I was screaming to let me go as he placed me in the back seat of his patrol car.

"Why are you doing this to me? I've done nothing wrong. I'm the victim of a mugging, and all I was trying to do was use his bathroom. Please, officer, won't you listen to me?" I continued to scream at him through the panel separating us.

He ignored me and talked into his shoulder mic. I'd never been arrested in my life and wasn't sure if that's what was happening now. I'd never been in trouble before. *What will my mother say?*

We drove and weaved through the busy city streets until we reached what I guess was his precinct. He got out and walked around to my side, instructing me to watch my head as he helped me from the car. I wanted to take my shoe and stomp on his foot but didn't want to add assault to whatever grievances I already had against me.

He took me by my arm and escorted me into the building. We walked past a huge information desk with multiple screens above. The desk sergeant took a look at me and rolled his eyes before instructing the officer where to place me.

"Now, are you going to behave so I can remove your restraints?"

Fuck you, I wanted to say but I simply nodded my head. My tears began to fall with no end in sight.

"Can you tell me your name?" he asked softly.

Wow! Did he have a sudden change of heart? I looked up at the clueless man before me and refused to give him my name. All I could do was cry. This lasted a few minutes, with the officer obviously frustrated with my hesitation.

"Look, lady, I can't help you if you are not going to cooperate with me. What's your name?" he asked again.

"Officer, you can't be serious right now. You want me to cooperate? Were those the words you just said to me? I have done nothing wrong but be victimized by the entire city! The hacker who emptied my bank account! My boss who threatened to fire me! The asshole who mugged me! The café guy who accused me of being a homeless prostitute loitering on his property! And to end my terrible day, you shoved me into the backseat of your car without ever asking me how you could help! I lost count on how many of my civil rights were taken away from me today. I don't deserve any of this, and you, sir, have abused any power you think you have over me. So, fuck you. I'm not giving you my name. You don't deserve to know it."

For a moment, I felt strong and empowered, but it didn't last long. He leaned in closer, probably not appreciating the verbal tongue lashing I just delivered, and he pushed back.

"I've run out of patience with you. You want to be a princess and throw a tantrum? Fine by me. You have two choices right now. Either you tell me your name, or you will spend the rest of the night in a cell with the real drunks and prostitutes and get a feeling of what spending a night in jail feels like. Trust me, you're not going to like it. Now, what's it going to be?"

I was exhausted, and my fight was gone. "My name is Willow Pierce," I quietly uttered.

Satisfied, he smirked and removed the handcuffs, calling over a female officer.

As I sat there, I thought to myself: *I should have stayed with Madeline to drink.*

CHAPTER Two

Valentin

"**W**ow! As I live and breathe, what brings the great Valentin Vasiliev to my precinct?" a familiar voice called out as I walked up to the desk.

I ignored his antics and greeted him with my usual "Don't fuck with me" expression. "Less of the dramatics, please, Frank. I'm here for work. What other reason would there be for me to be here?"

"Gee, I don't know, Mr. Fancy Pants. We don't get too many big-time lawyers down here slumming it up with us regular folk."

"Hmmm, well, when the son of one of the said lawyer's *fancy* clients gets busted for public intoxication and disorderly conduct, I have to slum a little and grace you with my presence. You know, show you how the other half lives," I mocked.

"Fuck you, you prick!" he replied.

We both laughed, and then my friend rounded his desk and pulled me forward for a strong hug.

"It's good to see you, Val. It's been way too long," he said.

"I know, and it's my fault completely. Poker next week?"

"Yeah, I guess so. I'll have to press my suit for the occasion."

"Do you even own one?" I asked, totally messing with him.

"Only for weddings and funerals. I guess I'll have to make a special exception for you."

"Oh, Frank, you're lucky I love you like a second father. Here, take this file. My client has made bail, and he's in holding, awaiting his ride."

"Sure thing," he replied and then took my paperwork.

Frank was a good man. Sure, we went at it and messed with each other, but our family would forever be grateful for his bravery when he took a bullet that nearly hit me when I was a teenager. The city was in an uproar during a protest, and we just happened to be in the wrong place, wrong time. Gunfire erupted in the streets, and I was almost caught in the crossfire. Out of nowhere, a cop leaped in front of me, taking one in the hip, thus ending his career as a beat cop. My family was in his debt and welcomed him as one of our own. He'd been a good friend even through the years when we weren't exactly on the same side of the law, but that was another story for another time.

I came back to present and focused on the reason why I was here. I placed my briefcase down and checked my messages on my phone while waiting for Frank to return. Out of the corner of my eye, I looked over to see the most beautifully broken girl crying in the corner of the squad floor.

She was alone at a desk, just crying into a mound of tissues on her lap. She looked beside herself. My eyes scanned her and saw that she was injured. Surrounded by upset officers and even angrier criminals, this woman stood out to me like an angel. A pure, white dove. She clearly didn't belong in a place like this.

I pocketed my phone and walked over to where she was seated. Her head was now down with a crown of thick hair falling over and covering her face. She tried valiantly to wipe away her tears on her tattered sleeve after she used up her tissues but then continued to cry.

I reached for a chair and sat down to get a better look at her. With my two fingers, I lifted her chin and found green eyes that were reddened and almost swollen shut. Surprised by my presence, she quickly sat up and shuddered back in her seat.

"I'm sorry. I didn't mean to frighten you," I said softly just above a whisper to calm her. "It's okay, I'm not going to hurt you," I spoke again with my hands raised in front of her, showing the poor girl that I wasn't a threat. "I want to help if you allow me to."

"Why?" she whispered. I could barely make out the word.

"Why what?" I asked, confused.

"Why would you, a stranger, help me when every single person I've come into contact with today has done the opposite?"

I was immediately angered and wanted to fuck up every last asshole who hurt this beautiful dove. I tampered down my emotions and looked directly into her eyes.

"I guess you met the wrong people, because unlike them, I do want to help you. Let's begin with cleaning these knees. It's clear you need some looking after. Please, will you allow me to help?" I asked again, hoping she would let her guard down and say yes. The look on her face told me that she wanted to trust me but was afraid. "Here, my card."

I handed it to her, and with shaky fingers, she accepted it and whispered my name, "Valentin Vasiliev, Attorney at Law."

She enunciated my name perfectly. I stood to my 6'3" height and extended my hand out to her. Without another beat of hesitation, she accepted it, and I led her away to a private conference room nearby with an attached bathroom. As I was leading her down the hallway, a female officer called out to me. I ignored her and found the room I was looking for. I opened the door for her to step inside, allowing me to inhale her flowery perfume.

"Everything you need is right through there," I said as I pointed to the bathroom. "I'll be right back, okay?"

"Okay," she softly responded.

The female officer was now directly behind me as I closed the door and stepped into the hallway. She was rambling on about procedures as I took a calming breath of my own before going on the defense.

"Are you fucking blind?" I shouted and then looked at her badge. "Officer Baker, have you even bothered to show any compassion to this woman? Did you tend to her injured legs? Or offer a cup of water?" As I waited for her to respond, I continued, "Yeah, you're finished. I'll take it from here."

I took another pause to see what she would do. *If she were smart, she would walk away and let me take it from here.* She instead chose to challenge me, and then I stepped further into her personal space, causing her to shift in her brave stance. I would never intimidate a woman, but I was growing tired of this bullshit and needed to get back to the broken dove in the bathroom.

Officer Baker rolled her shoulders and stood attentively. "I'll be at my desk."

Good choice. "You do that," I responded.

I knocked before entering, and she called out for me to come in. She had washed her face, which was now clean of makeup. It didn't appear she had much on but now I could see her skin perfectly. Her face was flawless. She looked so young. Her hands were cleaned too, and she was about to apply a wet paper towel to her knees when I stopped her.

"Here, allow me. There's a first-aid kit in the bathroom. I'll go get it." I left her for all of a second and returned with the metal box. "Are you thirsty? Can I offer you a bottle of water before I get started here?"

"Yes, that would be nice."

"Good, you need to drink all of this before you slip into shock. I'm not convinced you're not experiencing some level of it. It appears you've been through a terrible ordeal today."

"Yeah, that's putting it mildly." She crossed her arms over her chest and huffed out an annoyed tone.

I didn't want to crowd her, so I gave her some space.

"I'm sorry. You're only trying to help, and I appreciate it. It's just…" she hesitated.

"It's okay. Say what you're feeling."

"I'm pissed! And to be perfectly honest, my knees weren't the only thing that got hurt today. I don't know what bothers me more: my knees or my pride? I have never been so mistreated than I was today, and that's saying something, having survived high school with the mean girls."

"Well, let's hope from here on out, your day will get better. Okay, this may sting a little, but it's necessary." After I wiped the dried blood and dirt away, I applied the antibacterial spray. She jerked her one leg and winced a little. "I'm sorry, I know it hurts. From the look of it, you really took a hard fall on these." I sprayed one more time and then applied the antibiotic ointment before covering them with large bandages. "There, all done. That wasn't too bad, was it?"

"No, it's good."

"Don't give up on the human race just yet. Nice guys do exist and are out there." I winked, and just as I did, her cheeks began to redden with a rosy blush. I couldn't miss a hint of a smile. I was about to say something more, but we were interrupted by Frank, who asked to have a word with me. *Yeah, I have a few for him too!* I thought to myself.

The progress I had made with her was now gone as she retreated back into her scared shell. I told her everything was going to be okay and not to worry. I got up to wash my hands and dried them before turning back to the woman I still don't know by name. "Will you be alright on your own for a minute?"

She looked so skittish but nodded in silence as she continued to drink her water. I walked out of the room and closed the door behind me before practically shoving Frank down the hallway, leading him away from where she could hear us.

"What the fuck, Frank?" I said seething in anger. "Is this how the

NYPD treats women? Yeah, #MeToo, my ass." I wanted to fucking hit something. He put his hands up in surrender as if he were trying to pacify me.

"Val, I only saw her for a second when she was brought in earlier. That's it, I swear. When you disappeared with her, Officer Baker talked to me. You can't just do as you please around here. We have rules, Val, and yes, they do apply to you. Listen, I just talked to the officer who picked her up. He thought she was homeless. The restaurant owner said she was loitering on his property and refused to leave."

"Yeah, maybe because she needed fucking help!" I raised my voice. "Are you fucking kidding me right now? I don't believe how this happened. Homeless? I've never felt so angry in all of my life. The injustice in thinking that she's just another poor girl living on the streets. I want to hit someone right now, and I think I will begin with the asshole from the restaurant."

"Okay, come on, Val. You need to pull it together. And besides, you hit someone? Yeah, like you would ruin your manicure."

"Not the time for jokes, Frank, and I will not calm down. A gross miscarriage of justice has been made here today, and your department needs to be held accountable for your irresponsible actions. Your patrolman...what's his name? Eaton. Is today his first day on the job? Did he take a minute to really look at who he was arresting and hauling away like yesterday's trash?"

"She wasn't arrested or charged with anything. He just wanted to bring her in to calm her down a bit and get her some help."

"Yeah, so that's the story he's telling. I don't believe it for a minute. It took me all of ten seconds to know she was not a vagrant. I think her French manicured fingernails was one of many giveaways on who she is. Certainly, it's enough to refute the restaurant owner's initial judgment of her."

"Okay, you made your point."

"No, I'm just getting started. Remember, I'm not just a lawyer. I'm a very powerful man, Frank, and what happened here today does not happen in my world, especially to women. A very innocent woman."

"Val, please be reasonable. They made a mistake. She's fine."

"I'm not so sure she's entirely fine, but I will not debate this one more minute with you. I have to be going. Give me the file, Frank."

"You know I can't do that."

"Sure you can, and you will," I replied, not fucking around and grabbing the file from his hands. "Make this disappear, you hear me?"

I opened it up and perused the single sheet of paper with minimal information on it. The only words I was focused on was her name: Willow Pierce. *Fucking amazing! Her name is as perfect as she is.* I took what I needed, folded and put it in my pocket, and then tossed the empty file folder back to Frank.

"I'll be leaving now and taking Ms. Willow Pierce with me. Do me a favor and have a conversation with Officer Eaton on profiling, because he doesn't know shit. Better it comes from you than me, don't you think?" And with that, I didn't spare a second glance at Frank.

I ran my fingers through my hair and took a few calming breaths before entering the room I had left her in. I called out to her, but the room was silent and vacant.

"Fuck! She left," I said as I balled my fists at my side. *Out in the city all alone while injured.*

She couldn't have gone far, but even if I left to search for her, where would I begin? Then I remembered what I had in my pocket. I unfolded the piece of paper and smiled. *Lucky for me, I know where to find you, Willow Pierce.*

CHAPTER Three

Willow

Once the door closed, I released a deep winded breath that I'd been holding since I met Mr. Tall, Dark, and Handsome. *My god! This guy was incredibly striking in his appearance and so tall that I had to crane my neck up to see him. Damn, he's hot, like supermodel in a magazine hot!* He had piercing brown eyes with hair dark as night. One thing I could be 100% sure of was the expense of his attire. His suit alone had to cost over $3,000, maybe more depending on who did the cut for him.

Where did this Adonis come from? Men like him don't just fall from the sky out of nowhere and right into my lap. It sure feels that way, though. He's the first male I would view as a real man. Most guys I knew from home were just immature lifeguards, bartenders, or the perpetual student not wanting to leave college and move forward with their life.

I'll call him TD, short for tall and dark. I'm sure I will never see him again, and if I do, he will probably not want anything to do with me after I just left without another word spoken between us. Why would he? When he is so powerful and commanding?

The more I think about it, the more I conclude he was just proba-bly being kind. Like checking off his list of daily good deeds. Yeah, I know how I sound right now. I was being way too dramatic and proba-bly a little selfish too. I don't even know him, and here I am passing judgment on him when all he did was be kind to me. I'm no different than the café guy and the cop today.

I blamed my behavior on the strong women in my life. Mom raised me all on her own when my father who couldn't handle respon-sibility took off when I was born. My mom got pregnant with me when she was sixteen years old, and if it wasn't for grandma being so sup-portive of her decision to keep me, who knows what fate life would have handed us.

Mom finished high school before she was showing and avoiding quite the scandal back then. Working two jobs in-between taking care of me, she managed to get through college and nursing school, earning her degree. She did a lot of tedious work in the beginning but then moved up with more schooling under her belt and now was a lead OR nurse at a trauma one hospital in New Jersey. She loves what she does. When she wasn't working, she spent days at the beach and drove into the city for Sunday brunch with me when her schedule allowed.

Grandma joined us too if she was here. The Pierce women were quite the trio, and I just loved us so much. We were very close and told each other almost everything. *I think gram is the naughtiest out of all of us.*

I already regretted my decision to flee the police station after the coast was clear. By the time I made it home, I felt sick to my stomach. I limped my way down to the entrance of the subway. It only took me so far, and then I had to walk the rest of the way to my apartment.

It was a very hot day, and the apartment was stifling. Per gram's instructions, I had to raise the thermostat during the day, and only at night I could lower it to a comfortable temperature. "We don't have friends down at Con Edison" she always said. I sometimes believed she had a secret alert on her phone that informed her when I overused the utilities. She would gripe for all of a second and then forget why she was nagging me in the first place.

I used the last of the bath oil and salts I had in the house and filled the tub to soak my sore and tired muscles. I sat on the edge to test the water, which felt perfect. I removed my tattered clothing, then looked down at my knees and couldn't help but to smile. I was reluctant to remove my bandages, which was stupid, because if I did, then it would erase all the kindness TD showed me today. Whatever he did worked, because my cuts were already healing. I had to remember to apply ointment on my knees before I went to bed.

I should have stayed to thank him. *Stupid!* Why did I run from him? *Stop it, Willow*, I scolded myself. *Torturing yourself is not going to make you feel better. He helped you with TLC, and it's all in a day's work for him being awesome.*

As for me, I didn't know what was going to happen tomorrow. My job was uncertain. I needed to replace my phone. *Yeah, where am I getting the money for that?* I could call my mom. She would help me, but I promised myself that when I left her house, I would be as independent as I could, sans living with grandma. Gram doesn't count because she's not here. Oh, and there was the task of getting my bank account straightened out.

Not facing the big bad world tomorrow is what I may do. Hiding under the covers is looking better and better.

CHAPTER
four

Valentin

Slowly nursing the scotch in my hand, I paced the vast living room of my penthouse apartment, waiting on word from Oleg, a guard I had appointed on surveilling Willow. I had to know she was safe, and without barreling through her front door, this was the best way I could think of...for now.

The following day, she had not left her apartment, and the next day she left only to walk up to the corner deli for a paper and coffee. She wasn't seen carrying anything beyond the two items. *Was she eating? Keeping up her strength? Is she in hiding in fear that whoever mugged her will come back? Yeah, there was no chance at that happening.*

I already had men on the street looking for her assailant. Once I confirmed where she was mugged, I knew the restaurant and street cameras could offer a clear view of who had hurt my dove and clipped her wings. *She will fly again, I have no doubt. She just needs the time to heal, and then I will go to her.*

I knew how I sounded but didn't care. I was the determined stalker that wanted to know every last thing about Willow Pierce. I also wanted my pound of flesh for those who hurt her. I wouldn't go after the young and wet behind the ears police officer who grossly misjudged the situation. What I would do is track down the asshole from the café. Yes, he was in my sight and would pay for what he did.

I finished my drink and then poured another before making the needed call. *I'm the biggest hypocrite and should feel ashamed for what I am about to do. I have worked tirelessly at distancing myself from my family and who they are, but I will not hesitate to use their resources to suit my needs when absolutely necessary.*

Frank is right. I can't dirty my hands in any sense of the word. I am a servant of the law, and I swore to live by that oath. You don't get any in-between, but experience has taught me well and I know how to bend where I need to. Just thinking those words turned my stomach, but it had to be done. Without second-guessing my decision, I dialed Sergei's number.

"Yeah," he answered on the second ring.

"It's me. I need a favor, Sergei."

"What level?" he asked.

"The in-person kind. Pay a visit to Café West on Park and Fifth. A conversation is needed with the owner. His name is Josh Rickards."

"Understood. I'll have an update for you soon."

I disconnected my call and hit the treadmill to calm my rising anger. Just thinking about that asshole from the café was making me see red.

Three hours later, the call I'd been waiting for had come in. My parcel was delivered. I stepped into the dark room, and Sergei met me with a warm embrace. He was like a brother to me and would do anything for me. *Why does he even question me when he knows he will always agree to any request I make of him?*

"He's in the back," Sergei said to me.

"Thanks, I'll take it from here," I responded, and as I turned away from him, he grasped my arm to halt my movement. I asked over my shoulder, "Problem?"

"Valentin, I'm worried. This was not sanctioned by your father. You know he will find out, and when he does, he will question me. I will not lie to him, not even for you."

"I would never ask or expect you to be disloyal to my father. You continue to be his faithful servant as you always have been. However, tonight, you are mine, and I do expect discretion. Are we clear on this matter?"

"Yes. One more piece of advice, if I may."

"Go on," I said. My patience was running thin.

"Try to remember who you are in there. You are the prince in your father's eyes, and you are not to get your hands dirty."

"How could I forget? It's the story of my life, but this is a personal matter, and I will handle anything that comes my way."

I opened the door and found what I was looking for. His eyes were covered, and his hands and legs were bound to a chair. He wasn't going anywhere. This building was old, dusty, and damp. It probably had layers of mold on the walls with the rats in the sewer. *This was a place you didn't want to die in. They would never find you, but that's not why I was here. A message needs to be sent. It will be up to Josh Rickards on how it's delivered.*

He called out to me, but I didn't answer back. I remained quiet as I circled the space he was trapped in. The only sound that could be heard was his erratic breathing and the sound of my boots as they got closer to him.

"Please, who are you? Why am I here?" he pleaded.

I reached for the only other chair in the room and placed it in front of him. I knew the taunting was making him nervous, probably to the point of pissing himself. *It's what I want him to feel and so much more.*

"Do you like questions, Mr. Rickards?" I asked him close to his ear.

"Who are you? What is this about?"

"Again, with the questions. Before I answer your questions, you will answer mine. I never repeat myself, but for you, I will make a one-time exception. So, here I go. Do you like questions, Mr. Rickards?"

"Yeah, I guess."

"Hmmm, you guess? You have given me a child's answer, and that's not acceptable."

"I'm sorry. Yes, I like questions. When you ask questions, you find out information. Is that what you want to hear?"

"It's a start, and your answer brings me to my next one for you. But first, allow me to tell you a story. Two days ago, a young woman was in your restaurant. She was injured after a mugging and sought your help, but you refused her and turned her away. She asked for kindness and pleaded with you for compassion, but again, you refused her. So, here's my question. Why would you do that?"

"I don't know what you are talking about, mister. I don't know any girl needing help."

"Hmmm, this is most puzzling to me, Mr. Rickards. This was only two days ago. Surely your memory is better than that. Let me see if I can help you."

A moment later, he shrieked in pain as the crowbar I was holding in my hand made contact with his left knee. As he cried out in pain and sniveled like the weak and pathetic human being he was, he begged for his freedom. I struck the back of his chair with the metal bar, startling him to attention.

"How about now? Do you remember the young woman?" I said again close to his ear, making him jump.

In a ragged and strained voice, he answered my question. "Yes, I remember her. I thought she was homeless and looking for a handout."

"You refused her? Yes?"

"Yes, I did," he whimpered.

"Even when she repeatedly asked for help?"

"I'm sorry. I was wrong. I shouldn't have done that. All she wanted to do was use the restroom."

"Yes, to clean her injured knees after suffering a fall. But no, you refused her. Let me ask you this. What kind of man does that to an innocent woman in need of help? How did you feel after you went home for the night after locking your doors? Did you think of her? Maybe a small thought crossed your mind, and maybe you felt a pang of guilt? Did you do that, Mr. Rickards?"

"No, I didn't. I'm so sorry."

"Yes, you've said that, but are you saying that because I just broke your knee and you are fearful that I will do the same to the other? Because, Mr. Rickards, I am not a man that likes to be told what you believe I need to hear. No, what I want is the truth. I want to know exactly what is running through your mind right now. No lies, Mr. Rickards. Tell me the truth."

"Yes, I'm afraid of you! But it doesn't mean I am any less sorry for my actions. I treated her badly, and I'm ashamed of it. If you want to break my other knee, I can't really stop you, now can I? But I am sorry. And if I had the opportunity to see her again, I would apologize. I swear it."

"Fair enough, Mr. Rickards, I believe you. Maybe one day you will have that chance, but it won't be today. I do want you to do something for me before we part ways."

"Anything, I swear it."

"Good. I'm pleased you see things my way. Do you remember what the young woman looked like? Beginning with her hair and ending at her feet. Describe to me what you saw."

"Please, I see so many people throughout the day. I mean, this is New York. How am I supposed to give you a detailed description of her?"

"Simple. If you value your ability to walk, you will tell me exactly what she looked like. I'll give you a minute to think about it, and if I am not satisfied with your answer, your right knee will suffer the same fate as your left."

I dropped the bar down at his feet that radiated a loud vibrating sound throughout the empty space. I left the room and sought out air that my lungs desperately needed.

"Is it done?" Sergei asked as he slowly approached me.

"It will be in a few minutes. No need to worry, my friend. He will be alive when I leave here. You are to drop him at the nearest ER entrance, and make sure you are not seen. Are we clear, Sergei?"

"I understand."

"Good. See that your crew does as well. No mistakes."

I ran my fingers through my hair in frustration. *Deep down, this is not who I am, but it is a brief glimpse of a monster I always fear could easily come to fruition. And if that ever fully happens, then all that I'd worked for would be gone.*

It wasn't difficult to figure out where this frightening side of me came from. I loved my father very much but he was a complicated man and a dangerous one if crossed. He came to this country with seven dollars in his pocket and vowed to give his family a better life. He now had ten times over and then some, but it wasn't always through the typical "American way." It was not a subject spoken at the dinner table, and no one was stupid enough to ever question him.

I have to believe that what I am doing is right and that my actions are justified. I will leave here and go home to wash away the sins I committed here tonight, and then tomorrow, I will go to Willow and repent at her feet.

I walked back into the dusky room where the stench of urine was evident. *Mission accomplished, but so messy.* Walking back over to Mr. Rickards, I took my seat to ready myself to hear his vivid description of Willow. I closed my eyes to picture my dove and then asked him to begin.

"She's petite in height and frame, can't weigh no more than 110 pounds. I'm guessing 5'4", give or take a couple of inches. She has long brown hair that comes down to the middle of her back. It was in disarray when she sat down at the table. I guess windblown, I don't know. Wavy but not really curly. She had been crying, and her face was smeared in black streaks from probably her mascara. She was wearing a pale pink two-piece dress with a belt at her waist. Her shoes were flat."

"Very good, Mr. Rickards. So it seems you do have a very good memory. But is there something missing?"

"Her knees."

"Right. Describe what her knees looked like."

"Please, no more," he whimpered, dropping his head down to his chest.

"Continue, Mr. Rickards. I will not say it again."

"Her knees were covered in blood, and she had streaks of blood running down her shins. She was dirty, and one of her sleeves was torn. Her hands were dirty too, probably from the fall she took."

"Ahh, yes, the *fall*. I do believe the right word you are trying to say is *mugging*, because she told you that she was attacked resulting in hurting her legs. Her smeared makeup and all those tears that followed were a direct result from being attacked. Do you agree?"

His lip quivered, and he answered, "Yes, to all of it."

"Yes, but knowing all that vital information, you still refused her. Judged her. Shunned her and threw her out like garbage. Now, think very carefully about what you say next to me. Will you ever forget her? And the treatment you showed her?"

"No, I will never forget her and my cruel judgment of her."

"What happens to the next defenseless woman that seeks out your help? Will you remember?"

"I swear it. I will never ever treat another living soul like I treated the woman who asked for my help two days ago. I swear it. I promise. Please, believe me."

"Relax, relax, I believe you. And as a thank you for you telling me the truth, your other knee has been spared."

"Thank you, thank you."

While he did visibly calm down, I stepped closer and squeezed his injured knee. He shrieked in pain as I instructed him to be quiet.

I crouched down as low to the ground as my body allowed and coldly whispered for only him to hear, "Yes, I kept my word as you did, Mr. Rickards. You see, you spewed filth and hate, and that cannot be ignored. So as you remember her appearance, you will also remember her voice. The sounds of her pleas and broken cries. Let them serve as two reminders for you to never speak to a lady in that way ever again."

He grunted in pain as I gripped his chin.

I said, "Understand? Yes? Good. I'm glad you have seen the error of your ways. You may not believe it now, but I have given you a gift tonight. I was merciful to you, and that in itself is a blessing, because if I would have unleashed my true wrath on you, then let's just say you wouldn't see the light of day tomorrow. No, Mr. Rickards, you would be in forever darkness, six feet under."

I shoved him back as he continued to whimper through his agony of pain, leaving him to Sergei. Not one eye was upon me as I left the building. They all knew and understood how brutal a true punishment could be.

Blood was left on the floors. The smell is in the air, and it seeps into your pores. It's tangible and inescapable once you unleash the buried darkness within yourself. I kept telling myself over and over again that I restrained that part of me tonight and only took it so far, but not too far that I couldn't come back from the precipice of my anger. *I have control. It is essential for me to exist as the man I've become.*

When I arrived home, I removed all my clothing, including my boots, to be incinerated, leaving no trace of what I did tonight. I scrubbed my skin under the scalding water to the point of pain. My stomach rolled, but I controlled my emotions and stepped out from the steam-filled bathroom.

I needed to breathe. I wanted to feel. I needed Willow. *Her eyes have cast a spell on me, dragging me under the surface where only purity reigns. I've traveled all over the world and met and bedded exotic women, but no one compares to the feeling I felt when I met the broken dove.*

I can't explain it, and I won't justify my feelings to anyone. I have to know everything about her. Where she comes from and who her family is. Who are her friends? Does she have a special someone she confides in? I was driving myself crazy with my rampant thoughts, but they wouldn't stop until I knew everything.

It was late, and I hadn't received a report from Oleg, not that I expected to since I was otherwise out of reach earlier tonight. I reached for my cell phone and dialed his number. Even if what he told me was no different from the last time we spoke, I still needed that assurance she was safe.

"Valentin, are you okay? It's two in the morning," he questioned with a tone on high alert.

"Don't worry about me. How's the girl?"

"She's been in her apartment the entire night."

"How can you be so sure?" I questioned.

"I promise you, Valentin, she's secure. Oh, wait a second." And then there was a pause, and the line went silent. I heard Oleg speak Russian to another as I was screaming into the line for him to come back.

"What the fuck, Oleg? What's happening? And why is Sergei there? I know I heard him."

"I'm sorry, I noticed movement, and I'm now following her."

"Where the hell is she going at this hour? And why is Sergei with you? If he didn't follow through with my instructions, I will have his balls on a platter!"

"Sergei is here. I will pass the phone."

"I'm here," Sergei said to me.

"Why are you there? And not where you are supposed to be?"

"It's done, I promise. The café owner was dropped off just as you instructed. I watched and waited until the hospital staff found him. They brought him in, and I left."

"No one saw you?"

"No, and neither did he. He was blindfolded until we reached the hospital. He must have passed out, but I assure you he was breathing when I left him."

"He better be for your sake, Sergei."

"I only stopped by to check on Oleg before going home, and we both spotted her walking down the steps of the brownstone. He's on her now."

"She shouldn't be walking the streets of the city by herself and at this hour. I'm coming to you."

"No, she's flagged down a cab. I will let you know where it takes her to."

"Stay on her, and do not lose that cab."

"I won't. I'll call you back."

Waiting was fucking torture. *Why was she out this late? Could she be meeting a man?* Again, my thoughts were uncontrollable, not knowing. Fifteen minutes felt like hours had gone by, and then my cell buzzed, and it was Oleg.

"So, where is she?" I shouted.

"The Garment District, at a wholesale distributor. It looks like she's buying fabric."

Why would she be there? Every feeling I had raging through me was pushing me out the door to be close to her, but I held myself back. *I'm not exactly in the right frame of mind, and now she's out there on her own, making me completely crazy. I have eyes on her, but I want my eyes on her, only mine. Fuck!*

"She's coming out," Oleg reported.

"Does she have anything with her?"

"Yeah, the fabric and two bags. She just got into a cab, probably going home."

"Stay on her, and call me once she returns to her apartment."

I waited and waited until I was out of my mind. I ran six miles on the treadmill and then lifted weights until my muscles burned. I was dripping with sweat and in need of another shower. I checked my messages and still had no word from Oleg. I was gripping the device so hard I thought it would shatter when finally the call I was waiting for came through.

"Yes," I answered curtly.

"She's back home, and from where I am positioned, I can see her perfectly. She's on the top floor."

"Be careful, Oleg. I will cut your eyes out if they wander to things that should only be seen by me."

"Valentin, I know better. I swear to you, she's fully clothed. From what I can see, it looks like she has a measuring tape around her neck, and she's working on one of those dressmaker things, like a mannequin."

A fashion designer? How intriguing.

"Very well. Stay on your post, and do not leave until you hear from me. Clear?"

"Crystal."

My left palm was against the cool granite in my shower as I worked my right over my hard cock, fantasizing about the enchanting broken dove working me over into a state of Hades, fighting between eternal paradise and the deepest depths of hell. I shouted out my release as I opened my eyes and saw green, her eyes pulling me back to paradise.

The wait to see her felt unbearable, just watching the clock as the minutes and hours ticked by. I let out a few breaths and tried to calm my nerves at the anticipation of seeing her tomorrow.

I've never felt this way before. A want so strong to be with someone that makes me feel so alive. It's completely out of character for me, but what the hell? You only live once, and no matter how much I try to reason with myself that this is crazy and fast, my heart is leading me to her, and I can't stop it.

I'll go to her and tell her how I feel. I'll tell her that I want to make her mine and try not to complicate it with questions and just run with it and see where it leads. There is something about the broken dove that I cannot ignore. When I looked into her eyes, I saw a sadness. If she takes a chance on me, maybe I can replace that with comfort and protection?

A person's eyes can say a lot about them. She's in need of healing, I understand that more than anyone. Maybe if she allows me to heal her, she'll be able to heal me too?

CHAPTER
five

Willow

After two days in hiding, I was going crazy and needed to get out. I couldn't call Madeline and get into all that happened, so I texted a white lie and said I would be in tomorrow. She had problems of her own and sent me a one-word reply.

After how we parted at the office, she probably assumed I had taken her advice and took the time to think about my future, never knowing what happened to me. I would talk to her tomorrow, but for now, I needed to create. I took my emergency credit card and, on an impulse, went down to my favorite all night fabric store and bought material I had no right buying. It was a mad decision, but I shoved all the sensible reasons out of my brain and decided this was the best course of action to feel better.

Artists love to paint. You have a blank canvas to start, knowing what colors will blend right and create the beauty. Writers love to write. All it takes is a blank sheet of paper, pen, pencil, or strokes of a keyboard to write the next best seller. Well, it's not too different for me. I'm a designer. I envision a design in my head, and then I start with a yard of fabric and sew it into an ensemble that I hope one day I will get to display on the runway during Fashion Week. Yes, this Jersey girl can dream and will never give up on what she wants until she gets it. So, magic hands, create!

By the time I finally stopped working, the sun was rising. Wow, I hadn't pulled an all-nighter in a while, but for some crazy reason, I did feel better, and so far, my dress was everything I wanted it to be. I placed it in the corner and just sat back to admire my work.

"Not bad, Willow, not bad at all," I said and then hugged myself.

It was still early, and instead of making coffee, I stripped down and climbed into bed naked, loving the feel of my soft sheets against my skin. Sleeping on cotton this soft felt amazing, another high-end purchase I couldn't afford but luckily it was a gift from my mom. She worked hard as a nurse and was on her feet for many hours. She valued her sleep when she could get it and always said, "A body needs rest, and it should never sleep on cheap bedding."

I was a nerd in school and got straight A's. I took all the pre-college courses that were offered, and by the time I finished high school, I left with my diploma and enough credits for my Associate's degree. I was awarded over $200,000 in scholarships toward my education, leaving my mom with no need for student loans. Yes, I was very fortunate and did not waste one penny that I was awarded. I worked incredibly hard in school, and then after successfully completing my education at the New York Fashion Institute, I was hired by Madeline.

Mom was currently in a good place in her life, so although she couldn't give me much growing up, she tended to go overboard with surprise gifts every time she visited. The sheets. The MAC lipstick I wanted, because of course, it was Christian Louboutin. Maybe it was the casing I loved so much, sparkly gold with a crown for the top. It was so royal looking. I only used this particular color on very special occasions. *Who knows? Maybe once this dress is done, I will get to wear it somewhere special and already have the perfect lipstick to go with it.*

"Okay, Willow, get your head out of the clouds and go to sleep!" I chastised myself.

Three hours later, I gave my body a long, deep stretch and jumped into the shower to get ready for work. Okay, not really *jumped* since my legs were still stiff from my fall, but at least the angry cuts and scrapes were healing. I'd been taking care of them carefully, because I didn't want to have any scars.

"Oh, come on," I groaned, waiting for a cab.

If I walked all the way to the subway in this heat, I would be a mess by the time I got to the warehouse. I had no choice but to hike it to the subway. And then out of nowhere, a cab appeared.

"Hi, are you in service right now?" I asked.

"I am, miss. Where to?"

"Seventh Avenue in the Garment District."

"Yes, I know it. I would be happy to give you a ride."

I eyed him suspiciously at first, but his cab appeared to have all the right credentials, and he seemed harmless enough. *Okay, get a hold of yourself. Not every guy in New York is like the café guy.*

"Thank you, sir, I would appreciate it," I said and then stepped inside of his cab, which was immaculate, by the way. It seemed almost new. It drove very smoothly, never hitting one bump along the way.

The driver was focused and quiet, but his accent was interesting. I wanted to ask where he was from and then decided against it. He must have caught me staring, because I caught a glimpse of him smiling in the mirror.

"I can turn on the radio if you would like," he said.

"No, I'm fine. I guess I was just daydreaming. If you don't mind me asking, where are you from?"

"Not at all, miss. I am from St. Petersburg, Russia. I was born there and came over to America as a young boy. I am now a citizen of this great land."

"That's amazing. Do you miss your country?"

He gave me a look, and then I regretted my question.

"I'm sorry for being intrusive," I said.

"No, it's not that. I guess I don't meet too many people that care about where I come from."

"I guess you don't know the right people." I smiled and then leaned back, remembering what TD had said to me back at the police station.

The rest of the ride was quiet but peaceful at the same time. Once his car came to a full stop, I grabbed my portfolio case and replacement purse with just the essentials I needed. He opened the door for me, and I reached for my cash to pay him.

"Oh, I couldn't. Please, miss, keep your money."

"As generous as that is, I can't allow you to do that. This is how you make your living. Please take it."

He appeared to battle with his decision, but he finally accepted my payment and wished me a good day. I did the same and made my way inside.

I waved to a few of the friendlier faces Madeline employed, but when I reached my desk, I found all my things had been boxed up. *What the hell? No, this can't be happening. Is she really firing me?*

"Nice of you to join us," she announced, walking in behind me.

"Nice of you to fire me and pack my things. How thoughtful of you."

"Calm your skirt, Willow, and you are not fired."

"Really? Then why are my things boxed up? You could have fooled me."

"I'm sorry I didn't give you a proper warning, but I've been on the phone all morning with distributors. I wanted this to be a surprise for you, but I ran out of time."

"Okay, Madeline, I think you need to explain what's going on here. And from the beginning."

"Let's go grab a coffee, and I will tell you all about it. Café West makes the best croissants, and they have a mocha latte to die for."

"Um, sorry, I'll pass."

"My treat."

"No, it's not that. I will never go to that restaurant again." My jovial mood had dropped down a few pegs after the mention of the café. All I kept seeing was that angry man kicking me out of there.

"What's wrong, sweets? You are white as a ghost. Come here, and take a load off." She gestured to one of the chairs that didn't have a box on it.

I sighed and then lifted my skirt to show her my legs. Although the cuts were healing, I was covered in bruises. I was fair skinned to begin with, and now all this ugly coloring added made my skin look awful.

"Oh, sweet heaven. What happened to you? Were you in an accident? Wait, you don't drive. What happened?"

"I was mugged."

"What!?" she shouted, bringing half the floor to attention. She leaned her head out the door and shouted for everyone to get back to work before slamming it shut, which made me jump. "Tell me what happened?"

"It was the day you told me to go home. I had already been preoccupied with my bank card being hacked, and I was stressing over everything. I guess I was distracted and not paying attention when some guy hit me from behind and knocked me to the ground, taking my purse and my phone. He shoved me pretty hard, resulting in this happening." I pointed to my legs, and her eyes began to water.

"I am so sorry, Willow. I should have never asked you to leave. This is my fault."

"No, it's not. You didn't hack my account and then mug me."

"Yeah, but I did unload all my problems and make them yours to deal with. You were right about everything. I would be crazy to let you go. You are this rising star, and I swear I will do everything possible to get you where you need to go or want to be."

"Thank you. I appreciate you saying that. I'm much better now."

"Is everything okay with your account? Do you need any money until it gets resolved?"

"Well, my paycheck would be nice, and after that, I have my emergency credit card and some cash I had stashed away at home. Don't worry. I won't starve, and I still have a place to live."

"Thank goodness for small miracles. I will call my accountant right away and have them deposit money into your account. Consider it hazard money for all the pain and suffering I put you through the other day. Are you sure you are alright?"

"Yes, thanks to a very amazing man I inevitably met. The café owner wasn't so considerate and neither was the police officer that brought me down to the police station. The owner kicked me out and thought I was homeless and looking for a handout. I looked dreadful, so he's got me there, but for him to assume the worst in me felt terrible. People do the best they can in life, and sometimes it's harder for others. This asshole just shunned me like I had a disease or something. And then it was worse with the cop. He brought me down to file a report, but because I was freaking out, he cuffed me. I had never been so scared in my life."

"What an ordeal you went through. Why didn't you call me?"

"I was so ashamed, and besides, I didn't have my phone."

"You texted me the other day."

"Yeah, from my old flip phone, if you could believe that. It's practically an antique, but it still works. I'm going over to the Apple store later for a replacement. I'm still on my mother's plan, and once I tell her what happened, I know she will help me get a new phone."

"Nonsense, let me. You're not the only one with an emergency fund. I have some money in the safe. Let me go get it."

"Madeline, thank you, but I will be fine. And don't get mad at me for asking, but three days ago you were in dire straits, ready to close your door. Now today, you have money to burn. What gives?"

"We really do need to catch up. Okay, forget about the asshole on

Fifth. Let's take the day. We can go get you a new phone and then grab lunch at Bryant Park. After what you've been through, it's the least I can do. Consider today your last day of freedom, because tomorrow I am going to work you down to your pretty fingers." She reached for my hand and grimaced at my cracked nail polish. "Okay, add manicure to the list!"

My crazy and wonderful friend took me in for a big hug, one that I desperately needed. She was eccentric and always over the top, but her heart was always in the right place.

Madeline called ahead to order some sandwiches from a deli she liked. I was good to walk, and by the time we reached the deli, our order was ready. We took our lunch to the park and found a somewhat shady spot to eat and catch up on the last few days.

It was an odd feeling I felt as my eyes scanned the park. It was like someone was watching me in a way that made me feel safe. I couldn't explain it. The park was busy on any given day, but today it seemed calm. I shook my head while rolling my eyes. What an imagination I had sometimes.

I finished eating and took a sip of my iced tea, when Madeline snapped her fingers in front of me to get my attention. "Where did you go off to this time?" she asked and then bagged up our garbage and tossed it into the trash.

"Pardon? I'm sorry. I didn't hear what you asked."

"I swear, Willow, it's like you have dreams in your eyes, and you're trying to figure out which one will come true first. You get all starry and detached, and it almost makes me jealous that you can just let go and escape to another place in your mind."

"Oh, don't be silly. Who doesn't have thoughts that sometimes play on a revolving loop in their head?"

"Ha! No one I know but you. I just take life by storm and let the chips fall where they may. Sometimes it's a gamble and other times its risk, which brings me to the reason why I was so excited when you first arrived at work. First off, I meant what I said. You are going to be very busy in the coming months, because I don't have to close my doors. In fact, I may be expanding! I received a call this morning from Zara. She told me that her distributor decided to go in another direction for the new line they were launching, and they wanted someone new and fresh on the scene. I'm telling you, kid, I almost hung up on her, because when I originally placed our bid for that deal, I couldn't sell you enough to her team, and now she comes crawling back to us?"

"What did you tell her?" I asked excitedly.

"I said I wanted to hear more, and it wasn't going to cut it over the phone. I was picked up in a big stretch limo, and we took the city by storm. She took me to Pravda, some Russian caviar bar and half French bistro. I'm telling you, kid, it was class, class, class, and after two of their signature martinis, I was ready to sign on the dotted line."

"Wow, it sounds fun, and I'm sorry I missed it, but you didn't sign anything when you were drunk?"

"Nah, I'm just joking, but the drinks and food were out of this world. It was definitely above my pay grade, but you only live once! And some of those Russian waiters were not hard on the eyes. Oy! I need to get out more."

While her story was very entertaining, she still didn't give me any real details to this big and wonderful deal. *And she says I get lost in my head! You can practically see the stars and dollar signs dance around her.*

"Madeline," I said softly.

"Yeah, doll?"

"The deal? What is it?" I laughed through my question.

"Oh, yeah, I'm getting to that part. So, remember the line of cor-sets you designed for the theater group out of SoHo?"

"I would hardly call that a line, but yes, I do."

"Well, an actress that wore that costume just happened to wear it again to some club on the Upper West Side and was photographed in it. That actress just so happens to be Zara's niece. She asked her aunt to get in touch with the designer who made the costumes for her play, because she just landed a Broadway leading role, and they want *you* to design and make all the costumes for the show! Of course, you will have a huge team to help, but *you* will be the lead! I mean, is this blowing your fucking mind right now?"

I shifted in my seat and then got up to walk around the small space in front of our table before turning back to Madeline.

"What's wrong? Say something," she called out.

"I'm not a costume designer and certainly not on the large scale to design an entire wardrobe for an entire cast ensemble." I almost felt sick saying the words to Madeline and seeing the disappointment on her face.

"Nonsense, you can do anything."

"I'm not so sure, and I think I'm going to have to pass."

"No, you can't."

"Excuse me?"

"You heard what I said. You will not pass on this amazing opportunity. It will not only put you on the world's stage, but it will help my company survive. This will only benefit you, because you are now my in-house head designer. I need you, Willow. This is what we've been waiting for, and if Zara had accepted our original proposal, this deal probably would have never been presented to us."

"You don't know that and neither do I. Just last night, I started a new design on a dress that could easily put me there just as much as the corset I designed. Look, I know you weren't expecting me to say no, but something about this doesn't sit well with me and it shouldn't with you. Golden deals just don't drop in your lap overnight. Before I make any decision, I need to know more, and I have to meet the magic backer with the deep pockets before I open a new spool of thread."

"Fucking A! I swear if I played for the other team, I think I might kiss you right now."

"Um...thanks?"

"Oh, you know what I mean. You are just so smart and level-headed. But Willow, it's time-sensitive here. I already verbally said yes. The contracts are due to arrive this afternoon. Please, just think about this really hard and what it can bring to your career. I'm talking about long-term career success."

"Okay, I'll think about it, but I make no promises. If they want me so badly, then they will wait. Now, let's get back to the office."

"Seriously? We've been out for most of the day, I think it's time to call it. I didn't get much sleep last night, and by the look of it, neither did you. I'm in a generous mood, so take advantage of it and go home and get some rest. I'll call Zara and ask for more time."

"I'm sorry, Madeline. Am I being selfish here? What person in my position would turn down this opportunity? And if I don't do it, where will it leave you?"

"I'll be fine and so will you. I've been in this ever-changing business for more than three decades and counting. My eyes have seen a lot and I've gained and lost, but there is one thing I will never regret doing."

"Yeah? What's that?"

"Taking a chance on some kid from Jersey. You're bright and level-headed. I know you will go where your heart leads, and no matter what, we will be okay."

"Thanks, Madeline."

We gave each other a big hug, and then I decided to walk a little to clear my head. I waved my friend off and walked around the park for a little while to think about this magic deal, wishing I could talk to someone that would give me an honest perspective and not just tell me what I wanted to hear.

My knee was beginning to throb, so I sat down at a nearby bench, closed my eyes for a moment, and then I heard his voice. TD was standing in front of me, blocking the late day sun.

CHAPTER Six

Valentin

A fter receiving the file on one Ms. Willow Pierce, I spent my morning reading every single word trying to know as much as I could about my dove. She was twenty-two with a birthday at the end of this month. She was educated with several degrees in business and fashion. She was born and raised in a New Jersey shore town by her single mother, Brooke Pierce, a nurse. Reading on, I learned more about her schooling, family, and then I got to the most current information, which were her financial report and place of employment.

Where she lived did not match up to what she made at MW Designs, but then her brownstone apartment was in her grandmother's name and solely owned by her. Her personal checking account had been compromised on the same day she was attacked, leaving her not one cent in her account. I closed the file and slammed it on my desk for a moment to compose myself. *Motherfuckers!* Of course, it would be impossible to ever know who hacked her account, but the thought of them leaving her without any means made my blood boil into an uncontrollable rage.

I called my house manager to bring me another coffee since the one I had turned cold, just like my heart after reading this file. Once my cup was refreshed, I took a moment to drink the glorious liquid and read on. I didn't function very well without it in the morning, and since it was barely sunrise, I needed it more than ever. I was usually out of the door already getting my morning workout in and then off to my office in downtown Manhattan, but not today. Today was all about Willow Pierce and how I was going to see her again.

I knew Oleg was on her detail, and he would be driving her into work this morning under the guise of a city cab driver. I would coordinate it perfectly where she would have no other options but to accept a ride from my most confident charge. I needed her protected, and I trusted no one other than Oleg. Probably Sergei as well, but he had pledged allegiance to my father, which sometimes made our relationship complicated like last night with the café owner. I knew he was being cautious, but I threw caution out into the wind and just didn't give a fuck on what consequences lay ahead for me.

After I finished reading the file and then the background check on her boss and owner of MW Designs, an idea came to my mind. Our family had connections all around the country—the world, for that matter—but what I needed was right in this city, and she owed me a big favor. Today it was time to collect on that promise.

I phoned Zara Hill, one of the city's leading distributors for everything fashion. She mass produced everything from handbags to accessories and sold them to mass markets all around the world and exclusively for smaller boutiques around the city. Yes, she was perfect for what I had in mind for my dove.

"I need to see you in one hour. Don't be late," I ordered.

I dismissed my staff and gave instructions not to be disturbed. I took a shower and got dressed, forgoing my workout. I scanned my closet and found the perfect suit to wear today. I couldn't miss the way my dove looked at me when we met. I didn't make the connection until after I read her file, but now knowing what she did for a living, I realized she was appreciating my attire, which absolutely thrilled me. *So, Armani it is, and I also have the perfect tie that is going to make my dove very happy.*

Zara arrived right on time and was led inside my home to my office. I was seated behind the desk and only looked up when she was standing directly in front of me. I gestured for her to take a seat while I finished my call.

"Thank you for stopping by," I said and greeted her in my usual direct tone.

"It's not like I had a choice in the matter after you summoned me here."

"Call it what you like, I don't care one way or another. I need something from you, and I want it done this morning."

"And? What might that be?"

I tossed over a fashion magazine to Zara, in which I had a page marked with a Post-It note. She looked over the page and then back to me. "And? It's a picture of my niece from her play last month."

"Look closer, Zara. What do you see?"

"The ensemble picture? What exactly do you want me to see, Valentin?"

"The outfit she is wearing. It's quite beautiful, don't you think?"

"Yes, it is. I had a local designer create the costumes for her play. We were all very pleased with the final cut, and Jade loved it so much, she wore it out to a club. And that's the picture you are so enthralled with."

"Don't give your niece too much credit. It's not the body I like but what she is wearing and the person who designed it. Tell me more."

"She's young and very new to the city. She works for someone I know down in the Garment District. She's on the smaller scale with not a lot of experience, but her work is good, and Madeline Waters seems to like her."

"So much that she hired her as a designer?"

"More like an apprentice. I was in a pinch and didn't have any time to lend to my niece after her costume designer quit, so I called Madeline and she gave me Willow. She was fast with the turnaround, and as you can see by the picture, her design photographed well."

"So, knowing what a gem you have discovered, why haven't you taken on Willow for yourself? Zara, you have one of the biggest show-rooms in the city, nestled right in the middle of Saks Fifth Avenue. Surely a brilliant talent like Willow Pierce could be a valuable asset to your team. Am I wrong?"

"No, but I don't poach from my friends, and Madeline has been good to me over the years. I wouldn't do that to her, especially when her company is struggling."

"Hmmm, is that why you purposely outbid her for a new accesso-ries line she was trying to land to keep her struggling company afloat?"

"How the hell did you know about that? You are a lawyer, Valen-tin, not a fucking psychic."

"How soon you forget who I am. I am a man of great power, and my reach in all things is very long. You do well to remember that and maintain your tone when speaking to me."

She looked affronted at first and then conceded and gave me an apologetic look. "It was business, Val, plain and simple."

"Business is never simple. It can be quite messy at times to ma-neuver around. Today, it will be simple, because you are going to call your 'friend' Madeline and inform her that the winning proposal was canceled and you are very sorry you didn't choose MW Designs in the first place. You will forgo the original deal and sweeten her taste buds with this one." I handed her the contract, and I watched in delight as her eyes widened with every page she flipped through.

"You can't be serious, Valentin. This is impossible."

"Oh, I assure you that I am serious, and there is not one single thing in my world that is unattainable. You will propose this deal to Madeline and bring her on board, along with Willow Pierce. If you fail, then I promise you, dear Zara, you will not like what I do next."

"What if she declines? Then what?"

"She won't, because you will not allow her to. Make it happen, Zara, and it needs to be done today."

She sat there in silence with tears in her eyes, just shaking her head, probably never expecting what I had just thrown at her. It wasn't my intention to make her upset, but nonetheless, that's exactly what I did.

"Zara, look at me," I commanded. She raised her eyes and fought back her tears, not spilling one down her cheek. "I have the utmost confidence that you will make this happen, and I promise you that it will be beneficial for all parties involved."

"I'm sure you are right, Valentin. You usually are, but it's what I fear will happen if I am unsuccessful at bringing them into the fold. I've worked too hard to get where I am to just lose it all and by your hands. Please, don't do this to me. We've been friends for years, and I've always been loyal to you and your family."

"Yes, right on all accounts. I don't wish to hurt you, Zara. I'll use your word and see how it flows coming from my lips to your ears. I believe you said business is simple, yes? Well, then it's quite simple. I financed your career for a number of years. I allowed you to use my bevy of contacts to suit your needs, and I remember clearly a conversation we once had. Let me see if I can recall it."

I tapped my chin a few times and then sat up and moved around my desk to stand in front of Zara, towering over her. I leaned down and lifted her chin and held her with my two fingers. I said, "I believe you offered me your body that night right in the middle of the VIP room in one of my father's many clubs. You practically dry humped me until I moved you off my lap. You were left frustrated and in need of a release, but that was not what I wanted from you, was it?"

"No, Valentin."

"Good, you do remember. So, what I did state was again very simple. If and when I ever needed anything from you, I would call up-

on you, and with no questions asked, you would deliver on that promise. Correct?"

Still holding her chin, she nodded her answer.

I continued, "Very well. I believe I have made my point here, and
you will deliver to me what I want. Let's not think of the latter right
now. I am confident you will succeed, because Zara, you really don't
have any other options here. It's time to collect."

After showing Zara the door, I went back to what really mattered:
Willow Pierce. Arranging for Oleg to drive her this morning was brilliant. It alleviated a great deal of stress for me, considering last night's
events.

It was quiet on the homefront with no word from my father. I
knew he was still abroad for another few weeks or so, which gave me
enough time to secure Willow without any interference from my family.

I stopped seeking his approval a long time ago, but Sergei did
make a valuable point last night. To involve one of his men without my
father knowing about it was clearly not the best move I could make.
But I needed to act fast, and again, this matter was personal and all on
me to feel the repercussions if any occurred. Sergei checked in with a
contact at Mount Sinai and was told Mr. Rickards was admitted and
held for observation due to injuries he sustained from a physical assault. He was released this morning.

My calendar was clear through Tuesday, which gave me today,
tomorrow, and through the weekend to make progress with Willow. I
looked at my watch, and it had been a few hours since Zara left. Surely, she would have made contact with Madeline Waters by now. I was
beginning to get restless, which was never good for a man like me,
when my private line rang.

"Valentin Vasiliev," I answered.

"Hi, it's Zara," she greeted me, sounding apprehensive.

"Yes, I know. Is it a go?"

"No, not yet. I just received a call from Madeline."

"And? What did she say?"

"The designer passed on it and said no."

I roared into the phone receiver. "She passed on all of it? Is that what you are telling me? What the fuck!?" I slammed the phone down and took a minute to try to understand why Willow would not see this for what it was, which was amazing. I guess I underestimated her. No, it had to be something more, and I was determined to find out what it was. "Zara, stay on it, and do not disappoint me."

I ended the call and was about to make another, when my cell buzzed in my pocket.

"Oleg, what's wrong?" I answered.

"Hey, boss, I'm over in Bryant Park, where your girl and her boss were having lunch. They stayed for a while talking, and the boss just left, leaving her alone in the park. She took a walk and looks like she's tired and is hanging back on a park bench. I looked in the binoculars, and her eyes were closed, leaving her wide open."

I held the phone to my forehead, taking in a deep frustrated breath before getting back on. "You do not leave for one second, and you keep her in your view. I'm on my way."

I parked my car and met up with Oleg. He still had eyes on her, and sure enough, my dove had fallen asleep right out in the very open for anything to happen to her.

She looked breathtaking, and her cheeks were sun-kissed. As I walked closer to where she was, my heart began to race just enough for me to feel the excitement and anticipation build on talking to her again. Once I was right in front of her and effectively blocking the sunshine from her view, I gently stroked her cheek, hoping not to startle her.

When her eyes opened, she took a second to focus on who she was seeing, and I heard her whisper, "TD." And then she said, "I was dreaming about you." Maybe not realizing what she had just disclosed but purely to my delight, she was now fully awake and clearly embarrassed. Sitting upright, she straightened her skirt and reached for her bag.

I saw my opportunity and went for it. "Dreaming about me? How lovely to hear. I'm flattered."

"You're here," she said, still looking overwhelmed by our chance encounter. But in my world, everything was strategically thought out and followed through.

"And so are you, for that matter. What a beautiful coincidence seeing you two times in one week and in a city as large as New York. And they say lightning doesn't strike twice." I tried to make a lighthearted joke, but she seemed guarded around me and that pleased me in a way because she should be.

"I'm embarrassed. I shouldn't be here."

"Why should you feel embarrassed?" I questioned, moving my hand toward hers.

"Well, for starters, I was already mugged once this week. Falling asleep in the park is not the wisest decision I could make."

"And the other reason? I believe you said you were dreaming about me? I would love to know what about."

"No, you wouldn't. Don't mind me and my rambling. It's been a stressful and long week, and today was no better. I think I should have just stayed home and not braved the big world for one more day."

"I disagree with your theory, because if you had, then we wouldn't be sitting here right now on this bench on a gorgeous summer day in the park. And…" I leaned in closer to stroke her cheek and said, "You are far too innocent to be out here on your own, and I am forever thankful to be here to watch over you. It's what I was trying to do for you the other day, but you ran from me before I had the chance to." I never stopped touching her and was content in knowing she was not pulling away from me.

She leaned into my palm and told me she was sorry for doing that. "That day was a blur to me, and the minute I left the police station, I immediately regretted my decision, so I'll say the words now that I should have told you back at the police station. Thank you for taking care of me, and I am sorry for leaving."

"Apology accepted. Now, how about I escort you home or wherever you wish to go?"

"I don't want to go home," she said and then leaned once more into the palm of my hand.

"Oh, okay. Where do you want to go?"

"I just want to sit here. I won't fall asleep again. I swear all I wanted to do was close my eyes for a second, but I guess I was more tired than usual."

"It's understandable after what you had to endure this week. How are your legs feeling?"

"My one knee is a little tender, another reason why I sat down to rest. I have some bruises, but they are healing. You did a great job tending to them, thank you again. I don't have much I can offer to show my appreciation, but can I buy you a cup of coffee?"

I took a minute to look into her eyes. She was so young and beautiful. *Surely too innocent for me, but I would never hurt her, just worship the ground she walked on.*

"Coffee sounds perfect. But first, will you grant me one request?" I asked.

"Yes, of course."

"Will you tell me your name?"

She closed her eyes, and I swore the color in her cheeks changed to crimson after hearing my question. She extended her arm out to me as if she was shaking my hand in a proper greeting. "Hello, my name is Willow Pierce."

Taking her hand in mine and bringing it to my lips to kiss, I said, "Pleasure to know you, Willow Pierce. My name is Valentin Vasiliev, but you already know that from the business card I had given you." I reminded her of that fact.

"I'm sorry but I didn't keep it, and I must have forgotten. Oh, what you must think of me." She pulled back her hand and went to stand but was a little wobbly in her heels.

"Hey, don't go. It's not a big deal. You know my name now, and I know yours. Unless you've changed your mind on coffee?"

"No, I haven't. Thank you for understanding."

"Thank you for the invitation."

I held her hand all the way back to my car and then grazed her back as I helped her inside the car. Oleg was nowhere to be found. I slid into the driver's side and brought my car to life. "So, where shall we go?"

"I've changed my mind on coffee. It has to be five o'clock somewhere. How about a drink instead?"

"Sounds good. I know the perfect place we can go." *And so it begins, Willow Pierce. I have every intention of making you mine and never letting you go.*

Tolerating the congested traffic was worth the headache because of the passenger who sat beside me. I parked my car in one of the many bays I owned down here in the garage. She looked around and then back to me.

"Where are we?"

"My apartment. I live on the top floor."

"Um, I don't know about this."

I leaned in to cup her face in my hands. "I promise you, Willow, you are completely safe with me. I will never hurt you. I just thought my place would be quieter and more intimate. If you are uncomfortable in any way, I promise to drive you home, but please give me a chance."

"You seem so easy to trust, and I don't know why that is, but it's just a feeling I've had since the day we met."

"You can trust me, Willow. I am a man of my word. Please, let me show you inside, and as much as I love your shoes and the way they make your gorgeous legs look, they also seem to be uncomfortable."

"Very observant of you. Thank you for the compliment. I'm very short, so the higher the better in my choice of footwear."

"Good, it's settled then," I said and quickly got out and walked around to the passenger side to open her door and help her out.

CHAPTER
Seven

Willow

Once I agreed to go up to his apartment, I felt a twinge of regret. I think it was my fear of the unknown, because let's be real here, he was a stranger. A kind one, but still a stranger. He never let go of my hand, and when he did, it was moved to the small of my back to guide me off the elevator and into his apartment. We traveled up forty-seven flights of his sixty-story building.

He accessed the elevator by using an antique-looking key, which just made him all that more interesting. We were greeted by staff at the double doors. They greeted him with pleasantries and welcomed me inside of his luxurious home.

"Good afternoon, Mr. Vasiliev," his house manager said as she smiled between the both of us.

"Hello, Marta. We will be dining out on the terrace this evening."

Dinner with Valentin? This is a surprise, but do I want to stay? Hell yes, I do!

"Do you have any requests before I begin?" I watched him turn and give me his complete attention. "Willow, do you have a favorite meal you enjoy?"

I was taken aback with the question and probably looked like a deer in headlights. "Thank you for offering, but I'm sure whatever you choose will be fine."

"Very well, I'll choose this time, and you can pick next time."

Oh my goodness, he's confident and very sure of himself.

"Marta, we would like beef bourguignon paired with green vegetables and roasted red potatoes. Please retrieve the 2003 Chateau Petrus Pomerol from the wine cellar, which I would like now."

"Yes, sir, right away."

"Please, Willow, make yourself at home." His hand returned to the small of my back again, but this time he pressed a little firmer when I hesitated. "Are you okay?" he asked.

"Yes, I'm fine. I guess I'm just wondering what's happening here right now."

"I'm not sure I follow. Please explain."

"Valentin, I am so out of your league it's almost embarrassing for you more so than me. I mean, look at where you live, and dinner on the terrace, and the fancy wine. I don't belong here, and I'm feeling a little overwhelmed."

"Hmmm, this is a first, and I have to say very refreshing to hear. Willow, I can't help where I live and the fine things I have in my home, nor will I apologize for my eclectic palette when it comes to fine wine. Having said that, I painstakingly disagree with how you feel about yourself and whether you belong here or not. And what bothers me more is that you may actually believe the words you are saying, and that will never do."

"I've offended you, I'm sorry. I'm going to go before I make a bigger ass out of myself." I could feel my skin begin to heat with every word I just said to this beautiful man. I was beyond foolish, and I had never wanted an escape more than right now.

As I pressed the button to the elevator, two strong arms were around my waist and pulled me against a solid wall of muscle. I gasped in surprise as he turned me around and held me in place. I wasn't going anywhere, and the intensity in his eyes was exciting me more than scaring me.

"Willow, please stay with me. I want you to have dinner with me. I promise it will not go any further than you want it to. I would love the pleasure of your company tonight, and the view from my terrace is amazing. Please, will you reconsider?"

"Yes, I'll stay. Thank you, Valentin," and once I said the words, his mouth was on mine, taking the most passionate kiss I had ever experienced.

When our lips parted, he held my face and kissed me, again and again, moving slowly to my neck. I cried out in pure pleasure as I felt him sink his teeth into my skin. He didn't hurt me. If I was being honest with myself, I wanted him to do it again. I wanted to be marked by this man, and the more I craved it, his arousal grew stronger. I was completely breathless when he finally pulled away and looked intently into my eyes.

"Did I hurt you?" he asked and then touched the raised bloom on my neck.

"Not in a way I didn't like," I said, and then he gave me a devilish smile that I felt all the way down to my toes. *This man was dangerous and intoxicating. With just one amazing kiss, he easily had the power to ruin me for other men.*

"Come, let's have some wine and talk."

I said nothing more and followed quietly behind him as he wrapped his arm around my waist.

"This is your terrace?" I asked.

"Yes, do you like it?"

"More than like. It's stunning and on the line of an exotic botanical garden. What's not to love about it? And you have the Empire State Building in your backyard."

"How do you do that?" he asked.

"Do what?"

"I don't know exactly. I guess what delights me is the way you look at things and give a very honest perspective on what your eyes see. It's rare to meet someone who is real, and you are truly the first person I have met that I can say that about."

I was about to say something in return when my cell phone began to ring. "I'm sorry, I thought it was on silent. It could be work. Will you excuse me?"

"Of course, I'll refill our glasses."

I waited until Valentin was far enough away, and then I answered an unknown caller. "Hello, this is Willow,"

"Hello, this is Zara Hill calling. I hope I'm not disturbing you, but I was awaiting your call about the proposal I had made on your behalf to Madeline. Have you given it any thought?"

"Excuse me while I fangirl a bit. I can't believe I am speaking to Zara Hill."

"Oh please, darling, I'm a designer and a businesswoman just like you, and I want you on my team. Please tell me you have good news for me?"

"To be perfectly honest, I'm kind of starstruck at the moment. Today has been the most unexpected, and I need to catch my breath and think about what this will all mean for me. I'm loyal to Madeline, and I know what level of commitment you will need from me in order to complete what you are asking. It's the biggest project I have ever worked on, and frankly, I'm a little nervous."

"I understand your caution, but I assure you that we will all work together to make us a great deal of money, and for you, Willow Pierce, this is an opportunity that has the ability to solidify your career and where you will take it next."

"I absolutely agree. This is why I'm nervous. It's a huge undertaking and responsibility. I only get one chance to get it right."

"Then get it right the first time and join my team. This is a time-sensitive deal, and with all due respect, I need an answer and will give you until nine a.m. tomorrow morning. If your answer is no, then I will move on and make someone else's dreams come true. Have a good night, Willow."

"Ms. Hill, hello? Fuck! She hung up." I didn't hear him return to the terrace until he placed the wine and our glasses down to the table.

"Problem?" he inquired.

"I'm sorry if you heard that. I may have just sunk my career before it truly got started."

"Here, I'm sure it's not all that bad. Come, sit with me, and tell me all about it."

"You really want to know?"

"Yes, I do. We are getting to know one another, and this is how we do it, by talking." He smirked again and sipped his wine, urging me to do the same.

"What do you want to know?"

"Anything and everything."

"I'm not all that interesting, but here it goes, and please try to keep up. It's a telling tale."

"You are delightful, just like a beautiful dove getting ready to spread her wings and take flight."

"That is probably the kindest thing anyone has ever said to me."

"If that's true, then you are not talking to the right people." He lifted my hand and again brought it to his lips to kiss me ever so gently.

I wanted more but continued talking to him. "I've been living in the city for a little more than a year. I live with my grandmother who is never there, so I practically have the apartment all to myself. I was born and raised in a small beach town in New Jersey by my amazing mother. After receiving my business degree, I finished my education at the FIT, and I've been working for MW Designs since then. It's a great opportunity, but her company has been struggling. I sometimes fear I'm staying on out of loyalty to our friendship. She's been great to me, but now out of the blue, I get the offer of a lifetime."

"What's the offer?" he asked, taking a sip of his wine.

"I've been approached to design an entire cast ensemble wardrobe for a Broadway show, and under the tutelage of Zara Hill. I'm at a loss for words, and if I don't say yes, she's going to leave me in the dust and instead make another designer very happy."

"If she were smart, and I know she is because I know Zara, she will wait for you. I believe this is her tactic to light the fire under your hesitation."

"You know Zara?"

"I do. We've been friends for years, and we went to school together for one year until I began traveling abroad. What are you afraid of, Willow?"

"What makes you believe I am afraid?"

"It's in your eyes. They tell the story of your life, and it hasn't always been easy for you. So what makes you believe this opportunity will be just that: easy? You have to work for everything you have, and you're right to be cautious, but that's also an admirable quality in someone who is so young. Your decision to weigh the pros and cons is wise, but don't mistake her patience for weakness, because Zara can be brutal when it comes to her business. She only wants the best, and for her to want you, well, that's a feat in itself and one chance I would not say no to. It's only my opinion but an honest one at that."

"Okay, I'll do it!" I blurted out. "Oh, my goodness! Where did that just come from?"

"It was dying to get out! I just led you where you wanted to go. How about you call her back and tell her the good news?"

"No, I have until nine tomorrow morning, and I certainly don't want to look too eager. She came to me, and I think some humility will do Zara some good."

"I couldn't have said it better. Cheers to you, Willow."

We clinked our wine glasses together and celebrated my new job. *Madeline is going to freak out when I tell her.* I wouldn't have reached my decision without Valentin. He made me feel alive just with the words he said.

"This was the best meal I have ever tasted, and the company was so much more. Thank you, Valentin, for a wonderful evening."

"It was my pleasure to dine in your company, Willow. Won't you stay for a nightcap?"

"Tempting, but I think it's best I say goodnight while I still have the willpower to walk out of here. You make it difficult to think straight."

"You, Ms. Pierce, are very good for a man's ego. May I ask you one last question before my driver takes you home?" I nodded. "Earlier today when we met again at the park, you said you were dreaming about me, and then you said, 'TD.' As delighted I was to know that I've been on your mind, is there someone else in the picture I need to know about? Because I want to see you again, and I do not share."

He's direct. I have a feeling Valentin Vasiliev is going to be a handful.

"TD stands for tall and dark, my nickname for you since I had forgotten your real name. Good night, Valentin." I winked and stepped inside of his elevator, leaving him amused.

CHAPTER Eight

Valentin

I steadied my breathing and got myself in check as I watched her leave. Damn, she was intoxicating. I didn't want her to go, but I knew I couldn't overwhelm her with the secret thoughts that occupied my mind. She was adorable when I asked her about the name "TD." She couldn't hide her shy smile. Before I knew what it meant, I hoped she wasn't going to tell me she had a boyfriend in her life and that was his name. In a short amount of time, I already felt too emotionally invested with the beautiful Willow Pierce to ever just step aside and bow out gracefully. No, she was special and worth fighting for. My rational side was telling me to wine and dine her and have a lot of dates getting to know one another. The other part? The one that wants to touch, taste, and take all of her, was in a battle with patience, a quality I'd never been good with but would try for Willow.

I knew I could have convinced her to stay the night if I had more time, but Zara calling and interrupting our evening doused cold water on my plan. Although by doing so, she ultimately changed Willow's mind, which was exactly what I wanted her to do. I would do everything in my power to help her along with her career.

Since she left, I'd been reading her file on repeat to commit every last thing about Willow to memory. She shared so much with me tonight, and I shared nothing about myself, but that would change once I saw her again.

It bothered her about my obvious wealth. It angered me that she spoke poorly about her worth. She was a thousand times better than me, and all that I had in this life would never come close to what she had to offer: her heart. *She will willingly come to me and give me everything I desire from her. The wheels are already in motion. Our kiss and touches between us tonight proved without a doubt that we have a fiery connection between us.*

Oleg checked in after he watched her enter her building and go up to her apartment. I told him that I wanted him on her detail until I said otherwise. No more subway rides or taxi cabs unless it was Oleg doing the driving. He succeeded in driving her today, so he should have no problem doing so tomorrow.

Although I practiced within the law, throughout the years, I had made my share of enemies because of what I did and the last name I carried. I'd never had any real harm come to me, but with Willow now in my life, I had to take every necessary precaution to keep her safe. Once we get photographed together, the news of our relationship would spread like wildfire.

I phoned Zara back and thanked her for her help. She was still in a melancholy mood from my earlier threat. "Your timing was impeccable, and it swayed Willow to come to her decision."

"Valentin, this is a big risk taking on someone with little experience. If this goes south, I will be a laughing stock in the industry and will lose the trust of my investors who invested a lot of money in my brand."

"You worry for nothing, and I want you to stop it right now. Willow does have what it takes, and I believe you will be pleasantly surprised by the work she creates for you. You have to be patient and put yourself in a mentor state of mind. I can remember some years ago when you walked in Willow's shoes. Same rules, different playing field. You remember that, don't you, Zara? Do not disappoint me. Good night."

The next morning, I was up at dawn and decided to run in Central Park. I got in close to ten miles before returning back to my building. I showered and dressed for the day and made plans to meet Willow for lunch. I was sure she had phoned Zara by now with her decision. If not, I would have heard from Zara.

Unfortunately, Willow did not drive in with Oleg this morning, but it wasn't his fault. She was picked up by her boss, and they drove in together just after eight a.m. I figured by noon, she would be ready for lunch, and it would give me an opportunity to see where she worked and meet Madeline.

I had been working in my home office for most of the morning when Marta knocked on my door. "Come in," I said without looking up from my screen. I was finishing up a legal brief for court next week and never liked to be disturbed when I was working. "Yes, Marta, what is it?"

"I'm sorry to intrude, Mr. Vasiliev, but you have a call holding on your private line. It was patched through to the main house, not sure why you didn't get it in your office."

"It came through. I chose to ignore it. Don't you see that I'm working?"

"Yes, I do, sir, but it's your father phoning from Russia."

"You can go now," I said and instructed Marta to close the door behind her.

I spoke several languages, including my father's language of Russian. He instilled his teachings of the dialect since I was a baby beginning my first words. I hated it, because the more I spoke, I developed a strong accent as if I was born there. Once I was out on my own in college, behind my father's back I worked with several speech therapists to control my accent and speak a clearer American. I developed a way to control both, but when my father was present, I was only allowed to speak Russian.

I released a breath and took the call, greeting him perfectly. I explained I was working and apologized for the delay. He understood and got to his reason for the call. My mother had taken ill, and their return trip home would be delayed. He explained it was nothing too serious, but they erred on the side of caution and didn't want to fly until she was well enough to travel. The businesses were covered, but his only concern was Sasha, my younger brother who tended to be on the reckless side, especially when he wasn't under the watchful eye of my father.

I waited for him to mention anything about Willow, but he didn't, and I was relieved. I would have that conversation when the time was right and he was home in front of me to hear it. Sergei would not say anything, nor would Oleg. They were the only two who knew about Willow, and that's how it would remain until my father returned.

We spoke for another ten minutes, and then I wished him and my mother well. I was saddened to hear about mother falling ill, but she was happier when they traveled home. It was not often, and it always carried a great deal of risk. My father, Alaric, was feared by many, and if you had enough balls to take him on, you ran the risk of not coming out alive. I believed it was that very fear Sergei warned me about on the night I taught Mr. Rickards a lesson.

The streets of the Garment District were bustling with tourists, shoppers, and vendors. If you worked in the fashion industry, this was the place to be. Somewhere in this chaos was my woman. My driver parked the car, and I stepped out to take a good look at the warehouse that housed MW Designs.

I expected to find a decrepit building, because most of them around here were in need of upgrades. The area had gone through a huge revitalization that cost millions upon millions of dollars, but some businesses were not so fortunate to cash in on that opportunity and lost everything they had invested in, leaving their properties abandoned.

The front of the building was all glass, showcasing the retail space for the public. It was behind the scenes that I was most curious about. After I checked in with the front desk receptionist, I was shown where to find Willow. The building had a top floor they used for design and office space. I walked around to scan the room until I found Willow talking to an older woman, who I assumed was her boss, Madeline.

The room had large pillars that I could easily stand behind and not be seen. No one was paying particular attention to me as I remained the silent voyeur watching Willow work. She was pinning fabric to a mannequin and was very animated in explaining to the fellow designers what she was doing.

"I'm telling you, kid, you made the right decision coming on board with Zara. I've known her a long time, and she is a straight shooter." I listened intently as her boss sang Zara's praises to Willow, or more like continued with the sales pitch.

"Look, Madeline, I know what is at stake here for you. We have to make this partnership work, or it's make it or break it. The bar has been raised, and I just feel that I'm the one balancing it. It's a great deal of pressure. I work at my own pace, but now joining forces with Zara, it's all going to change."

"You know, Willow, this is nerves, nothing more. You're not always going to feel this way. Once you get your first line under your belt, it's like riding a bike."

"Yes, but this is not a runway show at Fashion Week. This is Broadway, totally different. My head is just spinning, and believe it or not, I do have other things on my mind other than work."

"Oh, really? Tell me more."

"Okay, don't freak out, but I met a man."

"Now you're talking. Where?"

"Believe it or not, at the police station on the same day I was mugged. He's a lawyer and just happened to be there. He was really decent and helped me out. I'm telling you, Madeline, that day was a complete shitshow from the start, and the only thing that was good was meeting TD."

"TD? That's his name?" she smirked at Willow, who still hasn't seen me eavesdropping on their conversation. I knew eventually I'd have to make my appearance known before I was discovered, but I was also curious to hear anything else she would say.

"It's what I call him. His name is Valentin, and he's totally dreamy. And he sure can kiss. I still feel him on my skin. It's not like I have all this experience with men, but this guy is in a league all on his own."

Oh, Willow, it's your inexperience that I valued most. You're so young and innocent and not jaded by the cruelties of this vast world. If you give me a chance, a real chance to show you the man I truly am, I would show you the very best of myself and make you happy, I thought to myself and I remained hidden.

I never heard her boss's reply. They were interrupted by a coworker, and it was the perfect opportunity to let her know I was here.

It warmed my heart to know she had been thinking about me. *And, my beautiful dove, you will feel much more than my mouth on yours. I intend to kiss every delectable inch of your porcelain skin.*

CHAPTER
Nine

Willow

"Is this ready to go?" asked Peter, who was our sample cutter and the very best.

"Yes, just give me one more minute on this hem, and it's all yours," I replied.

"It looks great, Willow."

"Thanks! Be careful with my baby."

"You got it."

Madeline jumped in, "Okay, kid, you had a temporary reprieve. Now tell me more about TD."

"I told you everything. He's older, sophisticated, and has a hint of an accent. I was too shy to ask him about it, but I think it's European."

"What does he look like?"

"He's very tall and towers over me. He has dark hair perfectly styled and combed back. Although I didn't get up close and personal, I'm assuming he has a beautiful, rock hard body underneath his clothes. Just a guess. He's so strong, and the way he held me was intense."

"Sounds like you have it bad for this guy."

"Who wouldn't? And if you saw him in person you would agree with me."

"Well, I guess my chance is coming sooner than I think, because based on your description, your prince charming is walking towards us right now."

I looked over my shoulder and sure enough, it was him. "OMG! I must look a mess." I quickly opened my desk drawer and reached for my compact mirror. "Will you look at me, Madeline? My hair is a mess, and I'm not wearing any makeup. Yeah, I have a chance with this guy."

"I would say you have more than a chance," he said so casually as he strode into my workspace and reached for my hand to kiss. "And what did I say about talking that way about yourself?"

I had to catch my breath and steady my rapidly beating heart before I could find the right words to say. He stared at me with his deep chocolate color eyes as if he was trying to look into my soul. I had lost all ability to function when Madeline bumped my shoulder.

"Aren't you going to introduce us?" she asked.

I blinked a couple of times and watched him return a mischievous smile. "Yes, sorry. Madeline Waters, this is Valentin Vasiliev, my…"

"*Boyfriend* is the word Willow is trying to say. It's a pleasure to meet you, Madeline."

"Likewise, handsome."

While Madeline flirted with Valentin, I was still trying to wrap my head around the word "boyfriend." I had one date with him, if you want to call it that, and now he'd slapped a label on us. *OMG! An "us" equals couple. Am I ready for that? He doesn't seem like a guy who is looking for casual. No, he wants a relationship with me. Why else would he be audacious to introduce himself as my boyfriend?*

Valentin was still holding my hand, an intimate act I found out quickly he liked doing. When my senses returned, he shifted, and his attention was back on me.

I asked, "What are you doing here? I would have thought you would be working?"

"I was, this morning in my home office. But now I'm here and would love to take you to lunch. Are you free?"

"Yes, she is," Madeline said over my shoulder, making him grin even wider.

"Hello? I'm in the room," I called out.

"Yes, and you have a guest wanting to take you to lunch, so go and have fun," she said.

"Are you sure? We have a lot of work to do."

"A girl has to eat, right? And the company is not half-bad either. Go! We will be here when you get back."

As Valentin stood confidently, assuming he could just interrupt my work day and sweep me off my feet, I on the other hand needed to take a minute.

"Madeline, would you please excuse us? I'd like to have a word with Valentin."

"Sure, kid, have fun." She winked and stifled her laugh as she closed the door. *Good to know I could entertain my friend.*

"You seemed to have charmed my boss. It's not very often she is as carefree as she was when she met you. Must be a great quality to have when it comes to women. Just knowing how to say the right things to make one turn their head in your direction and bend at your will."

"Hmmm, here's the thing about what you just said. I'll admit, I can be charming when I want to be, but there's only one woman I would like to turn in my direction, and she's standing right in front of me. Don't overthink it. It's just lunch." He extended his hand out to me and gave me a devilish smile.

There was a part of me that wanted to squeal like a teenager and hug myself, but I restrained myself and simply said thank you. I grabbed my purse, and we walked out together and into his waiting car.

He opened the door for me, and I slid across the bench seat as Valentin moved closer, taking my face in his hands while ravaging my mouth in a delicious kiss.

"I missed you, beautiful dove," he whispered in my ear and then placed a trail of warm languorous kisses down my neck.

He smelled amazing. It was so hard to think around him. I was slowly giving in when back at my office, I wanted him to work for my attention without expecting me to just fall into his arms.

When I couldn't think of anything to say, I simply said, "Hello, Valentin." I blushed, barely containing my emotions. "Did you want to do that back at my office?"

"Say it again."

"What? Your name?"

"Yes, my dove, I love how it sounds coming from your mouth. It gets me hard." He must have sensed my reaction to his words and pulled back just a little to look at me. "I'm sorry, was that too forward? It's difficult to manage how I feel when you are this close to me."

"It's fine. You just took me by surprise. May I ask you a question?"

"Baby, you can ask me anything."

"Why do you call me 'dove'? Does it have significance for you?"

"Yes, it does. What it represents is you. A dove is pure. A symbol of innocence, gentleness, and when I dream about you at night, it brings me a great deal of peace until I can see you again. To talk to you. To hold you. To kiss you. I want all of those things with you, and so much more if you are willing to give me a chance."

"Is that why you told Madeline you were my boyfriend?"

"Yes, because it's going to happen. It's what I want."

"And what you want, you usually get?"

"Among other things, but yes, that's the way it works in my world."

"Valentin…"

"Shhh, you don't have to give me an answer now. Let's just go to lunch, and we can talk."

"Okay, where to?"

"I know of a place. I hear the food is excellent."

I didn't notice the name of the restaurant until Valentin was holding my hand and guiding me inside. I grabbed his other arm to make him stop.

"What's wrong, dove?"

I was trembling and felt the color slowly drain from my face. "I don't like this place, Valentin, and I won't eat here. Please take me somewhere else or drive me back to work." I tried to be strong in my stance, but his eyes burned into my body, and it was like being pulled under his control. The scariest part was I think I liked it.

"It's alright, dove. You are safe with me, and no one will ever hurt you again."

Again? How would he know about what happened to me with the café owner? Did he read my police report? I shrugged off the doubt and trusted Valentin. We stepped inside, and the hostess showed us to a table in front of the window. He pulled out my chair for me, and I smiled at his kind gesture. *If Valentin is anything, charming is at the top of his list.* I nervously looked around the restaurant and didn't see the owner. I wasn't very good at hiding my feelings, and it was becoming virtually impossible to hide them from Valentin.

"Relax, dove, I've got you. Why don't you look at the menu? What are you in the mood for?"

He had a keen ability to read my expressions, so I was hoping he had a gateway to my thoughts as well. The only thing I wanted in my life was a fashion career, which was why I worked so hard in school and everything personal in my life took a backseat to all of that. Now, this gorgeous and charismatic man wanted me, and I wanted him too with every fiber of my being. *Should I just tell him? Or judging by the way he is looking at me right now, does he already know?*

He placed his menu down on the table and balanced his chin on his hands. *Again with the magnetic eyes. I swear if I don't stop staring,*

I'm never going to be able to pull away. I swear he was sex on a stick.

I asked, "Have you decided what you want?"

"I believe I have, and I'm not talking about lunch."

The temperature suddenly rose in the room, and Valentin flashed me a look of satisfied pleasure. He brought my hand to his lips and issued me a silent promise to be continued.

"Welcome to Café West. Your waiter will be right with you. I apologize for the delay."

I didn't need to look up to see who was at our table. Valentin's hold on my hand tightened a bit and then addressed the man who was at our table, not knowing he was the asshole who threw me out when I needed help.

Once their eyes connected, and Valentin acknowledged him with a simple "Thank you, Mr. Rickards," the owner stepped backward, and he looked almost fearful. He certainly didn't look the same from the last time I had seen him. *Had he been in an accident?* He was wearing a walking cast and used a cane for support.

"It's quite alright, I'm suddenly in the mood for something else, and it's not on your menu. Darling, shall we go?" Valentin extended his hand out for me to take, never taking his eyes off the owner.

He had to recognize me, right? I had already humiliated myself once already with this guy. I wasn't about to do it again and not in front of Valentin.

"Yes, let's go. The food here sucks anyway, and I heard they have a rodent problem," I said louder for his patrons to hear me. I earned a wink from Valentin, and he took my hand and led me away from the café. *Good riddance, asshole!*

"That was fun, but we still have to eat. How about dinner tonight? My place, say seven?"

"I think that sounds perfect," I responded.

"You're perfect," he said and kissed me sensually on my cheek. He placed a call to have some food delivered for me back at work. "Be a good girl and eat all of your lunch. You are going to need all of your energy for our date this evening."

And with his parting words, I knew there was no turning away from him now.

CHAPTER Ten

Valentin

"Y ou look pleased with yourself," Oleg said as I walked inside my apartment, where I had instructed him to meet me.

"As a matter of fact, I am. I saw the café owner today. He looks well."

"I agree, considering the beating you gave him the other night."

"He deserved it and was lucky to have only suffered a beating. I was in a generous mood that night."

"What are you doing, Valentin?"

"Pertaining? I think you need to be more specific?" I said and poured a couple of shots. "Za zda-ró-vye! Now, what's on your mind?" I questioned and knocked back my drink before pouring another.

"With this girl, Valentin. She's barely legal, for Christ's sake. She has no place in your life, and once your father finds out about her, he will make sure she never does."

"I will handle my father."

"You don't get it, Valentin! No one handles Alaric Vasiliev. Many men have tried and failed."

"Oleg, my life is not yours to worry about, and it goes double for my father. This is the life you have signed on for. It was never for me, and this is why I've worked my entire adult life distancing myself from it."

"Yes, that may be true, but when you need a favor, we both know damn well who you call. Isn't that right, Valentin?"

"Watch it, old man."

"Or what? You'll have me tied to a chair and beaten within an inch of my life? Sorry, but I've already danced to that song and dance many times in my life. Don't you get it? I've looked out for you your entire life since you were young, and I'm doing the same for you now. Sure, I can watch over her and pretend to be the friendly taxicab driver but my first priority is you, and I don't want to see you get hurt."

"I appreciate your concern, but I'm fine. This is my family, and I have never dishonored it, nor will I ever. My father knows I would do anything within reason for him, but he also knows that I am my own man and will not be told who I can love and share my life with. It's time to let old ghosts rest, my friend. Tatianna was never meant to be mine, no matter what two men promised to each other. She's living her life and is happy, so please allow me to do the same."

"Very well. The subject is closed."

"Good, let's keep it that way. As for Willow, you will be her security until I say otherwise. She may believe she can handle this city all on her own, but we know better, don't we?"

"Sadly, you're not wrong. I promise to keep her safe."

"I expect nothing less." I took my old friend into an embrace and slapped his back a couple of times. "You're a good man, Oleg. Thank you for always having my back."

"Always, Valentin."

I looked all around my empty apartment that stood high above the busy streets below. My view was spectacular, a view worth millions, and it was all mine to enjoy. Up until meeting Willow, I never believed I would want to share this life with anyone. I chose to be satisfied with that line of reasoning but secretly yearned to find the "one," and now that I had, everything had changed. I stared at the same view I'd been looking at for the past two years, but today, it's as if I was seeing it for the first time. *I want more and I want it with her.* It's just that simple, and that is the way I will convey it to my father when the time is right.

The rest of the afternoon I focused on Willow and the incredible night we were going to have. I knew it was fast, but after all the hot flirting we did with one another this afternoon, my dove made her intentions very clear that she wanted exactly what I wanted. *And it will happen as soon as I get my hands on her. She will be under me in my bed and will be staying the night, so I can wake up to her beautiful face and do it all over again.*

My driver sent me a text that Willow had been delivered and was on her way up to me. My heart was filled with anticipation waiting for her to step out of the elevator and into my arms. I was holding two dozen long-stemmed white roses for her. They reminded me of her, and what I was most looking forward to seeing was her blush upon receiving something so simple as flowers. This beautiful girl needed to be cherished, and it was something I was very good at doing.

At the sound of the bell, the doors opened and out walked Willow Pierce in a dress that left very little to one's imagination and had the ability to bring me down to my fucking knees.

"You look..." I was having trouble articulating the right reaction to her.

Then she let me off the hook and did it for me. "Pretty?"

"I think you can do better than that. How about 'stunningly gorgeous,' and that's for your choice of shoes. I haven't begun to find the right adjective for your dress."

"You are too sweet, and thank you. You look very handsome and relaxed. Am I overdressed?"

"No, you're perfect. I figured you have seen me in a suit, so I nixed the jacket and tie and went with a shirt and slacks. Do you approve?"

"Not that you need it, but yes, you look amazing. Are those for me?" asked Willow, as she directed my attention to the bouquet of flowers I was holding.

"Only for you," I winked and took one single flower from the arrangement and handed it to her but not before placing a kiss down to her hand. "Thank you for joining me tonight."

"Thank you for asking."

"I would have been a fool not to. Come, let's have some champagne and hors-d'oeuvres. I'm not sure what you like, so I had my chef prepare an assortment of choices for you."

"It all looks amazing, and I'm not sure what to try first."

"Try one or try them all. Each selection has a unique flavor for even the pickiest of palettes."

"Okay, I'm intrigued. Choose for me."

"Oh, dove, I would be happy to. We have cold and hot selections. The first platter is a smoked salmon with blini."

"Blini?"

"Another word for crepes. For the hot selection, we have Vareniki which are Russian pirogies. It is amazing, and the cherry sauce gives it just the right amount of sweetness to its creamy cheese and potato filling."

She loved the food selections and appreciated my talented chef. A few moments later, I noticed her sitting quietly. "Feeling flushed, Willow?" I teasingly asked as I began to stroke my finger up her soft and silky leg.

"Will you tell me something, Valentin, and please be honest with me?"

"Yes, of course, I will. I will never lie to you, beautiful dove."

"How old are you?"

"I'm thirty-two, soon to be thirty-three at the end of August. And you?"

"Something tells me I think you already know, but I'm twenty-two and about to have a birthday at the end of the month. Am I wrong, Valentin? Did you already know how old I was?"

"And if I say yes? Then what?"

"Then it raises several more questions."

"Okay, ask me anything."

"Are you sure you're ready for that? I tend to be sometimes too inquisitive for my own good."

"How about we simplify and just say you're a little curious. And why wouldn't you be? A stranger out of nowhere enters your life in a not so orthodox manner and literally trips over his own feet hoping to convince you to go out with him."

"And when I do, I insult him in his own home."

"No, you insulted yourself more than me. Why do you do that? You are beautiful, talented, and gifted. What you see in this apartment is just furniture and some overpriced artwork on the walls. There's no point in denying that I am a wealthy man and I do like the finer things, but nothing is finer than the woman in front of me. I have been enchanted by you since the moment I've met you, Willow. I know I must sound like a crazy man, but it's the truth."

"You don't even know me. I'm just a girl from New Jersey trying to make it in the big city."

"And by telling me this, do you think it will make me want you any less?"

"I don't know. I just know that I have never met anyone like you before, and all these feelings I have been having is making my mind want things I never entertained before meeting you."

"Willow, you're not alone in this. I'm feeling the same way you are, maybe more so. Have we talked enough? Because I really want to kiss you."

"You may not want to after I tell you one more thing about me."

"Impossible," I said and pulled her right onto my lap, with my arms around her body. I was over the questions and answers for the evening, but I endured it for her.

"I'm a virgin, Valentin."

And you don't know how happy that makes me, sweetheart.

She continued, "It's not because I didn't want to. I came close a few times, but in the end, the guy was not the one, and I decided I didn't want a mistake like that on my conscience."

"Thank you for telling me. Can I kiss you now?"

"You still want to?" she asked incredulously.

"Like my next breath."

Finally, she let go of all the bullshit that was occupying her headspace and allowed me to kiss her without holding back. I knew what I was capable of when it came to fucking women. It was a take, control, and release. *Willow is not the only virgin here tonight. I plan to make love to her all through the night and give myself over to her completely.*

I held her face as her hands found my waist. My need for her was reaching an all-time high, and I was going to lose my fucking mind if I didn't get her naked and into my bed. Without another thought, I lifted her in my arms and carried her upstairs to my bedroom. My bed was raised high on a platform with four steps leading up to it. I placed her on the highest step as if she was standing on a pedestal. I took her mouth again and then stepped down, leaving her where she was.

"Undress for me, Willow, and do it slowly."

Her cheeks flushed, and she bit her lip at my request. She was like a blossoming flower, her petals began to slowly open and she was mine for the taking.

"So beautiful, my dove. Don't be bashful. Show me your body."

With perfect submission, she pulled the thin strap tied around her neck, and with one tug, it fell down her chest, revealing perfect breasts with pink pebbled nipples. I strode over to where she was standing in perfect attention for me, and my two hands traveled up her legs to her center.

"Is this for me, dove?" Her arousal was strong, practically soaked and ready for my mouth to devour. "Out of all the choices we had to eat tonight, your pussy is the only flavor I want on my tongue."

Her hands found the sides of my head and pulled me closer to the junction of her thighs. Her dress was bunched up around her hips, giving me the clear path to begin my feast on her body. Her head thrashed back as she voiced what she wanted.

"Please, Valentin, touch me," she called out again.

I stopped and stepped back to admire her. She was exquisite. I used my two fingers to lift under her chin.

"Patience my dove, I'll get you to where you want to go," I said as I continued to fuck her pussy with my tongue, in and out of her soaked core until she was nearly on the precipice of coming all over my face.

She was close, so very close. My balls were rock hard as I held back and gave her the release she needed to take all of me. She nearly fell back onto the bed, but I caught her just in time.

"You are so beautiful when you come," I said and then removed her dress, leaving her jeweled encrusted stilettoes on.

I stripped out of my clothes quicker than I could say "Willow," and then I was above her, with my hands holding hers. "We are going to take this nice and slow, and if you feel the slightest discomfort, I will stop. Am I clear?"

"Yes," she answered breathlessly.

With her permission, I entered her aroused core with one finger, moving it in a circular motion. Once she was used to the feeling, I added another, and then a third until she bucked her pelvis up against my dick that was already leaking pre-cum from its bulbous head.

I reached for a condom and sheathed my dick. What I wanted was to take her bare but she wasn't ready for that, not for her first time. I knew I had to be gentle, but the sounds coming from her mouth were proving to be difficult.

I covered her mouth with mine, believing I was the one in control, but it was my dove that was dominating me. Her hands broke free and traveled to my back, where her nails raked over my slicked skin.

"God, I fucking want you!" I gritted my jaw and let out a feral growl, moving down to her breast, suckling on her erect nipples. I licked, bit, and sucked until she shoved against my chest, asking me to finally take her. I repositioned my dick at her entrance and entered her body as gently as I could without hurting her. We both cried out in pleasure and pain. I felt her body shift from innocence to vixen with every move I made inside of her.

She wasn't a virgin anymore. No, she was fucking mine. My woman. Mine.

"My beautiful dove. You're mine, and I'm never letting you go."

She didn't correct me and continued to move under me as our bodies became one. We reached our climax together as Willow bit down into my shoulder, riding out her orgasms.

"Holy shit! Oh my god!" she said as she opened her eyes and looked into mine. "Valentin, that was…" She was a delight. I didn't want to pressure her by saying anything more, so I remained silent waiting for her to talk. "Thank you for being my first. I never imagined I would feel this way, and I'm finding it difficult to explain it all to you. And to hear you say that I'm yours has left me overcome with emotion, emotions that are very new to me."

"For me as well. You're exhausted and need some rest. Go to sleep and allow me to hold you for a while. We can talk later."

"Okay," she answered and then closed her eyes.

She was asleep on her stomach, exposing her smooth, soft, naked back. I was on my side just watching her sleep as I stroked my fingers along her spine. *I must have worn her out. I pray to God I didn't hurt her too badly. A virgin? A fucking virgin!?* I knew I was rough with her, but the sounds of pleasure she was making made me lose my fucking mind and take her as deep as I could. I was in complete heaven.

"Hey," I whispered as she began to rouse from sleep.

"How are you?"

"I'm wonderful but I should be asking about you," I held her face and leaned in to kiss her, looking into her eyes for anything else she might be hiding from me.

"Valentin, I'm a little sore but that's to be expected for my first time having sex. I'm happy."

"Correction, my dove, it was more than just sex here tonight. And I plan on showing you so much more once you're ready."

"What a romantic," she smiled and then buried her face in the crook of my neck, sighing contently, and then I heard a faint rumble from her stomach.

"Come, I need to feed you."

"I'm stuffed, Valentin. No more. I'll get fat, and then you won't want me anymore."

The sound of her deprecation of herself was grating on my last nerve. I hated with a vengeance when women didn't see the value they had within themselves, especially my woman. *It's going to stop right here right now.*

"Willow, I need you to look at me right now, and don't take your eyes off me," I demanded in a stronger tone that under different circumstances I wouldn't have used with her.

She asked, "Is something wrong?"

"Yes, I'm afraid there is."

"I understand, Valentin. I'll get my things and go home."

This is what I'm fucking talking about. How could she believe after everything we just shared that I would ask her to leave? As if I would ever allow her to?

"Stop it!" I growled and then picked her up and tossed her over my shoulder, where I slapped her bare ass, causing her to shout at me.

"Valentin! Are you insane? Put me down!" she shouted again, but I ignored her. She was going nowhere. She struggled in my arms until I placed her down in front of the floor length mirror.

"What are you doing?" she asked and then began to sob.

"Shhh, don't cry, Willow. We have a problem that needs rectifying. It's one I believed we already worked out, but now I'm not so sure. Tell me why you are so hard on yourself? Just look at yourself and see what I see every single time I look at you. You are nothing but amazing. I knew it from the start. Now I just need to make you believe it too."

Once the words left my mouth, she visibly calmed and relaxed. "I'm sorry, Valentin, I don't know why I talk this way."

"Yes, you do, and you are going to tell me the truth, or we will be doing something entirely different than I originally planned for us tonight."

"Okay, I guess it comes from years of feeling not wanted. My mom raised me on her own and worked incredibly hard to keep a roof over our heads and food on the table. My grandmother is amazing, and if it wasn't for her generosity I wouldn't be able to live and work in the city. However, although they were wonderful throughout my growing up, I still wanted my father. I wanted a father to take care of me and my mom."

"What happened to him?"

"He took off after I was born and waived his parental rights. I have no idea where he is in the world, and if my mom knows, she would never say. I missed out on all the daddy/daughter dances and just having a dad. Anytime I would try to talk about this with my mom, she would change the subject, and then it would be forgotten but never by me."

"Come, let's go to bed." I wrapped her in my arms and kissed her softly.

"It hurt for a long time, and I guess it still does in a small way. And there's you."

"What does that mean, dove?"

"I guess it means if the man I share DNA with didn't care enough to stick around, then why would an amazing man like yourself want to? I'm sure you are not hurting when it comes to finding a woman's attention, so here begs the question once again. Why would you want to be with me when you could probably have anyone in the world bow at your feet? Someone who is elegant and confident? A woman who when she enters a room, all eyes are on her to see what she will say or do next? Why me, Valentin?"

"Oh, my beautiful dove, allow me to enlighten you. You are so much more than who you see staring back at you. If anyone is going to be doing the bowing, it's going to be me worshipping and cherishing you every chance you allow me to. I won't lie and say I haven't enjoyed my fair share of a woman's company but that's in the past. My entire life changed the minute I laid eyes on you, and I never want to take them off you. You are all that I see and want. I'm afraid I have fallen very hard for you, Willow Pierce, and when I say 'You're mine,' no truer words have ever been spoken before. I can't let you go, and if by some chance you managed to, then I will follow you and do everything possible to win you back. It literally pains my heart when you are sad and speak so poorly about yourself, so please for the sake of my well-being, stop doing it. All I ask is for you to trust and allow me to try to show you how you should be taken care of in a way you deserve."

"I've never met anyone like you, Valentin."

"Good, because you are mine now and will never have the opportunity to meet anyone else."

I made love to the beautifully broken dove who had completely captivated my soul. I meant what I promised myself when I met her. *I will spend every day showing her how special she is. I will heal this girl and make her whole, and her love will do the same for me.*

CHAPTER
Eleven

Willow

After the most incredible night of my life, Valentin held me in his arms and indeed cherished every part of my body more than once and left me in a state of complete relaxation. He fed me plate after plate of various breakfast selections, and once I was done, he carried me inside to his shower that was bigger than my kitchen back home in New Jersey.

When he slept, I took some time of my own to watch him sleep. He looked younger and relaxed with not a care in the world, but I knew better than to believe that. You didn't get to where he was without suffering some collateral damage. He was a prominent and wealthy lawyer and lived a lifestyle I could have never imagined for myself. We talked a little about his upbringing and his family, which he wasn't exactly forthcoming with. When the shoe was on the other foot, he wasn't so eager to share, but he promised he would as we got to know each other better. *I guess if I'm his, then I should know it all.*

His? I'm still trying to wrap my head around all of his dominance.

What will my mother say? My grandmother will probably adore him right at first glance but I believe my mom will be a harder sell.

His accent came out a little this morning when he was inside me again. He said a few words of endearment in Russian and wouldn't tell me what the words were, but he smiled and assured me they were beautiful just like me.

And the compliments and nicknames? He's so intense when he speaks to me and although I asked him why he called me "dove," he also used the word "broken" last night when I had upset him. He called me his "broken dove," and then once I put together what that truly meant, I got as close as I could to hold him back. This beautiful man wanted me for some crazy reason, and as we laid in each other's arms, I made the choice to say yes and be with him for however long he wanted me there.

Our second date, as Valentin put it, turned into the entire weekend spent at his apartment and mostly in his bed. It was Sunday night, and I needed to get home and regroup. I would never tell Valentin that but I think he knew and just wasn't letting on. He had clothes delivered and, wouldn't you know, they were all in my size. He said he was keeping my panties, and would not be returning them. *Why does that make me so happy?*

Valentin was true to his word and drove me home Sunday night. He even walked me to my door and wanted a tour inside. I knew his plan and practically shoved him out, but he was quick and held my arms behind my back while kissing me. I was caged against the wall with no room to move, and the fire ablaze on my insides was giving Valentin everything he needed to practically take me right there.

What would the neighbors think if they saw us together or, heard me writhing against him? Our hallway lovefest moved quickly to my bedroom where Valentin took me hard and never relented until he gloriously came inside of me. He wore a condom but voiced his distaste for having to use them. He didn't ask me if I was on birth control, and I was relieved that the subject hadn't come up. I was already so overwhelmed with adjusting to sex. I knew it wouldn't be too long for Valentin to ask, because clearly, he had no issue voicing what he wanted.

He remained inside of me, as I struggled to keep my eyes opened. He was still hard and began to move again, making me cry out from the pleasure. My body was quivering all over as the next wave of orgasms ripped through me. He lifted himself up on his elbows and slowly began to pull out of me, causing my insides to ache. He tied off the condom and tossed it in the trash.

"I want you forever. I want everything with you. I want to fuck you bare and feel you come undone as you experience another first with me. When you're ready, I promise I will make it special for you," he said, kissing me hard and making my lips sting. "Rest, you need it. I'm going to take a shower."

"Valentin, will you wait?" I asked as I reached for his wrist to halt him from leaving.

"What is it?" he asked and sat beside me.

"How do you know that you want me forever? Some couples spend their entire lives together and do not know what they want. But you...you seem to have it all figured out."

"I can't speak for anyone else. I just know how I feel, and it's something I have never known before meeting you. Rest. We will have plenty of time to talk."

He kissed me hard on my lips and then walked into the bathroom, closing the door behind him. I sighed and felt my heart beat faster under my palm. I ran my finger across my bottom lip and still felt him there. I was high on Valentin. His promise excited and thrilled me all at the same time.

We talked more about my home in New Jersey and all the things I liked to do when I was younger. He, on the other hand, traveled the entire world by the time he was thirteen. I couldn't even imagine what that was like, experiencing one adventure after another at such a young age.

After several attempts at saying goodbye, he finally did and told me to lock the door behind him and then go to sleep and dream about him. *Yeah, that won't be a problem once I do fall asleep.*

But I was energized and wanted to work. I moved the design mannequin to the workspace I was using and took a good look at the dress I was trying to put together. It began as a high neckline design and then I scrapped it and started over with Valentin in mind. Every single time he touched and kissed me, his hands went to my bare neck.

Valentin Vasiliev was immensely alluring, and I was having difficulty resisting his charms. *What woman would want to? I believe even the blind could see him and would not be able to walk away.*

Shit! How the hell do I wrap my mind around this relationship I have found myself in? Face it, Willow, you have been caught in his web and are his for the taking, I thought and then deeply sighed knowing how true that was. I tried to concentrate, but it was no use. All I was focused on was my Russian, and that was dangerous.

I can't even say how many times my mother would sit me down and talk to me about men and caution not to lose yourself in a relationship. What the hell did she know back then? She was sixteen when she had me. Hell, she wasn't even old enough to get her driver's license but she had a baby. Fuck! Why am I doing this? Valentin is not my father, and I'm certainly not my mom. Double fuck! My mom was amazing. She always had my back and didn't deserve me ranting about her, even if it was within my own head.

I knew it was late, and I was sure Valentin wouldn't be happy knowing I was walking at night on my own, but I needed to clear my head. This was the best way I knew how to do that. I grabbed my key that I always pinned on me and some money for a coffee at my favorite all-night deli.

I walked a few blocks and passed some people going about their way. Once I crossed the intersection near the deli, a strange feeling overcame me, like I was being followed.

My heart was beating so fast. I felt unsure all of a sudden and needed to get off the street and get to somewhere safe. I couldn't explain it and never felt this way before. I guess after the mugging, I was now more aware of my surroundings, which was never a bad thing to have.

I looked around and over my shoulder, but no one was there. I stopped at the corner and waited for the light to turn green, so I could safely cross the street. Chills began to run up and down my spine, making me shiver when it was eighty degrees on a summer's night.

This is crazy. What are you doing, Willow? You're from Jersey for Cripe's sake. You're tougher than this. The mugging and all the bullshit that followed has me rattled. The dirtbag got away, so why fret over something I can't change? I'm not going to live in fear and give anyone power over me. I stopped scolding myself, and when the light turned, I headed for the deli for my coffee. While I was there I picked up a few fashion magazines and enjoyed my midnight caffeine fix.

About a half hour later, I was beginning to get tired and headed for home. As I walked back to my apartment, I felt anxious again, which was beginning to piss me off. I always listened to that voice in my head, and I wasn't going to stop now, especially if I was going to continue to live here in the city. Having said that, strong or not, something was off, and I knew I had to listen to the danger warnings that were ringing loudly in my head.

I looked around and didn't see or hear anyone, but a presence? Yes, this I felt. I still had several blocks to walk back to my apartment, and I was closer to the deli than to my place.

I promised him that I would go to sleep, but my overactive imagination kept me up, and now I was in a precarious situation. *I'm scared and I can't shake the troubled feelings that I have which compelled me to do the unthinkable.*

With shaky fingers, I hit his number on my phone and prayed he wouldn't be too angry with me.

"Valentin, I need you."

CHAPTER Twelve

Valentin

Knowing my dove was home safely tucked away back at her apartment, I took some time to check in with my brother. I heard he had been causing quite the commotion down at one of our family-owned vodka bars, giving me a reason to make an unexpected visit.

I didn't make a habit of coming down here too often and although this club was legitimate, I still didn't wish to be seen here. It was a Sunday night, and the place was buzzing with all walks of life partying it up in the New York club scene. The bar was packed. I made my way through the crowd and went upstairs to the private rooms.

Sergei met me at the top of the stairs, and it was as if he was welcoming me home. Anytime a Vasiliev was present and in their company, it was a sign of respect to greet me properly. I returned it to our top captain and looked around for my brother, Sasha.

"Where is he?" I asked, looking around to the VIP rooms the top floor held.

"He's down the hall, the last door on the right with the big 'do not disturb' sign on it."

I tilted my head slightly, giving Sergei a questioning expression.

"I know what you're thinking, Valentin. This is what I was told when I got in tonight. Andrei says he's been up here for a while now, running up the bar tab."

"I'm sure he is, but let's just alert the bartenders that he has been cut off. Am I clear?"

"You got it," Sergei picked up one of the house phones and dialed down to our bar manager to give him the cut off for Sasha.

I walked down the long corridor to find most of the VIP rooms occupied with private parties. The rooms had been custom designed to fit one's lifestyle. Basically up here, anything goes. When I reached the room where Sasha was entertaining, I twisted the doorknob, and sure enough, it was locked. I gestured to Sergei to come over and unlock the door. Once he did, I stepped in and found a girl on her knees sucking off my brother.

"Hey! What the fuck?" he shouted without looking up to see who had the balls to interrupt the blowjob he was in the middle of receiving. When his eyes locked onto mine, he knew the party was over.

The oblivious girl was still getting him off until he shoved her off of him. She looked mad as hell and shot daggers at me, not knowing who I was.

I simply said, "Get out," and with a huff of disgust she pulled up her dress to cover her nakedness and stomped off. "Sergei, see that she gets safely downstairs and placed into one of our cars. Tell the driver it's a personal request from me."

"Yes, sir."

I closed the door and then turned around to face Sasha, who still had his dick hanging out. "Well, shove the snake back into your pants, and clean yourself up. You've been quite busy tonight now, haven't you?" I took in all the drug paraphernalia on the glass coffee table.

Lines of white powder were present and nearly two empty vodka bottles scattered on the floor along with condom wrappers.

"Valentin, I didn't know you were stopping by tonight. I'm sorry for the mess."

"Seriously? I think you can do better than that feeble excuse. Look at you. You are a disgrace. Have you been getting high since this afternoon? And who brought all the party favors? I do love how you decorate the room with your shit!" I roared in a tone that had him jumping back.

"I'm sorry, brother. I just was having a little fun."

"While papa is away?"

"Yeah, amongst other things. I didn't hurt anyone, and I did lock the door."

"As if that justifies your reckless behavior. Your bar tab is over a thousand dollars, which you will never honor because you believe our last name gives you a free pass. Well, Sasha, it does not. You are out of control, and I should drop off your sorry ass at rehab."

"Come on, it's not that bad. So I did some coke. Big fucking deal! Get off my fucking ass, and go be righteous somewhere else." He was clearly under the influence of drugs, because in his right mind, he would never have had the balls to raise his voice to me. I slowly walked over to him and with my two hands grabbed him by his neck, easily lifting him off the floor so his feet were dangling.

"Do you want to repeat yourself? I don't believe I heard you correctly."As Sasha struggled for breath, Sergei returned and took in the scene that was happening before him. I continued, "Nothing to say, Sasha? You have my full attention."

"Please, Valentin, I'm sorry," he struggled to say.

I dropped him down to the couch, and he fell to his knees gasping for air, cursing in Russian. Just the sight of him in this condition worried me. He had always been a loose cannon and in desperate need of structure in his life. My father was too soft on him, but he was their miracle baby who nearly died during childbirth, so our parents doted on him and spoiled him rotten. This was why my father wanted me to check on him. He had to know he would be up to no good. Sasha was still coughing when Sergei handed him a water.

"Oh, the dramatics, Sasha. If I would have truly choked you, you would be dead on the floor. Now get up! I will not tell you again."

He didn't look at me and just did what he was told. I towered over my brother and held his face, keeping him still. "Sasha, you are my only brother and I love you dearly, but if you continue to behave in this destructive manner, you will leave me no choice but to take matters in my own hands. Do you want this?"

"No, Valentin."

"Whether papa is here or not, you are my responsibility, and I will not have you fuck up your life and shame our family. You need to get your shit together, or you will no longer have a choice. Do you understand me? Don't shake your head at me. Use your words."

He clenched his jaw and enunciated very slowly, "I understand, Valentin."

"I truly hope you do, Sasha, because I am running out of patience with you. Sergei, get him cleaned up and taken home. I want Viktor with him tonight in case any emergencies occur. We can't have a repeat of Aspen."

"Valentin, I don't need a babysitter. I'm twenty-five years old."

"Yes, you are, and you behave like an adolescent going through puberty trying ecstasy for the first time. This conversation is over. You will go with Sergei and do as you are fucking told!" I shouted and then backhanded him across his face.

I immediately regretted my actions and would atone for them later, but for now, I needed to get my brother in check. I released a deep breath and silently counted to ten in my mind before addressing him again.

"Go with Sergei, and we will talk tomorrow."

He said nothing more and walked out too ashamed to give me a parting glance.

I wanted to be with my woman, and I was frustrated that I wasn't. I should have kept her tied to my bed and not allowed her to leave. My mood had been fucked up ever since I brought her home and left her at her apartment. I should have never left and stayed with her. *Fuck! I want to see her.* In that very moment of thinking of her, my phone was ringing with her name written across the screen. *Yes, this is perfect timing.*

"Hello," I murmured. "I was just thinking about you," I practically purred into my phone. I didn't hear anything in return and then I said, "Willow? Are you there? Talk to me." I kept speaking, but she wasn't responding to me. *Was this call by accident? And she doesn't realize she dialed me?*

And then I heard her say, "Valentin, I need you."

Four words she fretfully said, and my mind shifted into a complete panic. *Where the fuck was Oleg?* I rushed out of the club and into my car, speeding away as fast as I could to reach Willow. *It is so late, and why in the hell is she out in the city at this time of night?*

"Just tell me where you are? Fine. I'm on my way."

Does she suffer from insomnia and has trouble sleeping? I can't think of any reason why she would have to go to a deli in the middle of the night. She certainly didn't have any problem sleeping when she shared my bed with me. I could question her later about all of this. For now, I needed to get to my woman.

I turned the corner and parked right out in front of the deli. She wasn't outside, which I was grateful for. Once inside the small space, it wasn't too difficult to find her. Willow was sitting at a corner table, wringing her hands out in her lap. I quickly walked over to where she was sitting, and the minute she saw me, she practically threw herself into my arms. She was trembling and afraid.

My first instinct was to hold her, and without saying any words to her, I simply led her away from the deli and right into my car. I didn't want to return her to her apartment but to mine, where she would no longer be taking any midnight strolls. She said nothing as I drove on, not even sparing a glance in my direction. I tried in earnest to get my-self in check. I had just found her and didn't want to risk losing her because of my temper.

I parked my car in one of my private bays and got out to go to the other side to collect Willow and bring her upstairs. I gripped her hand and led her inside the elevator that would bring us upstairs to my place. After a pause, she finally looked at me and asked me to talk to her.

"Please, Valentin, this deafening silence is killing me. I hate it. I was never a fan of it."

I swallowed hard and let out a few deep breaths. "I promise we will talk once we are inside of my apartment."

I continued to get my breathing under control, not revealing to her how much she scared me tonight. As she tried to tug her hand from mine, it only brought me closer to her. Before the elevator opened to my floor, I grabbed both of her hands and held them with my one as I issued a warning of my own to her.

"There's one thing you should know about me. I hate distance, es-pecially with someone I care about. I'm not a fan. Please don't pull away from me, Willow. Not ever, even if it's in the simplest of ways. You're mine. You agreed, and by doing so means I can touch you as much as I please. It also means giving me the pleasure of holding your hand."

Her eyes widened, and she was clever enough to not shy away this time, understanding a little bit more about the man who had claimed her as his own.

The doors opened, and I released her hands to take one back and lead her into my home. I wasted no time talking and lifted her into my arms and carrying her upstairs to my bedroom.

"You do like carrying me, don't you?" she said.

"One of my favorite things when it comes to you, my dove."

With the change of scenery and the close proximity to my woman, I was calmer and was able to address as to why she was out so late. I placed her down on my bed and removed her sandals and then her shorts, if you want to call them that.

"These will never do," I whispered, removing a scrap of material before making my way up to her tank top.

She was gorgeous and on display in my vast bed. I wanted her so badly, but we needed to talk first. I quickly removed my shirt and pants, leaving just my briefs on. I climbed into bed to join Willow, and then lifted her on top of me, pulling her close in a sitting position. My arms wrapped around her small frame, holding her still where we were eye-to-eye with one another.

"Now that I have you where I want you to be, you will tell me why you were out in the city late at night and all on your own to where you risked getting hurt. What were you thinking?"

"Valentin, I needed to figure some things out, and I usually work to clear my mind, but even doing that did not help, so I took a walk instead."

"What's on your mind that you put yourself at risk?"

"You," she answered bluntly.

"I would never hurt you. You know that."

"I'm not so sure, Valentin. In just a short time, you have completely taken over every part of my being and have now called it yours. Dreaming of you? I haven't stopped since meeting you. Missing your touch? How can I not when you have marked my skin. You are everywhere, and it's a lot to take on."

"Is that a bad thing?" I responded.

"I don't know, and having to explain it to you right now while we're practically naked and I'm trapped like prey you are about to strike at, leaves my mind with a thousand thoughts that probably won't make sense to you right now."

I loosened the hold I had on her and moved my hands to her face to pull her down to my lips. I needed to taste her and feel her tongue inside my mouth.

"Open for me, and let me in."

She did with no hesitation as I continued to massage our tongues together. One easy tug, and her underwear was gone, leaving her soaking pussy to rub against my hard erection. My balls were full and ready to explode if I didn't get a release soon.

She sensed what I needed and slid her body down my thick legs and reached for the waistband of my briefs to pull them down and take my dick into her mouth. She held my balls and worked them over with her hand as her wet mouth took all of me down her throat. I threw my head back into the pillow until I could take no more and gripped her hair, tugging it with every swipe of her tongue sliding against the slit of my dripping cock.

"Yes, suck it, baby. Suck me until I fucking explode inside of your mouth," I commanded as she continued to pleasure and take me all the way to the back of her throat.

I was unrestrained with animalistic tendencies that could tear Willow apart and claim her soul piece by piece. Yes, I wanted all of her and desired no other. She took what she wanted from me tonight and fulfilled a dark need inside of me that now made me burn and nearly combust with pleasure. I was close as I felt my balls tighten. I pulled and pulled on her hair and with a pop breaking the suction she had on my cock, Willow opened her mouth wide, and ribbons of white hot cum shot into her mouth. I cried out into ecstasy as she drank every last drop of me.

Before she could collapse on my chest, I easily flipped her to her back and fucked her in the way I had promised the last time we were together. I was still erect and sank into her pussy, fucking her hard, practically splitting her in two.

"This is what you do to me, my beautiful dove. Eyes on me as I take your body, my body to fuck and give you and us pleasure. Say it, dove. Say the words," I demanded as I continued to pound her flesh.

"I'm yours, Valentin. I'm not going anywhere," she screamed, telling me exactly what I needed to hear to bring us over the edge with one another.

Shockwaves raged through my body as I came so hard and deep

inside of her, sending ripples of pleasure down my spine. Our bodies were slicked with sweat as we remained connected with each other. I didn't want to move, nor did I have the strength to do so.

"I'm dead. You killed me with orgasms," she said.

"What a way to go," I replied.

Her eyelids were heavy with exhaustion as they began to slowly close. I knew she was exhausted, and I didn't try to keep her awake. I leaned down and placed a gentle kiss to her lips, telling her to sleep.

I pulled out from her body, seeing my cum leak out from her swollen folds and knowing I took her without a condom. *Did she feel the difference? She didn't stop me. And would she let me do that again? Now that I have, I don't think I could ever fuck her with anything between us. She'll be sore tomorrow and will not be able to move without feeling where I've been, but I don't care. She needs to know who she belongs to, and as mine, she will never be so reckless as she was tonight. Never again!*

I only managed a couple of hours asleep while the rest of the time was spent watching Willow. She looked peaceful with not a worry at all marring her beautiful face. I wish I could mirror the sentiment, but with dealing with my brother and then having to leave one crisis to handle another, I was wrecked. I had court this morning, and I was exhausted. Today would also be busy for Willow with day one of working with Zara. I had this fierce need to keep Willow here with me. It was my practice, and I could easily pass off what I had to do to one of my junior attorneys. It was a filing motion, nothing too complicated to handle.

Willow was still asleep as I carefully edged out of my bed without waking her. I walked into my closet to put on a pair of jeans and then reached for both our cell phones, leaving her to sleep while I went downstairs to do some work.

My first phone call was to Cyrus. He was the best choice to handle my business this morning in court. I e-mailed my paralegal with everything she needed to give to Cyrus. After receiving a confirmation text from him agreeing to go in my place, I was relieved not having to worry about it.

Secondly, I needed a way to keep better tabs on my woman, and since Oleg did not check in and failed on her detail last night, I needed to take care of monitoring her myself. I didn't want to not trust her but when it came to her safety, she was severely lacking in this area and far too trusting to walk alone at night. She may try to live up to the stereotypical personality of a tough girl, but she's anything but, and it's another reason why I loved her so much. She was an innocent under the guise of acting tough, and it was fine if she wanted to keep up appearances for her career, but not with me. *I want the real Willow always. I will settle for nothing less, not when she is so much more.*

I checked my phone for any messages and saw I had several. One was from Sergei, telling me Sasha had been secured. I knew he would be with Sasha, taking care of him. I will deal with Sasha as soon as I work out my issues with Willow.

The second was from Oleg who regrettably explained what happened in his detail of Willow last night. I chose not to read on and would deal with him later. I scanned my contacts, finding the person who was more important than Oleg at the moment. I dialed, and he answered on the second ring. No matter the time, he would always answer my calls.

"Mr. Vasiliev," he answered. "What can I do for you?"

CHAPTER
Thirteen

Willow

When I opened my eyes, I expected to see light but the room was dark with the expensive drapes covering all the windows. I was at Valentin's and alone. He brought me here last night after I had called him. If my memory failed me, then I undoubtedly had my body to remind me of exactly what happened after he brought me back to his home.

He had been angry and didn't try to hide his emotions. He didn't voice the words, but his actions spoke volumes. I was already accustomed to reading his body language. He was a man who probably had a million expressions, and I was sure he would have no problem showing them to me as he so easily did with my body last night.

I moved my hand down between my legs and still felt the remnants from our lovemaking. No, correction, *hard fucking*, because that's exactly what it was. Valentin used my body to satisfy his wants and needs, and all I could do was submit and be played like a fine-tuned instrument. I needed to pee and then required a much-needed shower. I sat up in his humongous bed and pulled my knees up to my chest, sighing out loud.

I gave myself a stretch and then wondered how the hell I was going to get out of this bed without breaking a limb. Again, humongous, and I was very short. I swung my legs over and saw that Valentin had moved the four-step platform to my side of the bed, making it easier for me to climb down. I smiled and was grateful for his thoughtfulness. *Will there ever be a time that he doesn't surprise me with a kind gesture?*

Once I was safely down to the floor, I found his bathroom and relieved my full bladder. Afterward, I stood at the sink in front of the huge mirror to wash my hands and take in my appearance. In just a couple of weeks, my physical appearance had been transformed from an inexperienced virgin to a sexually active woman who had been literally claimed. *All that is missing is a collar around my neck and an insignia burned on my ass. Okay, a slight exaggeration, but I'm not just dating a guy from the shore. I'm dating Valentin Vasiliev, a sophisticated and wealthy man.*

The shower was too tempting for me not to use. I ignored some of the reminders that he left on my skin and soaked my sore muscles under the invigorating sprays from the massaging rain shower head.

I half expected Valentin to join me, but he never did. I combed out my long tresses and left it to air dry. Curiosity got the better of me, and I began opening the many drawers of his vanity. The entire right side held beauty products—all the ones I happened to favor and use daily. *Another act of kindness*, I dreamily thought as I used the moisturizer for my face and the lotion to cover the rest of my body. A few sprays of my favorite perfume, and I was ready to find Valentin. Of course, hanging on the hook of the closet was a soft linen robe. *Hmmm, let me see if it's in my size.* I removed it and immediately touched the fabric, loving it against my skin. *Wouldn't you know? The robe fits perfectly. Yes, he's over the top amazing and gets the boyfriend of the year award.*

Boyfriend? When it comes to Valentin, that label just seems so small for a man of his stature. I looked around all the wealth that was part of him and sighed again. This was one of the many reasons why I needed time to think last night. *Can I handle all of this? How will I fit in and not look like a lost rescued puppy he has swooped in and saved? God! Willow, pull yourself together. Isn't this the attitude that he has fucked out of you already?*

Another deep breath, and I set out to find Valentin. I opened the bathroom door and crashed right into the solid mass of muscle that made me weak in the knees and happy in his arms. When my balance returned and senses too, I looked into his mesmerizing eyes and lost all ability to speak. Yeah, he had that effect on me. As if he had a secret passageway to my thoughts, he just smiled and crossed his arms over his broad chest.

I may have stared more than I should have, but how can I not when he's shirtless and only wearing faded jeans. Even his feet are gorgeous. My body gave me away every time with this man. I usually bit my lip out of habit when I was nervous, but with Valentin, I think it was more out of anticipation and need.

"Good morning," he whispered flirtatiously.

"I, um…"

He chortled as he stepped closer, effectively backing me up against the door. "It's okay, we don't need words right now, not when our bodies are a universal language."

With his skilled hands, he slowly unknotted the sash to my robe and pushed the fabric open to reveal my naked breasts, full with my nipples erect. His hands were velvety soft, probably never worked a hard day in his life. His nails were perfectly manicured, not a cuticle out of place. Everything about Valentin was perfect. I remained still as he unfastened his jeans and slid them down to his ankles, kicking the denim away.

His tongue rolled over my neck, setting my skin ablaze with heat. I wanted him so badly while he just took his time until he was good and ready to take me. I cried out after I felt him enter me with his fingers pushing in and out with torturous pleasure. If this was his way of punishing me, I'd gladly welcome it. I just wouldn't tell him that.

He lifted my leg and wrapped it around his waist, with his two hands cupping my ass. With ease, he entered my dripping core and then pulled out only to delve in deeper, so deep I felt the pressure on my backside. He was close, we both were, and just as I thought it, I felt him erupt, filling me to the brim with his hot cum. He never stopped thrusting until every last drop was spilled. His hands gripped the sides of my face as he crushed his mouth to mine, making me open for him. Valentin was unrelenting and continued to kiss me until we both needed air.

Still no words spoken, he pushed the robe off my shoulders and down to the floor. It was one erotic moment to the next as he never dropped my leg the entire time we fucked. He lifted the other one until I was in his arms and carried me back into the shower. So many multifaceted sides to this man whom I had irrevocably fallen in love with. I was just not ready to tell him yet. I shoved my rampant thoughts out of my head and let Valentin take care of me. He was so attentive. I loved it.

Once he took the time to dry me from head to toe, he rained down on me with a gentler touch of kisses. *Oh, dear lord in heaven, I don't think I can do it again.*

One more kiss to my lips, and as if he was reading my thoughts, he said, "Don't worry dove. I'm not that much of a beast that I don't recognize the signs that you're tired and sore. I'm sorry if I gave you even the smallest amount of pain."

"I'm fine, and I'm not that sore."

He smirked. "Sure you're not. I have clothes for you on the bed. Get dressed, and then meet me downstairs. I'm sure you have already discovered the bathroom is stocked with everything you need. I'll be waiting for you."

He sure has great taste was my first thought after seeing what he had chosen for me, a Valentino butterfly lace mini dress in red with a price tag of $3,750. *Oh, let's not forget the nude pumps to complete the look!*

It took me some time to get my hair right, unsure about what style Valentin would like, but then I smiled because I could wear a paper bag and he wouldn't complain. I kept it down with big barrel curls. My makeup was light with a touch of pink to my cheeks and a clear gloss to my natural ruby lips. Mom always said I would never need Botox, not with lips like mine. I guess I now know what she was talking about.

Standing in front of the floor length mirror, I spun around to do the princess thing, because that's how I felt in this dress, this apartment, and in his arms. *Okay, no more delaying the inevitable. You have a man, your man who has made you his. He's waiting for you downstairs. For however long this lasts, I'm going to enjoy him.*

He was on his phone when I reached the bottom of the stairs. He turned and smiled, raising a finger up toward me. I poured a cup of coffee and fixed one for him, placing it down on the table. A second later, he disconnected his call and strode over to kiss me.

"You look beautiful, dove, and this dress looks perfect on you, as I knew it would. Hungry? You must be since you probably haven't had a decent meal since we parted yesterday evening."

"You don't have to worry about me, Valentin. I'm fine."

"Hmmm, but I do. It's become my life's mission to worry about you. But more so, I want to just love and take care of you, but you make it challenging for me, and that's what we need to talk about."

"I knew you'd be upset, but I didn't know how much until I saw it in your eyes when you came for me. I'm sorry to have done that to you, and I promise to try to be more careful."

"And just how do you plan on doing that?" He looked intently at me, waiting for the perfect answer.

I shrugged my shoulders, not really knowing what to say. "I don't know, Valentin, it's been ingrained in me for so long that I have to take care of myself and be as strong as I can. You know, the single mom rule of life. And now after meeting you, I've been completely swept off my feet, and it's a whirlwind of all the feelings a little girl dreams of when she's playing dress-up or pretending to be the princess in the tower waiting to be rescued. I don't need rescuing. I can take care of myself."

He was quiet, so very quiet for what felt like an hour, and then he just reached for me and I went willingly into his arms. Breathing me in and getting high off my perfume, he nuzzled my neck and said, "My beautiful dove, I know how strong you are, but did you ever think maybe it's me that needs the rescuing?"

I gave him a half-hearted smile and waited for him to go on.

He said, "What you don't seem to realize is that I've been waiting for you, and time doesn't matter If I've known you for years or a couple of weeks. My heart can't tell the difference either way. I want you, Willow, and I've made no secret of that fact. The bigger question remains: *Do you want me?* And before you answer, forget about what I have and just look at the man in front of you. Just the man who just an hour ago was inside of you, making you feel things you have never experienced with another. A man who will throw down his life if it meant saving yours."

"Oh, Valentin, yes, I want you. How could any woman resist you?"

"I don't give a fuck about other women. The only opinion I care about is yours. Tell me why you needed to think last night? And then put yourself at risk by walking alone at night?"

"It's what I do when everything else fails to calm me. I was in the middle of designing a dress, and I just got so lost in thought and wanted some air."

"Okay, fair enough. And the reason you felt you needed to call me?"

"I got scared. I felt someone may have been lurking in the shadows, and because I was closer to the deli, I went back and called you, even knowing it would upset you. After being mugged once already, I didn't want to make any more mistakes."

"Oh, baby, what you need to understand is that you didn't make a mistake. What happened to you was not your fault, and you fought back the best way you knew how. That took courage, my dove. What happened after that was unfortunate and has been dealt with accordingly."

"The café owner limping with a cane? That was your doing? Wasn't it?"

"Yes, but you already knew that. The minute I saw your eyes when he approached our table, it was clear you had quickly put two and two together. You see, I already staked a claim on you on the day we met, and no crime against my woman would ever go unpunished. Does this frighten you knowing that I was capable of such violence?"

"Before meeting you, I probably would have said yes."

"And now?" he asked softly.

"I say no. Thank you, Valentin. I…" Tears were filling my eyes as the words were right there. Three words were all I needed to say, and then once he heard them, I would be bound to Valentin forever.

"What, baby? What are you trying to tell me?" His hands were tangled in my hair, sending tingles through my scalp.

"I think I'm falling in love with you. There may have been a small part of me that tried to fight my feelings, but the closer you edged into my life, the weaker my resolve became."

"Say it again, dove."

"I'm falling for you. I know it's probably too soon, and I'm sure that thought has crossed your mind as well, but it's real, and I wanted to say the words before I chickened out. It's scary, but if it's what you want with me too, then I say let's go for it and see where it leads."

"Yes, I want you, Willow, and thank you for telling me."

"Your welcome." I voiced the words as many times as he wanted me to, and then we made love, binding us together with hearts, bodies, and souls.

Later that evening, Valentin took me to the Russian Vodka Room which his family had business dealings in. I got to enjoy the dinner that we didn't eat the other night. The European delicacies were indescribable to my virgin palette of finer cuisine. He explained in detail every course we sampled.

"This was delicious, I can't eat another bite," I said.

"Why? Because you think you will get fat?"

"Funny guy," I winked and then finished off my wine. "No, you ever hear of leaving some room for dessert?"

"I love the way you think, but unless it's in the form of a slice of Medovik, that's the only dessert you will be enjoying tonight. You can't lie to me, so don't ever try. I know you're sore and need to heal up for a few days before we make love again. Now, what would you like?"

"What's Medovik?"

"My apologies, it's a layered honey cake. It's very delicious."

"Yum, I can't wait to put it in my mouth and taste it," I replied suggestively, causing his arousal meter to skyrocket. *He is too adorable. I'm not sure how he would respond to such a word reserved for teenage love, but he is.* "May I ask something else?"

"I'm breathless with anticipation. What is it?" he responded.

"Just curious, but where am I sleeping tonight?"

He smiled, which caused my cheeks to heat and my cheeks to blush again. *Damn, what this man does to me!* He slowly shifted in his seat and moved closer as he reached for my hand, bringing it up to his lips to kiss.

"May I offer you some advice?" he said.

"You may," I answered, as his lips ghosted over mine.

"This advice will prove helpful for you moving forward, so pay attention, for I am a man who never repeats himself twice."

Oh, shit! My thoughts got away from me.

"Never ask a question you already know the answer to," he whispered.

There he goes again, charming the panties right off me.

His hand moved slowly under my dress, causing me to let out a pleasurable moan.

"You feel it? Don't you, Willow? It's our connection. So, to answer your question, you'll be coming home with me tonight." He paused, delivering a devilish smile. "If I have my way, you'll be staying…permanently."

CHAPTER
fourteen

Valentin

I had just finished with morning court sessions and was done for the day. I didn't have anything of importance pending on my calendar, so after returning to my office to finish my notes from the court, I took a minute to relax and recall the last few days and nights spent with Willow.

It was borderline obsessive, this I know, but letting my dove go this morning was easier than I imagined after the tumultuous night we shared together. I showed her sides of myself that were unrestrained at times that could have easily shifted to dangerous. I hated knowing she was unprotected, and today I would deal with Oleg and his failure to abide by my strict instructions to guard Willow.

My woman amazed me at every turn, taking all of me without a shred of doubt in her eyes. I wasn't lying when I told her how strong she was, but also there was a part inside of her that was fragile. Her heart had been damaged with disappointment from a father she had never known, and she carried the scars of that abandonment. When I held her in my arms and breathed her in, her heart and body were in desperate need of tender loving care, and I would do everything possible in my power to be the one who met her every need and desire.

Because I had her phone, she didn't see the missed calls and text messages from her boss, Madeline. Zara knew better not to barrage her with frivolous bullshit that didn't demand her immediate attention. I answered for her by informing her persistent boss that she would not be in today at all due to a personal matter that could not be explained at this time. I assured all was well, and she would see Willow on Tuesday. Madeline was smart enough to read between the lines, and simply replied, "Okay." I was satisfied she would not be bothering Willow again today.

I looked at my phone, which was now effectively monitoring hers. My tech guy easily installed monitoring software and linked both our phones. This way, if another breach of her security failed, I would always know where she was at and could get to her at any time. I vowed not to be too intrusive when it came to her personal calls received, unless I deemed them as harmful; then I would intercede.

With all we discussed and the lovemaking that followed, locating her phone was the last thing on her mind. When she left this morning, she simply picked up her phone where she left it when she first arrived and placed it in her new messenger bag she now was using, courtesy of me. In fact, an entire wardrobe was now hanging in a walk-in closet attached to mine.

The rest of her things could be moved over later, but with everything she needed here, there would be no reason to return to her grandmother's apartment. When I told her she would be staying here on a permanent basis, her eyes gleamed with excitement and desire. The subject was dropped until breakfast this morning when she asked if I was serious about the moving in part.

It only took a passing glance between us to show her just how serious I was. *I want her in my home and in my bed. I see no other op-*

tion. She asked for time to think about it and to discuss it with her grandmother when she returned home from her trip, which would be in the next week or so, just in time for her birthday.

I wanted to tell her no and close the subject forever, but the rational part of me knew better. No matter the pillow talk we shared, she was sensible and coming down from the high. She knew she couldn't just rush forward with something as important as moving in with a man she'd only known for a couple of weeks now.

The provision of clothes and personal items was just an incentive to entice her to want to stay with me without worry. I hoped she would stop questioning our relationship and follow her heart where it was leading her to go: home with me.

Her family was another obstacle I'd yet to take on, as well as my own. The way she spoke of her mother and grandmother was no less than hero worship. It was already evident they both possessed a strong influence over her, which raised another fear I had that she could be swayed to leave me if they did a good job at convincing her to do so.

I was never in a position to win over a family's affection, nor did I have to. My last name held so much power that's all that was required. On impulse, I took a gamble and revealed my truthfulness to her about what I had done in regards to my dealings with the café owner who had deeply offended her.

I expected her to be afraid and run from me again. She surpassed my wildest expectations and stayed and explained her reasons as to why she wasn't. It only pulled me closer to her and increased my need of wanting this woman in my life.

Oh, my beautiful dove, you're mine and there is not one person that will stop that from happening, not your family, nor mine. I will go to the ends of the earth to make us possible.

I sighed in contentment, and then after time spent daydreaming about Willow, I eventually got back to why I was at work in the first place and finished all I had to do. I took a quick meeting with my paralegals and the junior partners, going over current cases and the completion of others. I was about to conclude when my cell buzzed in my pocket. I glanced at the number and immediately recognized who was calling.

"Will you all excuse me for a moment? I have to take this." I gestured to my phone and stepped out and away from the conference room.

"Oleg, where are you?" My attitude already shifting to rage, directed all at the caller. He was speaking in his fluent Russian accent and gave me his thousand apologies as to why he had failed in his duty and pledged allegiance to me.

"I will be there in thirty minutes. You wait for me." I disconnected the call and held the cell phone to my forehead, sighing and valiantly trying to get my temperament in check.

I returned to my staff meeting and finished up with my agenda. Everyone had their assignments for the week and with my caseload lightened and tasks handed off, I could concentrate on Willow, which took precedence over anything else.

Oleg was seated at a table in a private room of the Russian Tea Room, another venture our family had interests in. The room had been secured, where we could speak freely amongst ourselves. I was still in my suit, which always gave off a feeling of intimidation. Men would greet me accordingly and then cast their eyes down until I addressed them again or at all, for that matter.

I would admit the tone I used when he called me earlier was harsh and downright cold, but he had nothing to fear from me. He was a trusted friend and I knew he would never knowingly do anything to harm me. My anger had dissipated, and once he saw me, he stood up to properly greet me but exercised caution.

"It's alright, my friend," I said. "Please, take a seat, and let's talk."

He gripped the sides of his face and said, "I don't deserve leniency here, Valentin. You warned me about failure, and it's exactly what I have done."

I allowed him to have his say, and then when I had enough, I slammed my hand down to the table and said exactly that. Leaning over, I pulled him up by his jacket lapels and made him see that he was not in any danger. I stared into his eyes for some kind of recognition that he knew he could trust and believe what I was telling him, but all I saw was fear. I shoved him back into the chair and ordered him to talk to me.

"What's going on here, Oleg? What has caused you to be afraid of talking to me?" I questioned and waited for him to respond. When he didn't, I became frustrated and reached for him again. "You need to speak. And be very clear with your words, or so help me god, I am going to do something you will not like."

"I'm sorry, Valentin, so very sorry."

"For?" I knew the guilt was eating him up alive, but I still needed to hear him say it.

"I lied to you last night. I was never on Ms. Pierce's detail." His hands were shaking uncontrollably to the point that he dropped the cup out of his hands, spilling the hot liquid all over the table and onto his lap. He didn't flinch and just sat there and did nothing, while I suspected the tea had burned him.

Instead of becoming enraged, I withdrew my anger and gave my old friend the chance to explain but not before warning him not to lie to me. I kept reminding myself to think of Willow and the kindness that radiated from her like the sun. *She's already begun to change me for the better. So, because of her, Oleg will be forgiven.*

"Judging by the way you are reacting, it seems you are expecting for me to enact a punishment, and I would say, quite a severe one you feel you deserve. Is this true, Oleg? Is this what you want from me? To deliver a punishment without ever asking any questions as to why? You know I am not that man. I am not my father. If you believe what I say is the truth, then you will talk to me now? My patience will only hold for so long before I actually do lose control."

"Valentin, you must believe me that I had no choice but to abandon the security detail for another I was requested on. He gave me no choice but to follow his order and to do as he asked of me. If it was anyone else, I would have said no."

I unbuttoned my suit jacket and loosened my tie. I took a minute to process what he was trying to make me believe, but I saw right through him and knew he was committing the one act I warned him to never do: lie to me.

"Whom are you referring to?"

"Come on, Val. Do I really have to say his name? You are the one that always advises to never ask a question you already know the answer to."

"Very well. If that's how you want to play this little game, let's assume I do know the answer...what then? You will give up some bullshit half-truth you expect me to believe? You'll beg for my forgiveness and make me believe it was a one-time error in judgment and I can still trust you? Has your loyalty shifted to another? Or, what pains my heart in asking, did I ever have it to begin with? Think carefully about what you say next, because your answer will determine how I will proceed."

"I don't have to think about anything, because other than last night, I have never lied to you, not ever, and I will never do so again. I knew she was with you for the remainder of the weekend, and I returned to the club to get some work done. Once you called me to say when you would be bringing her home, I finished up and turned the club over to Andrei. Before I was about to leave, I received a call on one of the burner phones. It was your father calling."

"And? What did he ask of you that you could not inform me of? Which begs the bigger question: why did my father choose you over his own son? Firstborn, or have you forgotten?"

"I haven't. Look, he wanted me to secure Sasha before you were to arrive at the club. I was given my instructions to get him out of there and bring him to one of the safe houses to sober up. I went to the house and got it ready for Sasha's arrival, but when I returned to the club, you were already there and not looking too happy with your brother. I stayed out of sight long enough until Sergei left, and then it was out of my hands by then. I left and returned to Ms. Pierce's apartment, only to find it empty and she was nowhere to be found."

"What are you saying, Oleg? You've been inside of her home? And without me knowing about it?" I was hanging onto a thread, because at any minute now, I was going to break his fucking neck.

"Yes, I've been in there, but no one saw me."

"When?" I seethed with anger.

"The day I drove her to work, and it was only one time. I was barely in there for a couple of minutes. I didn't plan on it, but knowing how she likes to wander so late at night, I decided to take the extra necessary steps to keep her safe. Once I returned to her building, I did a thorough search of each floor, marking all the exit doors. On her door, I placed a monitoring device that would be blind to anyone walking by. She would never suspect it, Valentin, and it would help me monitor her departures. On my eyes, boy, I would never do anything to put you or the ones you care about in danger. I would only turn on the app connected to the camera once I knew she was secure inside her home. It was for peace of mind for you."

"Enough! Shut up and be quiet for a goddamn minute. Did Sergei lie to me too? Is Sasha where he is supposed to be?"

"Yes, I've just come from there. Sasha is a little rough right now with going through the detox, but he'll be fine. It was just a small relapse. He asked for you before he passed out again. He wants you to know he's sorry."

I scoffed. "I know he is, and that's the problem we both know and have known for a long time. Sadly, my father does too. So, just to be clear so I don't get any of the details misconstrued here...my father called you for assistance because he didn't believe that I could take care of my own flesh and blood? My brother. Is this what you expect for me to believe?"

"Yes, that's exactly what I want. He knows you would never hurt your brother."

The rage I had tampered down was slowly rising, and it was about to emerge in a matter of seconds. When I saw the duplicity in his eyes, I flipped over the table, causing Oleg to thud his back against the wall. I palmed my eye sockets with such force it made my head hurt. He said nothing, which was wise considering how I felt at the moment.

"Does my father know about Willow? And the extracurricular jobs I have employed you on?"

"No, Val, I swear it. This was about your brother, nothing more than that. He's worried for him, that's all."

"And *I'm* not? How many times do I have to prove my loyalty to this family? Is it because I don't carry a fucking AK-47 strapped to my back?"

He was now on his feet and standing directly in front of me. "I don't know what you want me to say here. I've told you everything."

"Yes, everything but the fucking truth!"

"I love you, Valentin, and I would never betray you. My presence was required on behalf of your father. What he does in this family are his decisions, not mine. If you have a problem with the way he runs this family, then you need to take it up with him."

"Oh, I intend to right after I deal with you. Don't ever forget who you are talking to. It didn't have to be this way, Oleg, and because I feel there is much more to this lie you are spinning, we are not leaving here until all is said. Get comfortable, my friend, because you are not going anywhere."

"Valentin, please don't forget that it was you who made it known to the world about how you feel about your family's dealings. I haven't forgotten who you are, and because your father loves you more than the air he breathes, he let you go to live your life. He knows you worked hard to legitimize the clubs and other business interests he has a connection to. However, there are still things that go way beyond your reach and control. Sasha is your brother first, and he has to be protected at all costs."

"What has he done?"

"Nothing we can't handle, I promise you. As long as he stays at the safe house to wait for your father's return, all will be well."

"Am I to know when my father will return? Because here's the problem I'm having with all you have said here. When I spoke to my father a few nights ago, I was told by him personally that he wasn't certain when he would be returning because of my mother's failing health. So, was he lying? Or are you? I do so despise liars, especially the ones who I have had blind faith in and yet when given the chance to make amends, still make a mockery out of the truth. Now, we can't have that, Oleg, can we?"

"I didn't see any other way, and I had no choice."

"You always have a choice and clearly, you made the wrong one. Tell me the truth now, or so help me god, I will rip out your tongue and shove it down your throat."

"Fuck! This was not how it was supposed to go down. I wasn't lying about speaking to your father. What was a lie was him asking me to take your place in watching over Sasha. He would never betray you like that and neither would I if it could have been helped. Your brother got into some trouble with some members from another family, and it escalated very quickly, leading to one of its members taking a bullet to his head. Sasha called me, and I promised to help him. I have done everything in my power to keep this away from your father and you, but I see I have failed on all counts of good intentions."

"Give me a name? Who was it, Oleg?"

"Avros Shirmanov," he barely got out above a whisper.

"Dammit to hell in the name of all that's holy. You stupid shit! Sasha has never done anything half-way. No, he had to fuck with the son of the world's second-largest Russian mob family. Another mess I'll have to clean up."

CHAPTER
fifteen

Willow

"These look wonderful. I guess the time off did you some good," Madeline remarked as she held up my sketchbook. "I mean it, kid, the designs are fantastic, and Zara is going to flip when she sees them."

"Yeah, we shall see," I responded.

"Is that doubt I'm hearing from you?"

"Maybe a little, I don't know. I haven't really been able to concentrate lately, and now with the stakes so high as they are, I'm scared I'm going to fall on my face in a big heap of failure."

"Wow, so cynical for such a young woman as yourself. I wrote the book on cynicism, kid, and it's not a good look to have. I never would wish that on you. Come on, you can talk to me. What's bothering you? Wait a minute, does this have to do with the guy? I mean, Mr. Sex on legs guy? Oh, honey, you don't have any problems."

"Shut up and be serious for a minute. Yes, it's about Valentin."

"Willow, just his name makes me want to throw away my vibrator and put myself back on the market again in hopes I find someone better than Hal Shorenstein."

I shook my head and just wondered why I told her anything. "I'm going to take a walk, and when I return I am going to put on my headphones and block you out."

"You can try, kid, but I'm not going anywhere! I love you too much to stop messing with you. Come here." She opened up her arms to give me a hug, and at that moment with my friend, I missed my mom so much.

I stopped for a coffee and walked without a destination in mind. I just needed to clear my head and think for a little while. I found myself back at Bryant Park, staring at the same park bench Valentin found me asleep on. The memory of that day came flooding back, and I suddenly missed him and wanted to be back in his arms. He made me feel so safe and wanted. *How does that happen? And to someone like me who wasn't looking for love and romance and was just satisfied enough reading about it in books?*

And what about all that happened with the café owner? He hurt a man because of me and the crazy thing about learning this information is I was grateful to him for it. Growing up with a single mom taught me many things, and one was to always have your friends back, especially when they were in need of help.

When my mom got pregnant with me, most of her friends moved on to begin college and do all the fun things a college freshman should be doing. My mom was caring for a newborn and taking online classes in-between feedings. Everything I am was because of my mom, and I tried very hard to make her proud of me.

Would she be proud to know that I condoned the gruesome beating of a man who just insulted me? Yeah, I'm sure that would go over well. Grandma would be another story and would probably side with me with no hesitation. Mom tried to handle everything with a conversation, whereas grandma wouldn't think twice about slapping you upside your head. Oh, I missed her. She sent postcards from every port she stopped in. The last one was from Bermuda. She wrote on the back, "Hanging with the beach bums. Wishing you were here" and closed it with hearts and hugs.

Holding my phone in my hand and staring at my mom's number, I released a breath and dialed her. I didn't know if she would be working or not, but if she was, I would leave a message.

"Hi, honey, what a great surprise. How are you?"

"Hi, mom, I'm fine. I just wanted to call and say hi." My voice broke a little. It usually did when I would hear her voice. "How's work?" I asked the first question that I could think of.

"*How's work?* What's wrong, Willow? And don't try to tell me nothing, because I hear it in your voice."

I could never hide anything when it came to my mom, another person in my life that could read me like a printed book and give a detailed account of my thoughts.

"It's nothing, mom. I just have a lot on my mind, and I'm swamped with work."

"Really? What's going on?"

"My boss landed a big deal with me designing a line for an upcoming Broadway play. I can't go into details right now, but it's a good thing."

She happily squealed into the phone and began asking me question after question until I said, "Mom! What did I just say? Listen, I have to go. I just wanted to hear your voice. I'll call you soon."

"Okay, hold on. Now I know you, little girl, and you just don't call me out of the blue in the middle of a workday to just say hello. Talk to me now, or I will hop in the car and drive in, and you know I despise shore and city traffic."

"Fine, you win." I laughed.

"I usually do, so spill. Who's the guy?"

"Why does it have to be a guy? Maybe I met a woman and we're having one hot affair? What would you think of that?"

"I would say tell me more and good for you."

"Yeah, you probably would. I love you, mom."

"I love you too. Now, who is he?"

"Someone who is way out of my league and will probably come to his senses any day now."

"Fuck that shit! Then he's an asshole who needs his eyesight checked. You are amazing inside and out, and if a guy doesn't know that after talking to you after ten seconds, you cut him loose and say, 'Take a hike.'"

"Okay, cool your jets, mom, and your Jersey street cred. He's no fool and makes his intentions very clear on who and what he wants."

"And that's you?"

"Yes,"

"Look, Willow, you are an adult and are smart enough to trust yourself in making good choices. I just don't want to see you hurt in something that is bigger than you can handle."

"I know, and I'm working it out in my own way. He's intense and a little scary, but when I'm with him, I feel so protected."

"How far has this gone, Willow? You haven't, ugh, I can't even say the words. This feels very weird."

"Yes, mom, I have. And I'm already in too deep with this man. One day he was just there and dropped into my life as fast as lightning strikes, and I've been trying to catch my breath ever since."

"Please baby, take this at your own pace. You don't want to get all caught up in this man and one day look in the mirror and not recognize yourself."

"Why? Because that's what happened when you loved my father? Is that why you always discouraged me from dating?"

"I was young and didn't know any better. He said all the right things, and I fell hard. When I told him I was pregnant, he stayed and said more right things. The moment you screamed your way into the world, he fled faster than a fugitive on the run. I guess I should have felt something after that, maybe anger or regret, but when I looked into your eyes, all I felt was love for you. I know I haven't been the best example when it comes to relationships. I'm sorry for that, sweetheart. I just never wanted you to go through what happened to me. A consuming love can be a dangerous one. I don't need to know anything more about this man right now. When you're ready I'll be here to listen. Just be careful, baby. I love you so much."

Tears flooded my eyes to the point I couldn't see. My amazing mother just made it okay for me.

"I love you, mom. I'll call you soon." And I disconnected the call and continued to cry, but this time around, they were happy tears.

Talking to my mom always made me feel better. Sometimes the conversation could become a little heavy to handle, but I also knew her advice came from a good place with the best intentions. Experience and personal growth had taught her many things, and she tried to pass those lessons to me. She was afraid for me, and I understood her reservations.

In a small way, maybe I was too. However, knowing and feeling the way I did would not stop me from taking a chance with Valentin. He was too charismatic for me to walk away from.

My whole life I'd played it safe. I never even broke a curfew or snuck out my bedroom window to go to a party with my friends. They had all the fun, while I stayed home to study and get the good grades my mom expected from me.

For once, I want to know what it feels like to be free. Free to just leap without a net but knowing you'll be safe, because the person you have placed your trust in will never allow you to be hurt. This is what I feel for Valentin Vasiliev, and I'm done agonizing over it.

It had been hours since I left the office, and it was too nice of a day to go back and stay indoors. I texted Madeline and told her I was going to work the rest of the day from home. I had my sketchbook with me and couldn't think of a better place to work than right here on this bench.

Who knows? Maybe Valentin will find me here again.

CHAPTER
Sixteen

Valentin

Avros Shirmanov, I kept repeating in my head until I finally said his name aloud. *Of all the men my brother could have taken out, he chooses a top lieutenant in a rival mob family and one who will be missed and vengeance will be wanted with blood spilled.*

"Oleg, I'm done fucking around here. No more lies. I need to know everything, and I mean all of it."

"I'm so sorry, Valentin, you will never know how much."

"Enough with your apologies. All I am concerned with now is my brother and how the hell I am going to save him from joining Avros. Begin, and let's hope you are as vivid with the truth as you are with the lies." I called down for drinks, needing more than just a shot to take the edge off. No, this called for the whole bottle.

"It all started with the oldest reason in the book, and it got messy."

"A woman? Come on, Oleg. He's not that stupid."

"You'd be surprised how a woman can turn a man's head and dazzle him with a golden pussy."

"Be careful with what you say next to me," I warned.

"I wasn't talking about you or your girl. She's not like them, and you are not your brother. He's young and impulsive, which is putting it mildly. He fucked up, Val, and knows it."

"Oh, is that right? I guess that's when I found him. He was doing his penance by having his dick sucked off."

"Impulsive, just as I said."

"No, more like stupid. Okay, let's break it down. He meets the Femme Fatale in a bar, where they drink it up and she lavishes him with attention. The party moves upstairs to one of the private rooms, and they fuck. Am I right so far?"

"Yes," he answered.

"Was she alone? Any spotters in the club on Shirmanov's payroll?"

"Not one. We meticulously scanned the security footage inside and outside the club. She came alone and took a seat at the bar. She was only in the club for under an hour when Sasha arrived. He made his usual pickups and then went up to the office to secure the deposits in the safe. He walked down to the bar and it looked as if he said something to her, and then they both left and went upstairs to his private playroom."

"And that's where we don't have any cameras installed, right?"

"You would be correct."

"What about the hallway? Clearly, you can see who enters and exits, right?"

"Yes, we can. About ten minutes later, Avros was spotted on the cameras and kicked his way inside. Our guys quickly followed, and it got ugly."

"Don't forget messy," I added.

"Yeah, that too."

"This was nothing more than a smash and grab, but for whatever reason, Shirmanov used his woman as bait. Sasha may be a lot of things but can be downright lethal when a gun is in his face."

"Or a knife. It doesn't matter, as long as he strikes first. Avros had a score to settle with your brother and chose to handle it on his own. Our families were not privy to their conflict, and I felt it was best if I handled it without alerting your father or you. I know you will never believe a lie is justifiable, but it had to be done. On my eyes, son, I swear that's my truth."

"I believe you, Oleg. So, where does that leave Sasha? What's the word on the street?"

"Avros was seen in Atlantic City the night before last and looking quite well."

"Or so you want his crew to believe?"

"Yes, and so far it has worked in our favor. Avros was always reckless, more so than Sasha ever was. He has shamed his father and his family more times than I can say. It was only a matter of time before he was called up to atone for his actions. What you must understand is that he came after one of our own. A son for a son. The Bratva take care of their own. It's always been this way, and Shirmanov would never dishonor our code."

"Not even for his own son?" I asked.

"No, not if it meant more shame and disloyalty. When honor is at stake, it's worse than death."

As proof to me that he would never lie again, Oleg took out his knife and handed it to me, accepting any punishment I would hand down to him. I refused him, which left him shocked. I would not spill blood here today, no matter how angry I had become with him earlier. I understood better, and I sympathized with the anguished choices he was forced to make.

We shall move past this indiscretion and never speak of it again. I had more pressing matters to deal with at the moment. First was my brother and making sure his sins stay buried, along with Avros and his whore.

Secondly, my beautiful dove. It had been too long of a day away from her, and once I checked my phone and saw no calls or messages from Willow, I needed her more than my next breath. It took me all of a second to locate her. Once I did, fury filled my veins once again.

I thought back to the conversation we had and how I practically cut my heart wide open for only Willow to see. I told her that I loved her and wanted her always. By declaring my hand so soon, everything I had been feeling was now out in the open. So she had to know at least on a small measure what I was capable of. Her safety meant everything to me, and today would be the last fucking day she walked alone in the city without protection.

"Are you ready to go?" Oleg asked as he walked over to me.

"No, change of plan. I want you to go to the safehouse, and bring Sergei with you. Inform Sasha that I will see him tomorrow."

I straightened my tie and put my jacket on, running my hands down the invisible wrinkles I knew were not there. I was fucking un-nerved and needed to get to my woman.

"Where are you going, Valentin?"

"Have you forgotten your place? Where I go and what I do is not any of your concern, Oleg. You remember that."

"My apologies. I just want to make sure you're okay, you know, after everything we talked about."

"It's over. Let's move on. I need to go, but as of tomorrow, you are back on Willow's security detail."

"And what of Sasha?"

"He's no longer your concern nor problem. I will handle my brother. You will do as I say, or we have a bigger problem than what already has transpired between us. Is it clear? Or do I need to speak slower?"

He had the audacity to look affronted but then relaxed his facial features and grasped my shoulders, a show of respect and care.

"You really do love her, don't you?" he asked.

"More than I can ever put into words, or even understand myself. All I know is that I need her safe, Oleg, and I trust no one more than you. Hear me when I say that today is over and we move on, leaving it where it belongs, and that's in the past. No good will ever come to you if this is what you choose. I haven't distanced myself from my family. You know that is not a reality I can ever walk away from. On the outside, the life I have looks very different from yours and it's upheld to a higher standard because of the career I have chosen and the circle I choose to align myself in. It's smoke and mirrors. Deep down in a place that is not shown to others, you and I both know it's a different way of life. Some days, it's a harder pill to swallow and I bear the burdens of my choices, but they are not yours to worry about."

"I understand."

"Good, see that you do. I am a Vasiliev, first born son to Alaric Vasiliev. I love my father very much." As I said the words, my accent became stronger and deeper as the darkness began to rise within me. "Oleg, his blood runs through my veins. I will never forget who I am, and my loyalty is never to be questioned. Not by you, not by anyone. Do you understand?"

"Yes, I do."

"Good, this pleases me. If this conversation was taking place with anyone else, you know your throat would have been slit and the person responsible for doing such a heinous act against you would not lose one night sleep over it. Don't ever lie or fail me again."

I took him in my arms and placed a kiss on each side of his face, leaving him to be on his own while I was in search of Willow. I had stayed longer than I should have when I should have already been reunited with my woman.

She was no longer at Bryant Park and, considering the late hour, I was grateful in knowing that. I checked my phone again, and the signal placed her at home. *Finally! She's home safe and hopefully behind a locked door. After everything that happened with Sasha, I could not risk anything happening to Willow. Not when I have just found her.* I knew this was my heart talking instead of the rational part I knew and trusted.

Love was a powerful emotion that could bring the mightiest of men down to their knees. I'd seen it happen with my father and how he felt about my mother. Their bond was unbreakable, and he had never allowed it to ever be shaken. It's what I wanted with Willow. *With each passing moment spent with her, I mean to bring her closer, so close that she will never leave me. I promised to give her time, but I knew that was more for her benefit than my own. It's been a fucked up day, and I just want to see her. I want to love on my woman and shut the rest of the world out, to be buried so deep inside of her that I don't know where I begin or she ends.*

I made some calls and picked up dinner and flowers, lilies to be exact. I was hoping she would like them and thank me properly.

I held the carryout bags along with a large bouquet of flowers as I took the elevator up to her floor. I knocked on her door a couple of times, expecting to see her at any moment. I waited a couple of minutes and then began to pound on the door. *What in the hell is going on here?* I knocked again, waiting for Willow to swing open the door and jump into my arms, but I was met with silence.

She's not here. "Where are you?" I whispered aloud as I stood in front of her door, allowing my anger to take over. I checked my phone, and it showed that she was here. I dropped the bags and flowers to the floor, and with all my aggression inciting me, I kicked down her door. I shouted her name over and over throughout the apartment, coming up short at every turn. This apartment was empty, and she was not where she was supposed to be. I pulled out my phone and dialed his number, wanting answers. The location software was supposed to be foolproof.

"Mr. Vasiliev, what can I help you with?" he asked all too eagerly.

With my phone to my ear, I rubbed my right temple, attempting to suppress my anger from reaching its boiling point. "I want to know why your software is failing."

Without wavering, he said, "No way. That's impossible."

"Why? Because you say so?"

"With all due respect, sir, I'm the best there is, and my shit always works. It could be the receiving phone with the glitch, but I know it's not here on my end."

Just as I was about to say more, voices could be heard coming from the hallway.

"Oh my god! I've been robbed," she screamed. I heard the fear in her voice, recognizing the same tone she used on the day we first met. She walked further inside the apartment, but she wasn't alone. A man was with her.

What. The. Fuck!?

I took in the scene before me and thought of everything I could possibly think of to calm the hell down. Or, I could rip his face off and ask questions later. I remained where I was standing, waiting for my dove to come to me.

She didn't.

Instead, she walked over to her broken door, assessing the damage and probably worrying about how she would pay for it. *Oh, my love, don't worry about a thing. I will have this fixed in under an hour, and then you will be coming home with me.*

"Willow, are you okay?" he asked, placing the fabric down and reaching for her face. He put his hands on her. I wanted to kill him for touching what was mine.

She looked at me for all of a second and then shook her head. "Yes, I'm fine. Whatever has happened here is just a misunderstanding."

"And what about him?" he gestured with his thumb.

I remained silent no more and stalked over to the unsuspecting fool. My fists were balled at my sides as his eyes were intently on me. "*He* has a name, and *I* don't appreciate not being acknowledged when I'm standing right here in the room. My name is Valentin Vasiliev, and Willow is my woman."

"Funny, she's never mentioned you. I guess you're not all that important to her."

My eyes glazed over with lifeless expression. It took me all of a second to react to his words by wrapping my hands around his fucking throat. I rammed him hard against the shattered door, restricting his airway.

"Valentin!!! Oh my god, stop it. You're hurting him!" she screamed and placed her small body in front of mine.

"And *I'm* not hurt? Watching the woman I love defend another man right in front of me?"

"Valentin, please, he's my friend. Stop this right now!" Her small hands could hardly be felt on my bigger and stronger arms.

My senses finally registered, and I released him but not before shoving him back. His body slid down the door with his bony ass landing on the floor. She immediately dropped to her knees and consoled him. Yes, she gave another man comfort while I stood there, not knowing what to say for the first time in my life. Feelings of betrayal ravaged through and pierced my heart. He was still gasping for air when she looked up toward me and delivered one last blow to my heart.

"I think you should leave," she demanded.

I closed my eyes and realized what I had just done. I lifted her up into my arms and tried not to scare her any further. The look in her eyes was shredding my heart. She was afraid, which caused her to push me away. I wish I could take it back, but the damage was already done. I felt sick.

With tears in her eyes and barely making eye contact with me, she said, "Please, Valentin, just go." She asked again, as her voice broke, just like my heart.

I let her go, but not before placing a kiss on her forehead.

"I'm sorry, love. I'm so sorry."

CHAPTER
Seventeen

Willow

"Yes, I'm still in the park, but I have to get over to the outlet before it closes," I said excitedly over the phone to Madeline.

"You are killing me here, kid! First, you disappear for hours on end, and then I get a text that you're not coming back. Zara arrives in two days, and she is expecting to see some mock-ups."

"Madeline, where's the faith? I have been working this entire time. It just wasn't in the office. I am jumping out of my pants on how these designs came out! It may just be my best work."

"Isn't that Casanova's job to remove you from your pants?"

"Ewww, you need to get out more. I will see you first thing in the morning. I'll bring the coffee."

"No, I'll buy a whole box of Dunkin, and then I'll be chaining you to your desk."

"I'll pass. How about we invest in a Keurig and just brew our own? I'll throw in the first box of K-cups."

"If it means you won't disappear tomorrow, done! I'll place the Amazon order now."

"I love you," I cheerfully said.

I made it just in time before the fabric store had closed, buying everything I needed for what I was envisioning. This time I had Madeline's card on me, and I breathed a lot easier when I saw the grand total. *It's going to be worth it as soon as she sees what I have in mind.*

My hands were overflowing with supplies when I ran into Tag, a friend from design school who was now modeling part-time.

"Need a hand, beautiful?" He winked and then grabbed practically all of it with no effort at all. He was tall and slender but worked out hard to maintain his body. This I knew from all the times he attempted to drag me with him to the gym.

Ugh! I hated working out, but I wasn't blind and did appreciate the male form, especially Valentin. He was stunning in and out of his expensive suits. Just remembering every inch of his golden skin had my pulse racing and my folds dripping with arousal.

I had no experience when it came to what I should be doing with a man. Valentin had been my first in everything sexual and patiently guided me through it all.

I surprised myself when I found the courage to give him a blowjob, another first for me. I was scared and nervous I wouldn't please him, but then he encouraged me, and the sounds emanating off him only fueled my own desires to keep going and take all of him. He came so hard down my throat that I believed I was not going to be able to swallow all of him, but I managed to, which pleased him even more.

The sounds from the city interfered with my daydreaming of Valentin, and we needed to cross the street.

"Yes, I would love some help," I said to Tag.

"You got it. So, how have you been? I live in the same building as you do, but I never see you. How is that possible?"

"Oh, I don't know, pretty boy. Maybe it's because you're out on the prowl, trolling for hot men and don't have time for your friends anymore."

"Shit, there you go using my best lines, because that's what I was going to say about you. Don't try to fool me, Willow. I saw someone leave the building late Sunday night, and him I would remember, so do tell."

"What? So you can try to steal him away from me with your seductive charms? Nope, not this one."

"In my defense, it was only one time, and Perry was clearly giving me the vibe."

"Yeah, whatever. You just stay on your side of the street and leave mine alone."

"Okay, but you'll tell me if things get rocky, so I can swoop in and make a move?"

"Sure, Tag, you'll be the first to know."

He shoulder bumped me, and we practically laughed all the way back to the building. Tag's family situation was similar to mine. Our grandmothers had been friends for years, and when we met in fashion school it was like a small reunion amongst old and new friends. Sadly, his nana had died only six months after he moved in. She had been sick but kept her cancer quiet from the rest of her family. She was a widow for a great number of years before dying herself.

She was Tag's father's mother, and he was the facilitator of her will. Her assets were divided amongst her four grandchildren, leaving Tag the apartment, the furnishings, and some money to live on to give him some room on what to do after he finished with his education. What a beautiful act of love that she had given him. He would always joke that he was her favorite because he was the baby of the family. I teased him, because he had the cutest dimples from the rest of his siblings, and what grandmother in her right mind could resist them?

"Hey, before we go upstairs, can I show you the proofs from my last photo shoot? I'm telling you, Willow, they are awesome. My agent is talking billboards, print ads, the works. Everything is finally beginning to pay off."

"I am so proud of you! I'm sure your family must be over the moon."

"Are you kidding? My ma has the neighborhood wired for any alerts she gets on me."

"Awww, it's because she's proud of you and wants all of your dreams to come true."

We entered the building and walked inside his apartment. He placed the supplies down and walked over to his desk to retrieve his portfolio. His smile was infectious as he handed me the book. I flipped through it, loving picture after picture of my gorgeous friend.

"Oh, Tag, these are fabulous. Dream big, right?"

"Exactly. Hey, Willow, who's watching over *your* dreams, making sure they come true for you?"

"What? Why would you ask me something like that?"

"Because you're alone, and you're back to walking again at night."

"Stalker." I punched his arm.

He pretended that it hurt but then got serious again. "I mean it, Willow. Are you okay?"

"He's a friend, and it's very new. He's been wonderful, and I'm trying very hard not to overanalyze and taint it with my bullshit worrying."

"You take all the time you need when it comes to matters of the heart, and I mean yours. You are the kindest and sweetest person I have ever met next to my ma, and that's saying something. Take all the time you need with the mystery guy or anyone after him. You are special, Willow, and any guy that ends up winning your heart is the lucky one."

I couldn't help the tears that began to fill and spill from my eyes. "Look what you've done. Crying is not a good look on me. You're lucky I'm not wearing any makeup today."

"Come here, little one. Someone needs a hug," he said, and then took me in his arms and squeezed tightly but lovingly. It was perfectly innocent, but I still felt a pang of guilt for being in the arms of another man, knowing Valentin would not be happy about it. I already had a clear picture on who Valentin Vasiliev was, and as much as it scared me, it also excited me and made me want him that much more.

"Okay, I really have to get upstairs and begin working on these patterns, or I'm going to be toast with my boss tomorrow."

"Alright, let me give you a helping hand."

The elevator dinged, and we stepped out, with Tag carrying all the fabric and supplies. What a gentleman. Just as we reached my door, I noticed the door hanging off its frame with splintered pieces all over the floor. I shrieked in fear when I saw all the damage. My grandmother was going to freak.

"Oh my god, I've been robbed," I shouted, and then I slowly walked inside the apartment, not knowing what I would find missing. Tag was right by my side, getting ready to attack just in case someone was still here. I loved him for thinking he could be my brave hero, but he was too handsome and needed his face for work.

Stepping out from the design area stood Valentin, taking me by complete surprise. I was shocked to see him inside of my apartment, and I couldn't read his mood because he just remained where he was standing. I turned around and looked back to my broken door and knew it had been Valentin that did this. *But why?* I asked all the questions in my head, afraid to hear the answers on what he might say.

When Tag walked over to join me by the door, he asked if I was okay and then gave a not so nice look to Valentin. *Oh, shit!* I knew well enough to know that wasn't going to go over well with my man. I quietly smiled to myself, knowing it was becoming easier to say those words and know the truth behind them. *My man.*

It only took less than a second for Valentin to react to Tag, and it wasn't in the best of ways. I didn't miss the way his hands curled into fists as he made his way over to me.

"*He* has a name, and *I* don't appreciate not being acknowledged when I'm standing right here in the room. My name is Valentin Vasiliev, and Willow is my woman."

His woman? Oh, yes, I am. And normally his dominating talk would have made me crumble to the floor and get wet down between my legs, but this was Valentin marking his territory. And I didn't like it in front of my friend, a male friend with sisters who wouldn't think twice about protecting me.

Tag didn't back down and challenged Valentin, which was not only stupid but dangerous too. "Funny, she's never mentioned you. I guess you're not all that important to her." He mocked Valentin.

In a blinding blur, Tag was grabbed and nearly choked to death, leaving me helpless to stop it. All I could do was scream.

"Valentin!!! Oh my god, stop it. You're hurting him!" I continued to scream and try to stop Valentin from killing my friend right in front of me. I cried and begged for his mercy. "Valentin, please, he's my friend. Stop this right now!" I shouted again and then attacked his arm until he finally released Tag, but not before shoving him hard against the wall. Tag was gasping for air and coughing to catch his breath.

Valentin looked sick to his stomach. *Was I responsible for this?* I couldn't handle much more right now and did the only thing I could think of: I asked him to leave, which nearly broke me just as much as I knew it did for him.

"I think you should leave," I tearfully asked him and then watched him close his eyes fighting to hold onto me.

I was still trying to comfort my friend when two arms pulled me up and off the floor. Valentin ran his hands through my hair and never pulled away from staring deep into my eyes. I wanted to wrap myself around him and beg for his forgiveness, because in a small way, I knew I had hurt him here tonight.

I knew he would only go if he saw the truth in my eyes. I painfully whispered the words and then broke him as if all the time we spent together had just been washed away. "Please, Valentin, just go."

This time he listened but not before kissing me on my forehead and looking absolutely broken. "I'm sorry, love. I'm sorry," he said and then walked out of my apartment and possibly out of my life forever.

I wiped away my tears and went back to Tag, who was now up and on his feet, a little shaky but standing. I hurried into the kitchen to fetch him some cold water. He drank it down quickly and then coughed a few more times before clearing his throat enough to talk to me.

"I take it that's the boyfriend? Or as he stated, your man?"

"Yes, and yes, but I'm thinking it may be over after tonight."

"I'm sorry, little one. I should have never talked shit to him. I shouldn't have gotten between you two. Sorry."

"Stop apologizing. He's the one that attacked you. Are you hurt? Any lasting damage?"

"Nah, I'm not that much of a diva. I can take a toss or two, but I prefer it's in the bedroom. Listen, I can call my uncle the contractor to come on by to fix your door."

"Thank you, but I'm sure someone is already on their way."

"Seriously? Who is this guy?"

"He's everything, and someone you don't want to make an enemy out of. Go home, please."

"Are you sure?"

"Yes, I'll be fine. I have very important work to do for my boss, and I can't let her down."

"I love you. You know that, right?"

"I know, and the feeling is mutual…in a brother/sister kind of way." We smiled at one another, and then he gave me a hug.

"I have to leave in the morning for Chicago for another shoot. I hate knowing how upset you are. I can reschedule it. Let me call my agent and see what I can do."

"No way, and risk being blackballed because they think you're a canceling flake? No, I'm fine. Go be a supermodel, and don't worry about me."

"Shit, when you put it that way…I'm going! I'll call you when I get back."

Just as I was walking Tag to my broken door, two men showed up, carrying toolboxes. Tag gave me a look, and I assured him that I knew who sent them. *Less than an hour, I'm impressed.*

"Sorry to disturb you. We're here to repair and replace your door. We also have new reinforced locks to install as well."

I answered back nonchalantly, "Sure, don't let me get in your way."

I waved them off and reached for my purse to get my phone. No messages from Valentin. My heart just sank deep into my chest seeing a blank screen. I didn't second-guess my decision and decided to call him. If he didn't answer, I would leave him a message. It would be up to him to call me back, or better yet, find me in the park at our spot.

It rang once before going straight to his voicemail. *He must have his phone turned off.* Old insecurities were returning, masking the happiness I felt and replacing it with negative fears. *He would never just avoid me.*

I wiped away my tears and bravely dialed his number again. When his silver-tongued and poised voice came over the line, all the tears once again threatened to spill over. I feared once I started, I would never stop. I took a deep, calming breath and after the sound of the beep, all the words I should have said when he was here began to pour out from me, and I prayed I could get them all out before time ran out.

"Hi, Valentin, it's me, Willow. Of course, you know who's calling you with caller ID and all. I mean, who doesn't have that nowadays. Ugh! I can't help but say stupid things when I'm around you. What I'm trying to say is sorry. I'm sorry that I pushed you away tonight when the look in your eyes was asking to stay. I know I hurt you tonight. It should come as no surprise to you that I'm new at being in a relationship. I don't have the slightest clue on how to behave. It's pretty much like standing in a four-way intersection and trying to figure out which road to take. Before I came home tonight and everything went wrong, there was not a minute that ticked by that I didn't think of you. I was almost hoping you would magically find me and sweep me off my feet. I guess I'm growing accustomed to being in your arms. But as much as I love being there, those same arms almost hurt my friend, someone I care very much about. You scared me, because I didn't know how far you would take it. Please call me back, Valentin. And by the way, thank you for sending the workers to fix my door. I...I love you."

By the time I changed out of my work clothes and returned to the living room, my door had been repaired. I inspected the door and its frame, admiring the good work they did here. It was actually perfect, and I didn't even think grandma would notice if it wasn't for the new lock replacement. The old door was leaning against the wall in the hallway, and you would have to be blind to miss the large size shoe-print right in the middle of it

"Okay, miss, you are all set. Here are your new keys for the top and bottom lock, along with an extra set."

"Thank you," I simply said and then locked the door behind him.

I checked my phone continually for any response from Valentin, but it was radio silent. I held my hand over my heart, clutching my phone and just cried until I had nothing left to shed. I hated silence. The cold shoulder act of rebellion would never work in any relation-ship I was in. I needed to express what I was feeling and not keep it all bottled up inside, another trait from my mom.

I could no longer obsess and stalk my phone. I had a lot of work to do in a short amount of time. I wasn't a big drinker, more like an occa-sional glass of wine, but tonight the whole bottle was required. I put my earbuds in, blasting Adele's painful collection of heartache songs. Ten minutes was too long, and I changed it up to Taylor Swift. At least her break-up songs had a happy beat to them.

I worked through the night, finally stopping around four to get some sleep. I was a walking zombie and felt myself about to crash. In between pouring the wine, I called him three more times. I knew it was foolish, but I couldn't stop myself. No long drawn out messages this time, just asking him to call me back.

I left my phone in the living room to charge so I wouldn't wake up to check it. I took a shower and made coffee. I unplugged the cord and swiped the screen to wake it up and found not one message. Not one.

"Please, Valentin, call me and say we're okay," I whispered through more tears. "I have to get to work," I said and then searched my closet for something to wear. My look was nice but on the simple side of comfort. I skipped the shoes, and as an act of rebellion, I wore my favorite pair of Chucks. I kept a few things at work and could easily change if any clients stop by. Zara was not due to arrive until tomorrow, so that left me today to finish and ready myself for her critique.

Looking over my designs, I knew they were good but were they enough for Zara? She could take one look at them and hate what I had done. *I'm sure I'm not the first designer to fall flat on her face in epic proportions, right?*

I refilled my travel mug and gathered my things to leave. *Oh, what the hell, let me check my phone again. Nope, still nothing. For the sake of my sanity and my career on the line, I have to force myself to put him out of my mind and focus. He's not an easy man to forget, but I have no choice.*

Not in the mood to be pushed and shoved on a crowded train this morning, I opened up my Uber app and called for a car. Thanks to Madeline, my paycheck got an increase, and although I didn't have money to burn, I had enough that I could afford this morning's ride. According to the app, a black town car was just around the corner, and my driver's name was Ollie. *Sounds harmless enough.* My app showed me that he was less than a minute away. I put my phone away, and as I took a sip of my coffee, the town car arrived. The driver was someone who had driven me before.

Coincidence? Or is this Valentin's way of watching over me?

"Hello, my friend," he said in a boisterous greeting.

"Good morning, Ollie. Going my way?" I asked, and then we both laughed as I stepped inside of his car. "So, the other day you were driving an NYC taxi, and today you are an Uber driver. And right in my neighborhood ready to pick me up. Crazy, right?"

"Small world, I guess, and the cab was a loaner. I didn't like the feel of the car, so I upgraded. Do you not like it?"

"I like it well enough. It's very clean, almost new in fact."

He said nothing more to confirm my suspicions on what was really going on here. I deeply sighed and then wiped away more tears. *Dammit, Willow, pull yourself together. This is just ridiculous to cry over someone who's been avoiding you. Yeah, that's what it feels like.*

"Oh, I'm sorry. I didn't mean to upset you," he said while looking at me in the rear-view mirror.

"You didn't, Ollie. I was already there."

"Is there anything I can do to help you?" He seemed to be genuinely concerned about my well-being.

Once we arrived, I gave him my thanks with a promise to leave a good tip. He said it wasn't necessary, but I told him that I was doing it anyway. I stood in front of the warehouse building door, holding my things and feeling lost. He hadn't left yet. I got the feeling that if I had stayed all day here on the sidewalk, then Ollie would too. This had Valentin written all over it, and to prove my suspicions were correct, I turned and walked back over to the car.

"Yes, Ollie, I believe you can do something for me. Will you deliver a message to Valentin from me?"

"I don't understand," he played his part well, but I knew better.

"Come on, give me a little credit. The ruse is up, and I know who you work for, so please tell your boss exactly what I'm about to say to you." There was no reply; he just listened. "Tell Valentin his silence is keeping his 'broken dove' broken, and the dove fears it will never be able to fly again. If this is not what he wants, then please tell him to call me. Don't worry, Ollie. He will know what it means." He looked at me sympathetically, and I knew I had been right all along. "Thank you. You've been very kind," I said and then found the courage to walk inside and not look back.

Somehow, I knew he would still be there watching me, because that's what Valentin wanted him to do. *Come on, Valentin, please call me back. Okay, breathe, Willow. It's time to kick some major ass today.*

Nine hours later, I was staring back at seven dressed mannequins, all in an original design by Willow Pierce. Madeline had given strict orders for me not to be disturbed today, and with two Keurig machines now in the office, my coffee running days were over. I didn't check my phone since putting it on silent this morning. He knew where I was, and if he meant anything he had said to me in all the time we've been together, he would man up and call.

I lifted the blinds, giving Madeline the signal to come in. The look on her face was priceless, and it made me want to just dance around the open showroom.

"Not bad, kid. Zara is going to be eating a lot of crow for a long time coming. She should have accepted our bid from the very beginning, knowing how talented you are. These are just amazing. I feel like celebrating, don't you?"

"No, not really."

I plopped down into my chair and did everything I could not to rain on her good mood. I'd been so busy working on the designs, I didn't share anything about Valentin to Madeline.

"Hey, why the long face? What's going on?"

"I lost him, Madeline. He's gone, and he's probably not coming back."

"I don't believe that for a second, kid. No, the man I met is crazy in love with you, and he's in too deep to just walk away from someone as wonderful as you."

"You didn't see the look in his eyes last night when he saw me with Tag. You remember him, right? He's my friend from school and lives in my building."

"Oh, yeah…model, right?"

"Yes, along with the ten other jobs he does. I haven't seen him in a while and ran into him down in the Garment District. He walked me home, and it was totally innocent, but tell that to Valentin."

"Um, does he know Tag is gay and sparkles like thirty-one flavors?"

"No, he does not because he didn't give me a chance to explain. I guess he was coming over to surprise me with dinner and flowers. Oh, Madeline, they were my favorite, lilies to be exact. I didn't even notice them until hours after he left. I couldn't even look at them. I just felt sick. I've called him numerous times and still no response back."

"Okay, enough of this moping around and feeling sorry for yourself. You are a superstar and in need to let your hair down and do some serious celebrating tonight. There's this hot new techno club in Chelsea I've been wanting to check out for a while now. Let's change and get all dressed up and go."

"I'll pass. I think I'm just going to go home and eat a gallon of ice cream."

"No, you are not. You are coming out with me tonight, and thanks to the art of selfies, I know the perfect way to remind your man what he's missing."

A few hours later after consuming too many shots, I was pretty much floating on air. I couldn't feel my feet from all the dancing I was doing. Madeline had called a group of her closest friends to come down and join us. I was surrounded by the most awesome group of cougars who could drink me under the table and make it look like tea time with the queen.

Madeline was bumping and grinding against me, fending off the guys she deemed not worthy enough. Every time I tried to leave the dance floor, one of her friends pulled me back in, until I finally saw an opening and made a dash for the bar. I waved them off, and they continued to get their groove on.

I stepped into the crowded ladies room to catch my breath and relieve my full bladder. I was surprised I was still standing after all the drinks I consumed, but that was the plan, right? Madeline dragged me out clubbing as if I knew anything about that and fed me drink after drink to forget about Valentin.

It took me a few minutes to find Madeline, who was now sitting in a booth with a man, who was shamelessly flirting with her. I smiled over at my friend as I approached them.

"Hey, kid, come and join us," she shouted over the loud music.

"No, you stay and have a good time. I'm calling for a car to take me home."

She was now out of the booth and on her feet, pulling me into a hug.

"Are you sure? I don't have to hang with these guys. I'll come with you."

"No, when was the last time you enjoyed yourself like this?" She tapped her finger on her chin, knowing it was longer than it should have been. "You see? Not even you can remember that far back. I'll be fine. Probably won't be in at the crack of dawn, but I'll make the meeting with Zara."

"Okay, be careful, and text me when you get home, so I know you're safe."

"I will. Thanks, Madeline, I needed this."

"Yeah, you did, but I'm not really sure it worked."

No, it didn't, my friend, but thanks for trying.

I made my way through the throngs of clubgoer's trying to reach the exit. I was almost there when the heel to my shoe snapped, sending me colliding into a railing that I latched on to break my fall.

"Shit!" I cried out, as I knew I had twisted my ankle. *First my knees, now this.* I was angry at myself because my head was all twisted over Valentin. I leaned against the railing on the ramp that led to outside. I took a breath and rolled my ankle back and forth to see if I could walk on it. It didn't seem too bad after all, and I tried again to leave the club.

"Hey, need a hand?" I turned around to see a couple of guys standing a little too close for my liking.

"I'm good. Thanks," I answered back.

"Are you sure?" the taller guy asked, and then his friend stepped up behind him, taking a look at my shoeless foot.

"I said I was fine, and my boyfriend will be right back. So please leave me alone."

"Boyfriend? Really? We didn't see any guy with you when you were out there shaking your fine ass. Come on, baby, let's get a drink. The night is young."

"If you don't leave me alone, I'm going to scream this club down. Now back the fuck off and go away."

I tried to be as strong as I could, but two against one never equaled a fair fight, and these guys were big. My car was probably gone by now, but I was probably safer outside near the bouncer than in here with these two assholes. I made my way up the ramp, and then my ponytail was pulled, sending me back into his arms.

"Get your hands off me!" I shouted as loud as I could, and then with my good foot, I kicked him as hard as I could.

"Fucking bitch!" he shouted back as I tried to run.

Before he could reach me, I was saved by Valentin, who had the one guy in a choke hold, sending him unconscious to the floor. He grabbed the other guy by his throat and punched him so hard in his stomach I thought he was going to cough up blood. With no effort at all, Valentin picked him up and thrusted him against the concrete wall. The man went down like a rag doll.

The club was so noisy and not one person even cared to see what was happening. *What the fuck is wrong with people?* I thought as I just stood there, shaking and wanting him to hold me.

He found me. He saved me. And then without a parting glance in my direction, he walked out, leaving me alone again. I stepped outside, and there was Ollie leaning against the same town car that he drove me to work in this morning.

What a colossal mistake it was coming here tonight. I took one look at Ollie and just broke down. He was older and distinguished, very European. I'm not sure what made me do it, but there was something about Ollie that I trusted. I wasn't frightened by him. He wrapped his arm around my shoulders and helped me inside the car.

"Come on, sweetheart. I'll take you home."

I cried all the way home and then some.

CHAPTER
Eighteen

Valentin

I played her message over and over again while I felt every twinge of pain shatter another part of my soul. She never wanted me to leave, but I knew I scared her after attacking her friend. I knew there would be no stopping my anger after I watched another man's hands on her.

She belonged to me. Friend or no friend, no one gets to touch her. I was incensed with countless thoughts running through my mind. I acted first on impulse and reacted so badly, forcing Willow to send me away.

I really didn't remember too much after leaving her apartment. My driver took me home, and I drank until I passed out, only coming out of my drunken haze with Oleg's hands shaking me awake.

"Valentin, open your eyes," he shouted.

My head was pounding, and my eyes burned.

"What the hell are you going on about, Oleg? And how the hell did you get in here?"

"Is that a serious question? Please wake up. I'm here about Willow."

His tone had changed to concern, making me fully awake and alert. I was on my feet, feeling woozy with the room beginning to spin.

"Oh, shit!" he said, taking me by the shoulders to lead me into the bathroom.

He opened the lid to the toilet, and I puked and puked until I had nothing left to dispel from my stomach. He handed me a hand towel to wipe my mouth. I crawled away and tried to sit up.

"You look like hell," he said.

"Tell me something I don't know. Willow? Is she okay?"

"She doesn't look any better than you right now. I picked her up per your instructions and took her to work, but we have a problem."

"What are you talking about?" The fog in my mind was slowly fading, and with every mention of Willow, I was becoming more alert and focused.

"She made me."

"No fucking way!" I balled the towel in my hand and tossed it across the room, in disbelief of what I just heard. "What did you say to her? As if you haven't betrayed me enough!"

"Val, that's not fair, and you know it. All my years of faithful service to you and your family, one mistake in judgment does not erase that and constitute betrayal. Furthermore, she's not a fool and is not as naïve as you believe."

"I don't believe that at all. She's rays of light that have brought my dark soul to life. She's a thousand things but a fool she is not."

"I'm sorry I misspoke. Listen, she asked me to deliver a message to you. Here, give me your hand and let me help you off the floor."

"No, I'm fine right where I am. What's the message?"

"Tell Valentin his silence is keeping his 'broken dove' broken, and the dove fears it will never be able to fly again. She said you would know what it means and you should call her."

Oh, my beautiful girl, using my words against me. Well-played, my love. Oh, I miss you.

"Oleg, have you checked on Sasha this morning?"

"I have. He's doing much better. He's eating again too."

"That's good to know. What about his meds? He needs to establish a regimen again."

"Yes, I know. I called his doctor and psychiatrist and brought them up to speed. He started the prescription this morning."

"Very good. Who's with him now?"

"Sergei."

"See that he stays with Sasha and doesn't let him out of his sight until I get there. Guards are on the property?"

"Yes, all secured."

"At least something is going right. Give me your hand. I may need your help after all."

"Always."

Once I was steady on my feet, he left me on my own so I could shower and continue to sober up. I stood under the sprays of hot water as I thought of no one but Willow.

Just to hear her say how sorry she was for hurting me made me sicker to my stomach than all the alcohol I had consumed. It wasn't her fault, though. *Last night is on me, and it's my sin to atone for. I've always been jealous and possessive. It's one hundred times greater with Willow, and I don't see myself letting that part of me go anytime soon. How do I make this right? She's not the only one that's scared and unsure of what to do. She makes my head, heart, and body spin.*

I should have returned to her once I knew the door had been repaired, but I wasn't in a good place, and I was more afraid that my dove was. My role in this family as firstborn son meant I had to be the best in all areas of my life. I had to lead and protect at all costs, no matter if I was directly involved or behind the shadows observing quietly. I'd been alone for most of my adult life, working hard and building my successful practice. My mother would like for me to meet and settle down with someone special and give her grandchildren. *It will happen with Willow. My heart connected with hers the minute we met and it's hers to have for all of eternity.*

I failed her last night with my impulsive anger. I allowed it to be stronger than I was and that would not happen again. I knew I was stubborn, always had been. With Willow by my side, I knew I would be able to be better, and it would be because of her alone. Last night was a mistake, and I punished myself enough for it. I had to get myself in order, so I can go to her and bring her home where she belongs. *And that's with me.*

I called my office to check in, and all seemed to be in order. I had no pressing matters to deal with and had no reason to go in. *They don't need me there anyway considering the foul mood I was still trying to free myself from. I would only bite their heads off and cause unnecessary problems that didn't exist.* My office ran very smoothly, and I wasn't going to do anything to put that in jeopardy. I was always available for my clients 24/7, and my office would call me if any emergencies occurred.

"Oleg, you're still here?" I questioned as I came down the stairs that led into my living room.

"We need to talk."

"I believe we said everything that needed to be addressed. I'll go see my brother today, and then..." I hesitated.

"Willow?"

"Yes, Willow. I will see her today."

"Valentin, you better do more than see her. You need to put her back together, and I mean soon."

"Yeah? And what business of this is yours? Willow is my woman, and I will handle her accordingly. All I need for you to do is stay on her detail and keep me informed."

"Sure, I can do that for you, but it's not me who she wants to look after her. She wants and needs you. You didn't see her face when I dropped her off this morning. The expression of pain was so apparent, it nearly broke me. She's lost without you, and it doesn't take a genius to figure out why. You got to her, Valentin, made her love you, and then you left without another word spoken. I understand more than anyone what yesterday did to you."

"Enough! I don't want to talk about my brother again. He's handled, and it will remain that way."

"And? What of Willow? Is she handled too?"

"Be careful, Oleg," I warned.

"You need to figure out your shit before you lose her. Whatever she meant by that message tells me she's serious."

I let out a deafening growl and tugged on my hair until I shouted out my frustrations. "I could have killed that man last night, and without probable cause. I felt rage, jealousy, and the need to mark her in such a way that any man would know who she belonged to. I have this animalistic side that just wants to tie her to me in every way imaginable and never let her go."

"Oh, Val, why do you take on these burdens? I've known you since you were born, and you have so much good inside of you. You have lived and breathed your family with honor. You are a good man, and the life you lead is the one you chose. Your brother, your father, and me...we didn't know any better. Go to your girl and make things right. She wants you, Val."

"Not as much as I want her, but I have to get myself under control first. I scared her enough last night, and I will not risk doing that again where she runs so far away from me that I will never get her back. Stay close to Willow today and call me if anything changes."

"You still tracking her phone?"

"Yes, and it's showing she's at work."

"Good, at least that's something. Will you be alright here on your own?"

"Yes, stop asking me. I don't need to be handled," I countered.

"Very well. I'll be going."

Fuck! It's not his fault, and all this misdirected anger is not helping. "Oleg," I called him back.

"Valentin?"

"Thank you."

I made the calls I needed to and then visited my home gym to work out for the next three hours. I was pounding on the punching bag until I had no strength left in my arms. I ran ten miles on the treadmill and did about two hundred sit-ups. My muscles burned probably from the tears that ripped through them as I pushed my body to lift more weights. I needed to feel this to serve as a reminder to what I had done to Willow. Flashes of her beautiful face were all I saw as I continued to punish myself for hurting her.

We will get through this. I know we will. She loves me. I see it in her eyes and feel it when I touch her. Once I know we are okay, a conversation will be needed, and I will have to put everything out in the open to show her who I really am. It's a risk, but she's worth it.

I entered the house where my brother was being held. It was for his safety to be here for a while until all calmed down out there on the streets. Oleg, Sergei, and Mical's crew had all ears to the street. Word was circulating that Avros ratted and was working as an informant for the FBI. It was quick thinking on my part, but I had to come up with something fast after we had Sasha moved.

Our families were always under the watchful eye of parties in our government, the FBI trying to get them up on RICO or the DEA hunting them down for drugs. My father in his younger years ran a pipeline for guns. I was just a boy back then and worshipped the ground he walked on. I guess in a way that still remained true. As I grew up, I saw him for the man he was and made my own judgments and chose to live my life outside of theirs.

Everything that happened with my brother had defied that and placed my own life and future happiness at risk. *I can't be two men for my father and one for Willow.* I had to straighten out my brother before he fell so low that I would never be able to reach him. He'd suffered a great deal, and when his mental illness was more powerful than he was, he became a prisoner trapped in his own mind.

A light tap to my window made me look up to see it was Sergei. I was so lost in thought I didn't hear him step up to my car.

"Hey, how is he?" I asked as he took me in for a hug.

"He's good, resting. The meds seem to be working and doing their job."

"I'm happy to hear that. I know he's waiting for me to make it all better. I just needed a minute to figure out how the hell I do that and keep this family intact."

"The hard part is over, Val. He's okay now. I promise you."

"I'd like to see for myself. Let's go."

The two-story log cabin home was far enough away from the city and was nestled into the woods, away from any roads. The property was well protected with surveillance monitoring at every entrance and exit. No one would ever be able to get on the grounds without a dozen tech guys knowing about it. I was at least comforted knowing if I couldn't be there for Sasha, then the family would.

When I stepped inside, the house was dark with all the window panels drawn to a close. The only light was coming from an opened bedroom door upstairs. I followed the round staircase, and I felt my brother's presence. He was waiting for me, and it was time to go to him.

I took the stairs and knocked gently on his door. He was in bed, halfway under the covers, quite the difference from the way I found him the other night at the club. I sat down beside him and brushed away the hair that was covering his eyes. He looked so young and—hard to believe—innocent while he slept.

"Hey, Sasha, wake up for me," I called out for him.

He stirred a bit and then gave his body a small stretch before opening his eyes fully to look at me. He wore such shame in his eyes, it nearly broke me to witness it. His lip quivered, and his body began to shake.

"It's okay. I'm here now." I continued to calm him.

"I'm sorry, Val. I know I messed up. I'm so sorry. I'm sorry. I'm sorry." He cried and buried his face into his pillow.

"Sasha, you need to listen to me very carefully. Pay attention, because I will only say this once. Look at me, brother." He did and wiped away his tears. "We know you were targeted by Avros. We also know why. Now, I need to hear it from you. Make me understand why you were off your medication. Make me understand why you continue to be reckless with your health. Make me understand why you continue to hurt this family."

He wept like the fragile human being that he was. Yes, I knew he was a man of twenty-five, but deep inside he was just a lost boy. I gave him his minute to let it all out, and that's all I was willing to give. It was all I could do without losing my control.

I held him by his shoulders. "Stop crying right now. You are a Vasiliev, son of Alaric, and brother to Valentin. You are so much stronger than you know, and you must find the strength within yourself to fight your demons. You must do this, Sasha."

"How? I want to die, Valentin. You need to let me go, so I can be free."

I slapped him across his face and pulled him to me. "No, you don't get to say those words to me, not ever. You will find the strength you need, and I will be there every step of the way to make sure you do. You will not hurt yourself or further shame this family. You will get well and stay on your medication. You are not broken, little brother. I promise you with all that I am that I will do everything I can to never have you feel that way again."

"I will, Val. I will for you." He sat up and wrapped his arms around my neck and held on with everything he had. "I love you. I promise to do better, you'll see. I'll make you proud." He repeated the phrases like a prayer, memorizing word for word until he was so exhausted he literally fell asleep in my arms. I placed him back down and tucked him back under the covers like I did when he was a child. I stayed with him for more than an hour and found some peace, hoping that wherever he traveled to in his dreams, he found the same.

"Sergei, I have other matters that require my attention, so I must be going. With the help of a sleep-aid, Sasha should sleep soundly for the rest of the night. I want an update in the morning, and then conference me in once the doctor arrives. Clear?"

"Yes, Valentin, you have my word that I will not let him out of my sight."

"I trust you, Sergei, and know what you say is the truth. You have my numbers and which one to use in case of an emergency."

"They won't be necessary, but I have them."

"And? What do we know about the other problem?"

"Homes and business were raided. Evidence of his betrayal was conveniently found in one of the clubs he does business out of. It's all in the hands of the feds. The breadcrumbs you laid out for them were the perfect bait. No one suspects a thing, and won't, not ever."

"We shall see. I have to go. You know what to do."

Driving into the city, a feeling of calm washed over me for the first time in a long while, knowing my brother was safe. He was going to be okay, and maybe this time for good. I was just pulling into Manhattan when my phone buzzed with Oleg calling. Somehow, I knew Willow would be the reason.

"Yeah," I answered curtly.

"Your girl, her boss, and a group of friends are all down in Chelsea at the new techno club, Vibes."

No. No. No. Of all the damn places her boss could drag her to, it had to be the meat market dance club. Fuck! I have to get her out of there.

"Do you see her?" I asked, as I hit the gas to go faster.

"Yes, she's in my view and…"

"What!? Spit it out, man!"

"She's not alone, Val."

"A man?"

"Several, along with other women. They have her surrounded and protected. It looks like they're all friends, mostly older, probably friends of her boss."

"It doesn't matter. I don't want any men in her close proximity. Watch her as if your life depends on it, because it does. I am on my way."

When I arrived at the club, I texted Oleg to meet me outside along the side entrance, where I parked my car. It was not wise for me to be seen out in the open, especially at a freaking dance club. *I'm a lawyer for motherfucking sake! This is not my scene and will never be Willow's.*

"Where is she?"

"She's in the ladies room. I saw her go in there a few minutes ago. I pulled up the specs on the inside of the club. The restroom she's in is located right near an exit. From the looks of it, I think she was ready to leave."

"Bring the car around to the front and stay there."

I entered through the front and went to the side of the club where I knew my woman was. I checked my phone and pinged her location that told me she was still in the restroom.

A few women stepped out, talking and laughing. I yearned to hear the same happiness from my dove. I hated that she was in this bar, but at least she was with friends who cared about her. I remained in the shadows, and when she finally emerged she looked wrecked, probably from dancing and drinking all night. *I hate this. God help any asshole who dares to fucking touch her.*

She was a little unsteady on her feet as I began to approach. I was going to reach for her when she had a mishap with her shoe, causing her to stumble.

Fuck! Now she's hurt and two predators are sniffing around where they shouldn't be. The taller one out of the two was clearly advancing on her. She refused him once, and he came at her again. The other said something, causing her to fight back a little stronger. I was proud of my dove and her strength. Just as she made her way up the ramp, the fucker put his hands on her and pulled her hair, making her stumble back into him.

Motherfucker! He's dead.

It took me a second to reach her. I pulled the bigger of the two out of the way with my hands around his throat nearly choking him to his final breath. I shoved him hard against the wall, and then he collapsed to the floor leaving his friend standing. He tried to lunge and take a swing, but it was laughable to believe he could get close enough to touch me. One hard jab to his kidneys, and he fell to his knees, gasping for air.

She looked over at me with tears in her eyes and fear written all over her stricken face. I couldn't handle Willow sending me away again. So this time, I left her.

Fuck! I got into my car and pounded the steering wheel as I screamed on the top of my fucking lungs. "Goddammit to hell! How in the hell have my blissful weeks spent with my woman suddenly gone to hell? Fuck! I want her back."

I pounded the dash as I drove like a lunatic back to god knows where. I finally parked in a lot and laid my head against the seat, wanting only Willow to comfort me.

When I calmed slightly, I texted Oleg to bring her home. She trusted him, and I knew he would take care of her until I could. I'd had enough of this renegade bullshit I was knee deep in. I pulled myself together enough to drive myself home and promising to get my shit together so I could be the man that Willow deserves.

The elevator took me up to my floor as I received the text I was waiting for. She was home and was safe. Closing my eyes, I sighed in relief as I stepped further into my darkened home that matched my fucking heart.

Yeah, asshole, who's broken now? It's certainly not my Willow. She was so strong back in that club, trying to be brave and solely fend off the assholes trying to mess with her. I knew what I was capable of and could have easily snapped both their necks and not bat an eye, but where would have that left me? I would be no better than any man in my father's organization, and I am damn well better than that. *I'll do better. Anything for Willow.*

I walked into the bedroom and turned the side table light on. As its glow began to light up the room, I saw her asleep in my bed, our bed. She was back to her natural-looking self with no makeup. Her hair was fanned across the pillow. Her long lashes swept across her face like feathers.

"Oh, my beautiful dove, I love you so much," I silently said and then leaned down to take her mouth in a gentle kiss.

Her eyes slowly opened and looked directly into my eyes, smiling. "You came back to me," she whispered.

"And I'm never leaving you again," I answered with a kiss, leaving us both breathless.

CHAPTER Nineteen

Willow

I had never cried so much in all my twenty-two years of life. *The pain I felt when Valentin looked at me with wounded eyes will haunt me forever if he doesn't come back to me. Where I saw love was replaced with sadness and pain, and I don't know how to reach inside of him and pull him back from the perpetual darkness he's in.*

He didn't just come into my life and turn it upside down to walk out and never be heard from again. He's so strong, confident, and beautiful. He chose me, and in return, I chose him back. We have to move past the huge misunderstanding that has left us both miserable. He came for me tonight, rescuing me once again. He's probably beating himself up over something no one could have controlled when you're faced with an uncontrollable circumstance. Those two guys wouldn't take no for an answer, and had he not been there, I could have been in grave danger.

It happens all the time to unwary girls just looking for a good time with their friends, never knowing the danger that surrounds them.

When I was in college, a guy slipping the date-rape drug into a girl's drink seemed to become the norm at parties. Most girls never said anything, because they never remembered being violated. Did they say no in their minds but had no power to stop the physical assault? It's disgusting, and it could have happened to me tonight. I was shocked to see Valentin but was never scared of him.

All these thoughts were making my head hurt, still swimming in alcohol. One false move, and I feared I would vomit all over the new leather in Ollie's backseat. I must have fallen asleep, not hearing the car come to a stop nor the door opening. I rubbed the fog out of my eyes and saw Ollie with his hand outreached for me to take.

"Come on, you're home." He smiled, and then I looked around to my surroundings.

"This is not where I live, Ollie. This is Valentin's home."

"No, my sweet girl. It became your home the minute he made you his. You belong here with him, the man you love and who loves you back with all that he has. He's been lost without you, and you are the only one that can bring him back."

I took his hand as he helped me out of the car and into the building. My ankle was sore and needed some ice to bring down the swelling. He wrapped his arm around my waist and lent the support I needed to get inside of Valentin's apartment. *I don't know his role in Valentin's life or what he does for him, but I don't care. He obviously cares for him a great deal and knowing what I do about Valentin, he wouldn't trust just anyone with me.*

"Okay, I want you to keep this ankle elevated for at least twenty minutes. Keep the ice pack on it. It's not that bad, and the icing will help. Here's some pain relief for a headache you are sure to have in the morning."

"Ollie, wait," I called out for him.

"What is it?"

"How are you so sure?"

He raised his hand up to stop me as if he knew what I would ask next. "Because I know him. You know when you gave me the message you wanted me to tell him, I'll admit I was confused and didn't know what it meant until I took time to really think about it. Once I did, it became so clear to me. Go easy with Valentin and give him a lot of room to make mistakes, because he will. But the man that I know him to be will learn from them and do better. There is so much more about him you don't know yet, and I can't be the one to share that piece of his life with you. It's his story to tell, and he will when he's ready."

"Okay, I can do that."

"I know you will, Willow. That's why I brought you here. He needs to hear the truth from the woman he loves."

"Thank you, Ollie, for everything. One more question?"

He smiled and waited for me to ask.

I wiped away a tear and tried to be strong. "He'll come back, right?" I couldn't stop shaking. *I don't know what I will do if he doesn't.*

"Yes, my child, he'll come home."

"When?"

"When he's done punishing himself. Take care, Willow, and take care of him." He placed a kiss on the top of my head, and then he was gone, leaving me to cry myself asleep and wait for Valentin to come home.

For a moment, I thought I was dreaming until Valentin kissed me and made it real. The roughness from his beard touched my face.

"You came back to me," I whispered.

"And I'm never leaving you again," he answered by kissing me breathlessly.

"I'm sorry, Valentin, I'm so sorry for upsetting you and making you worry."

"Shhh, it's over. I'm here, and I'm not going anywhere. I left you twice, and I will carry those mistakes with me for the rest of my life. I promise you I will never do that again and risk seeing anything in your gorgeous emerald eyes than love. It's what I'm seeing right now. Am I wrong?"

"No, you're not. I love you, Valentin, and I've missed you so much. It's only been a couple of days, and it feels like months. Make love to me. Make me yours."

The need for this man is slowly devouring all of me, and there is not anything I could do to stop it, nor do I want to. It is the overwhelming, electrifying, and combustible energy that wages war on your heart and soul, and it makes you feel so alive. It's what my mom always feared would happen to me, because it did for her and she got her heart broken for it. What I have with Valentin is so much more than we know and understand, but we'll learn together.

He lifted me into his arms, kissing me fervently as he carried me upstairs to his bedroom. "Can you stand?" he asked. "The ankle," he specified. "Does it hurt too much?"

"No, I'm fine. Ollie took care of me."

"He's a good man. Sometimes I forget that. Come, I need to get you clean, baby. I have to wash away his touch and erase my mind of watching another man put his hands on you."

I broke down in his arms and released all the pain that was inside of me. "I'm sorry. I don't know what I was thinking of going there tonight. Madeline just kept pouring shots down my throat, and I let her because I was missing you."

"It's my fault for not coming to you sooner. I should have the minute I heard your message, but I had other things plaguing my mind and couldn't separate the two."

"Are you okay?"

"Yes, I am now. Let's shower. It will free us both."

A rosy vanilla scent invaded my senses. It was decadent against my skin. He bent down to the granite floor and began moving the body poof up the inside of my thigh. Electric tingles pricked at my skin as he repeated the same washing to the other leg, making me want with need. My insides quaked, and I closed my eyes, willing Valentin to touch me there.

"You need something, don't you dove?" he whispered seductively, knowing exactly what he was doing to my body. "You're practically shaking, you're so wet for me. Isn't that right, dove?"

"Yes! Valentin, please touch me," I whimpered, as he settled his mouth over my throbbing clit, plunging his tongue deep inside of my core, causing me to cry out his name.

His hands gripped the insides of my thighs, keeping me in place as my back thudded against the shower wall. My hands instinctively touched the sides of his face, pulling him closer. The orgasms that racked through my body were barely keeping me on my feet. He would not relent until I came once, twice, and for the third time until I could barely stand.

Never stopping his perfect mannerisms, he moved his hand to my backside, breaching the tight entrance of my ass. I screamed again as he slowly and tortuously moved his finger in and out, passing through the tight ring of muscle. It was an unknown sensation that sent me over the edge and into a heavenly haze of pure pleasure. *He hasn't even fucked me yet, and I've never felt more sated.* On cue, he growled into my neck and sucked on my skin, bringing the blood to the surface.

"Not today, dove, but soon I will mark every last inch of your delectable body. Your glorious round ass of perfection will be taken, and you will love every fucking minute of feeling my dick inside of you. You are mine, Willow, and there is not one thing about you that I will not claim and own. You are mine to do with as I please, and that is to pleasure and worship you, to fuck you until you scream my name. This pussy is mine. No one will ever be where I've been. Do you understand me, Willow?"

I cried at the merciless dominance he exerted over me and submitted willingly to only him. "Yes! Valentin, I'm yours to do as you please. Everything I have is yours. Please, don't make me wait any longer. Take me," I rasped. "Take me now!" I didn't recognize what was coming from my mouth as I never dreamed I would ever feel this high with a man. This was Valentin loving me and keeping every promise he has ever vowed to me.

"I'm going to fuck you with no barrier between us. Are you on any birth control?"

Remembering his earlier promise, I didn't care about anything but pleasing him. I just needed to answer his question, and once I did, there would be no stopping Valentin and all the naughty things he would do to my body. I couldn't wait.

"No, I never needed it," I replied.

He shot me a scandalous expression, sexy man that he was. I knew I had unleashed the beast within him, and I would take it all, because I knew he would never hurt me.

"I love you, Willow, my beautiful dove. I am going to fill you with my cum, and I don't give a fuck to the consequences. To see your belly grow with my child would be God handing down a blessing to us both." And without another word expressed, he entered my swollen pussy and fucked me so hard, causing my vision to blur. As he came, he howled my name. "Willow!!!"

Was last night a dream? I thought as I slowly opened my eyes, and then I turned my head to see Valentin watching me. *He always watches me. What is he looking for when he does this? It has to be pretty boring to just watch someone sleep, but he doesn't seem to mind. I think deep down it satisfies him and brings him peace.*

I gave my body a stretch. I was deliciously sore from last night's activities. What we shared with one another was very real, because I can still feel his touch all over my body, inside and out. I happily sighed and then placed my hands on his face to kiss him. "Good morning," I said, smiling through my kisses.

"Good morning, dove. How did you sleep?"

"Ahhh, I think you know. What time is it?"

"Half past six. What time are you meeting with Zara?"

"How did you know that was today?" I questioned.

"You told me so. Don't you remember? Problem?"

"No, I just don't recall it, and we were fighting."

"Come here, love." He pulled me on top of him with his hard erection pressing into me. "You will never know how sorry I am for how I behaved with your friend at your grandmother's apartment. We're going to have a conversation about that, I promise you, but I know today is a big day for you. You don't need any distractions."

"Valentin, you are not keeping me from my work, and I welcome you to distract me anytime you like."

"As much as that delights me to hear you say that, I have a lot of work to catch up on myself. Will you come to me tonight when you're finished with your work?" He asked me so sweetly, how could I ever say no to him?

"Yes, I will, but I'm not sure how late I will be working. Can I call you this afternoon when I have a better idea?"

"Sure you can, and I look forward to hearing your voice. Don't worry about interrupting my day either, my assistant already has your name. Unless I'm in court, there is no reason why I will not be able to speak with you."

I buried my face into his chest, not wanting him to see me bite my lip and blush. Oh, the thoughts running through my mind right now were making me want things with this man I never believed I could ever come close to having.

"Willow, please look at me," he requested. "I don't ever want you to feel that you have to hide your feelings from me, not when your eyes are so expressive. They tell me so much about you. Every time I look into them, I feel as if I'm being taken through another window to your soul, a place you haven't shown anyone but me, and it gives me hope that you want us to happen just as much as I do."

"Oh, Valentin, of course, I want you. I didn't know if I was coming or going when I didn't hear from you. All my calls went unanswered, and I believed I had lost you. And then Ollie showed up and drove me to work."

"And your message to me? How did it make you feel saying those words?"

"Sad and afraid."

"Why?"

"The thought of you ending what we had and never seeing you again made me feel so small and broken. It's like we're standing in the middle of the street with a line separating us, not knowing what's on the other side. You are daring me to cross over and take a chance, but I hesitate because I'm cautious and overthink too much, whereas you are strong and brave."

"Oh, baby, you are so much more than who you just described. I see it, why don't you? Whoever is responsible for the way you under-value yourself should suffer the way you have. I hate it, Willow, and it is not a trait I want you to have. You have the power to overcome these negative feelings, and when you feel it becomes too much, lean on me, and I will make it better. I promise you. I love you, Willow Pierce, and want nothing more than to spend the rest of my life with you. Every word spoken last night was my truth, a bearing of my soul laid out wide open for only you to see. I need you so much right now. I want to be rough with you and bury my cock deep inside you."

He held my face and gripped it slightly tighter than he usually does. His dark brown eyes were glazed over with fiery desire. "Please, dove, tell me you want me too?"

I couldn't move with Valentin holding me in place. "Yes, I want you too. Please fuck me."

The dirty talk was another first that I had no clue how I sounded, but he seemed to love it, and it only aroused and awakened all of his senses. He flipped me over to my stomach and raised my ass high in the air. My face was flat on the pillow, and before he entered me, I felt a hard slap to my backside, causing me to cry out. My hips were held by his hands, and he took me again and again until we nearly shattered together. I was propelled so high and then I came so hard that I had to bite the pillow to stifle my feral cries of pleasure. Valentin followed my orgasm with a powerful thrust inside that filled me with his cum. He was a sex machine that continued to slam his pelvis against my ass.

My arms began to weaken as hot cum oozed out of my vagina and slowly ran down my thighs. He was considerate and met my every need. He placed a soft kiss to my naked back and began to pull out of my body, making me wince a little.

We collapsed beside each other and tried to catch our breath. Not giving me a minute to do so, he pulled me close where he could hold me. My face was on his chest, and his long legs were over mine. He huffed out a breath and then took my mouth in an arduous kiss.

"Look at me, Willow," he demanded after catching my eyes closed. "Never turn your eyes away from me. Do you understand?"

I trembled slightly, "Yes, Valentin."

"Don't be afraid. I will never hurt you, never in a way that doesn't bring us both pleasure. I need you to understand that. There is a difference. I would not be the man that I am if I didn't know that."

"I know. I trust you. You didn't hurt me, I swear it."

With complete honesty laced with raw emotion, he expressed exactly what he was feeling and what he wanted from me. As much as he craves and demands everything from me, I don't want him to feel bad when I do submit because I don't. I have never felt more alive than when I'm with him. I kissed him with every bit of strength I had left to show him that I was all in and not going anywhere.

I said, "I. Love. You. No more silence between us. I'm here with you, and it's where I want to be. Do you believe me, Valentin?"

"Yes, with all my heart."

He took me again so gently I wanted to cry in his arms. He made me feel so incredibly special and wanted. With ease, he carried me into his shower and took care of all my needs. Once I was dressed for work, the thought of leaving him if just for more than a few hours had made me a little sad, but it didn't last long. Observant to the change in my mood, he kissed away my sadness and promised to personally pick me up from work when I was ready to come home.

He stressed the word *home* because he didn't want me returning to my grandmother's apartment. Every time he made his intentions clear, he never used words like *my* or *I*. It was *ours* and *us*. No more separation between city streets and addresses. He wanted me here with him…permanently.

"Have a wonderful day, and good luck with Zara. She can be a handful, but she's smart enough to appreciate fine work, especially when it's right in front of her."

Every time he mentions her, warning bells ring loudly in my head. Who is she to him? And do I need to be worried?

My eyes were focused everywhere but on him. I felt the temperature drop in the car as my body gave me away, showing Valentin that I was upset. Jealousy was a new emotion for me, and I didn't know how to handle it. He sensed it, of course, he did. He held me by my shoulders to turn me around and used his two fingers to lift my chin. We were so close, and I knew my eyes would betray what I was trying to hide from him.

"What's troubling you? Have I said something to upset you?" he asked softly.

Just ask him, Willow, because you will hate yourself if you don't, and today is just too important to fuck up.

"You'll tell me the truth?" I bravely responded to him.

"I will strive to always be as honest as I can with you. What has you doubting that promise?"

"I know you told me you've been friends with Zara for a number of years, but…"

I hesitated and struggled to find the right words to say without angering him.

"Ask me, Willow," he demanded, still gripping my chin.

"Have you slept with Zara?"

Without faltering he answered, "No, not ever. We have been friends for a long time, I told you this."

"She's very beautiful," I whispered.

"Yes, she is, but not as beautiful as you are, dove. Please don't be threatened by her or doubt my feelings for you. You are the only woman I see. Now, get to work and be amazing. I love you." He kissed me soundly, effectively showing me our conversation was over.

"Should I be whispering to you this morning?" Madeline asked as she walked into my office carrying two coffees.

"Nope, I feel fantastic and ready to be amazing today," I stated confidently while accepting the coffee and taking a sip. "Hmmm, this is good. Vanilla, my favorite."

"Yeah, that may be true for coffee but certainly not when it comes to other vanilla things in your life. Judging by the mark I'm seeing on your neck, looks like it got pretty rough last night. How's the sexy Russian? Tie you up lately?"

I nearly choked and dropped my coffee. "Madeline!" I sounded appalled and then reached for a mirror and saw exactly what she was referring to. *Oh my god, when he said he wanted to mark me, he wasn't lying.* "I need a scarf to cover this up. I can't meet Zara looking like an overzealous teenager that got carried away with her boyfriend. This is so embarrassing."

"I think it's sexy, and I'm sure your man doesn't care one way or another. I'm glad you two worked it out, right?"

"Yes, we're fine. We still have some talking to do, but I'm good."

"You know I love teasing you. Kidding aside, you'd tell me if you weren't okay, right? You're so young and innocent. I don't want to see you hurt."

"Why? Because the man I'm falling in love with has the ability to shatter my soul and leave a million pieces of me scattered all over the street?"

"Yeah, something like that," she giggled.

"I have it covered, don't worry. Now, enough on my love life, we need to kick some major ass today and impress Zara."

"With what you have come up with, I'm not worried. And besides, we still have some time, and I want to tell you about my night."

"Okay, I know you're dying to, so go on."

"Harry took me back to his place. You know, the one I told you about?"

"The rooftop apartment in the meatpacking district?"

"The very same. He has the entire top floor to himself. God, I love that street. It's filled with so many queens filling up the streets, makes me want to put on my kinky boots and party with them."

"Okay, veering off track here."

"Yes, back to Harry. He was amazing, and you will never believe what he has installed back at his place. I mean, it shocked me a little but I was so hammered, I was willing to try anything."

"What did you do?"

"He fucked me in a swing!!! A sex swing! Never tried it. Always wanted to. And I did it. And I loved it. Should I call your man up and have him install one for you?"

I rolled my eyes at my friend.

She said, "You don't fool me, Willow! And drop the unknowing eyes, because I know exactly what kind of man you're sleeping with, and I would bet everything I own that he doesn't do *vanilla* and will be introducing you to a hell of a lot more than just the basics. Hey, I'm just preparing you."

Lord! She's exasperating at times.

I screamed, "Enough! You've had your fun, and all at my expense. Zara will be here soon."

"Did I hear my name? Okay, darlings, show me what you've got!" Zara called out as she walked in, looking every bit the supermodel she was.

Please tell me she didn't hear our conversation.

CHAPTER
Twenty

Valentin

"Good morning, Mr. Vasiliev. I wasn't expecting you in today," my assistant said as she followed me through my office. She placed a hot cup of coffee on my desk and took my briefcase from me.

"Change of plans. By the end of business hours today, I want this desk clear, and what I mean is no current and open cases that directly involve me." I rounded my desk and sat down behind it. "Coffee is delicious as usual. Thank you."

"My pleasure sir. Shall we get started?"

"Yes, let's get to work," I replied and then began running through all my pending cases.

I reached out to several of my clients to touch base and to set future appointments for lunch and regrouping. I had always given my full attention to where it was needed, and they needed to know their business was always our top priority. I worked through my usual lunch hour and made every possible effort to complete my tasks. Once I finally had a minute to take a breather, all my thoughts were back to Willow.

I rested my eyes and leaned back in my chair, sighing in contentment. For the first time in days, I was at peace, a feeling that was not always easy for me to obtain. I only had two speeds I operated on. One was fast, and the second was faster. I worked more hours in a week than most do in two.

I had given all that I could to my family and honored every request that was ever made of me, especially when it was for Sasha. He was safe and well on his way to recovering, and with any luck, get his life back in order. It was all I wanted for him, to be sane enough to live a productive life.

And now, after meeting Willow, it was time to focus on me and what I wanted for my life. I couldn't tear my eyes away from her sleeping form. She was home and back where she belonged: in my arms, where I intended to keep her. The way she submitted and so easily gave me complete trust to do as I pleased to her body was a gift. I was so in love with her and wanted our future to happen. I knew without a doubt that it would.

I opened the photo app on my phone and looked at every single picture of my beautiful dove, another secret I kept to myself. She was too hard to resist with her perfect curves, round breasts that fit perfectly in my hand, and her ass. Oh, just remembering how I promised what I would be taking from her, and how soon it would be, set us both ablaze. She was perfect and submitted beautifully.

Willow was my compulsion on every level. I knew it, and so did she. We needed to have a conversation to set the record straight on a few things of importance. First thing will be her good friend "Ollie." It didn't take long for Willow to connect him to me. I practically put a spotlight over his head while trailing her.

A knock on my office door brought me back to why I was in the office in the first place.

I sat up and fixed my tie. "Yes, come in."

"I'm sorry to bother you, sir. He wasn't on your calendar, but he says he's a friend."

"Does this friend have a name, or are we playing twenty questions?"

"Forgive me, sir. His name is Pavlo Shirmanov."

Friend, no. Enemy, yes.

I cleared my throat and told her to send him in. *Okay, let the games begin.* He was older than my father and had been ill with early onset Parkinson's, but that information was only privy to his most trusted comrades. He'd been stable so far with the medication he took, but his condition would worsen over time, leaving his organization up in arms, especially with Avros no longer a living heir to his throne.

"Pavlo, to what do I owe this unexpected visit, and here at my office?" I said, as he approached closer and placed two kisses on my face.

"You are very smart, Valentin. I always knew this about you. You are quick on your feet and quietly manage your family without ever making an appearance at the table. Your father should be very proud and honored to call you son. It's what I wanted for my Avros, but I knew he never had it in him to even come close to the hopes and dreams I set forth for him. A disappointment who has brought shame on my family in more ways than I can explain."

"This is very enlightening, Pavlo, but what does it have to do with me?"

"I think you know why I'm here."

"No, I really don't, and you need to get to your point a little faster. I'm a busy man, and I detest my valuable time being wasted."

"As do I, son, but this meeting is not a waste of your time nor mine. Avros is dead. His body was found in a shallow grave off an abandoned road in Atlantic City. My clubs were raided, along with the bathhouse turned upside down. They tell me my son was a rat and gave over valuable intel that has the ability to dismantle my organization. As you can see, I'm still standing and not in a federal prison, as you may have planned for me."

"Pavlo, you have painted a colorful picture, but unfortunately, your suspicions of me and my family do not have any merit here. Whatever conflict and dishonor that has been brought down on your family was not at our hands. And you don't come at me with your baseless conspiracy theories to threaten me with. Now, as a show of respect to my father and for your family's loss, I will absolve you of the transgressions you have conveyed here today. But know this: you approach me again and make false denunciations against my family, you will pay dearly for that offense. Have I made myself clear?"

He got up from his chair and said nothing as he began to walk to the door. He hesitated and then looked over his shoulder and said, "He was still my son, Valentin, and I loved him just as much as your father loves you and your brother. I've heard you, and you have heard me. We will not speak of this again. Thank you for your time."

I remained where I was seated, never taking my eyes off him. He grew weaker right before my eyes, looking older than he was.

His lips were moving, but I couldn't hear all that he was trying to say. His words slurred a bit, and then he finally managed to get out a Russian phrase I knew very well. "Little thieves are hanged, but the great ones escape." He then paused and asked, "So, which one are you?" and then walked out of my office, never looking back at me again.

I sat back in my chair and balanced my chin on my hands, needing time to process all that was said here. His tone was provocative while attempting to get a rise from me, but I was too strong for his twisted mind games.

He was scrambling, because he knew his son had placed his organization at risk, and he was running out of time to choose a successor or die without one. It would leave the ones under his command to break free and take on new business endeavors without the umbrella of protection from a family.

Our family was protected, no matter what Pavlo may have believed. He couldn't touch us, not ever, and would never get close enough to try. He was delusional in his thinking that I would allow that to happen. Hits had been contracted before, and they were handled accordingly, as this one would be if he decided to go rogue in his final days. We would be ready to crush the Shirmanov dynasty, piece by piece.

I dialed Oleg's number quickly once I was leaving my office. I took a private elevator down to the parking garage, where Oleg was waiting for me.

"Were you followed?" I asked, while taking in our surroundings.

"No, I switched out cars, and no tails were on me."

"Okay, let's take every necessary precaution in the coming days to see what Pavlo may or may not do. I do know I will not be able to return to Sasha, nor will you, until I know it's safe and we won't be followed."

"Does he suspect anything? Or was this him trying to rattle your cage?"

"I would say a little of both, but I'm not a hundred percent certain. We need to lead him in other directions and far away from Sasha. I may have no choice but to call my father and bring him up to speed on all the current events I have protected him from. If he believes for one second all is not well, especially when it comes to Sasha, he will rain down hell on all who have threatened the state of our family. I will not let that happen. Our family has come too far to legitimize our business interests. My father has to be contained and know there are no threats against us, or the outcome will be swift and unforgiving."

He sighed, "A bloody war."

"I won't let that happen. Come, I need to get to Willow."

He paused. "Valentin, as if you can stop it. I know you believe you could, but in the end, your attempts will prove to be unsuccessful. Remember who you are, because what you are suggesting is far from the man standing before me. You must understand and hear me. You can only carry this family so far before they retreat and break free. Don't underestimate your father. He's always a few steps ahead of all of us, men in power usually are. Do what you must, but in the end, he will make the ultimate choice or sacrifice. It will be out of your hands, and there will not be one thing you can do about it unless you take your rightful place and lead with him. It's the only way, son. Your father set you free and has long accepted your decisions. Don't forget that you walked away from this life, determined to stand on your own without the stigma your name brings. Your future hangs in the balance, and it is divided by the love you have for your father and the love you want to have for your future with Willow. Walk away now, Valentin, while you still can. I beg of you."

CHAPTER
Twenty-One

Willow

Zara studiously examined all seven mannequins that were on display for her perusal. She tapped her chin as she continued to eye them with critical eyes. She took some notes on her tablet and tapped her sky-high stilettos together like Dorothy in Oz.

"Madeline, we've known each other too long for me to stand here and placate you or your designer, so this is what I think. The designs are good but nowhere on the level that I require for this show."

While Madeline nursed her obvious hangover and downed Tums like candy, I addressed the elephant in the room. I tried in vain not to allow her critique to place doubt in a place I had no room for, so I took another approach.

"Okay, Zara, why don't you tell me exactly what you're looking for? I followed your requirements down to the letter and created what I believed was what you asked for."

"Yes, you have. But something is missing, and I will not attach my name to anything that I don't deem to be perfect."

"Fair enough, but I can't give you anything more than what I have already done."

"Hmmm, you are a tenacious one, I'll give you that. Young, confident, but very naïve if you believe an opportunity like the one I have practically handed to you on a silver platter will come again so easily."

"I disagree with your assessment and vehemently encourage you to look again."

I turned around to see Valentin stepping inside the room and not looking too happy at the moment. His tone was cold and his eyes were pinned with Zara's, who didn't look all that well with his unexpected appearance.

"Valentin, what a surprise," I said and walked over to properly greet him.

In the foul mood he appeared to be in, I expected him to slam his body into mine and take my mouth just as hard, but he surprised me by gently kissing me on my lips and then holding me close for a hug. I felt the warmth of his body engulf me until Madeline subtly began to clear her throat. Always the gentleman, he addressed Madeline with his impeccable manners.

"Ladies, please forgive my intrusion on your workday. I figured by now you'd have the champagne open and celebrating."

"It's what we were hoping for as well, but it seems we have reached an impasse with Zara, and I may need something a little stronger than champagne," I said, holding onto my thick skin and not willing to back down to her.

"Hey, I have all the boys' right here in my desk drawer," Madeline said. "I have Jack, Johnnie, Captain Morgan, oh, and a bottle of my favorite vodka. I think even a rooskii like you can appreciate this fine drink on your fancy palette."

Has she lost her fucking mind? Talking to Valentin in that way is just appalling, although I couldn't miss a hint of a smile crossing his face. I hurried over to Madeline, hooking my arm in hers, and led her down to an empty conference room away from our guests. I needed to have a word with her, or several for that matter.

"What has gotten into you? Who are you right now?" I yelled.

"Me? What about you? You, pulling up your big girl panties, believing you will actually work again in this business after talking to Zara Hill like that. Little girl, you have a lot to learn, and smacking a gift horse in the mouth is not the way to do so."

"Okay, Madeline, I've had just about enough of the song and dance you want me to do with you. I get it, you've helped me and gave me a start, which I have thanked you for a thousand times over. I've been loyal and have produced excellent work for you and this company. You have been off the rails for weeks now, and either you want me here or you don't, but I'm not going to be your fucking doormat."

"So, you're going to walk? Wow, you get a little taste of what it's like on the other side, and you just kick the little people to the curb. Fine, I see how it is." She threw her hands in the air and walked away, slamming the door. I was left alone, wondering what the hell just happened here.

When I returned to where I had left Valentin and Zara, it appeared they were in a heated discussion. Never one for eavesdropping, I quickly made my presence known. "Am I interrupting anything?"

"Are you alright?" he asked, cupping my face in his hands.

"Yes, just a disagreement which I'm sure will blow over once Madeline calms down." I turned back to Zara and made my apologies. "I apologize for the scene you had to witness and I'm sorry you and I couldn't reach an agreement on the designs." I stretched out my hand as a sign of closure, but she didn't take it.

"No, it's me who owes you an apology. It wasn't fair of me to come down on you so harshly when all you did was deliver exactly what I had requested."

I looked over at Valentin, who was smart enough to remain silent. After all, this was my place of work.

"Change of heart? I have to say this surprises me a great deal considering how you felt ten minutes ago. So, what happens now?" I asked.

"We run with what we have and move onto accessories, along with footwear."

Now I knew this had Valentin written all over it. I should have trusted my gut from the beginning, but I ran with it although I knew something seemed off. *This bitch put me in my place quicker than you can say "Louis Vuitton," and now she's all sugary and sweet and making my teeth hurt.*

"I'll leave the accessories line to Madeline since it's her area of expertise. I'll have enough on my plate with the costumes," I said.

"Yes, you will. I'll be in touch."

Yeah, I'm sure you will, I thought as I took in the exchange between Valentin and Zara. *Yup, I'll be hearing from you Zara, because it's exactly what you've been told to do.*

Madeline locked herself away in her office. She could be in there all night licking her wounds, while she left me on my own to clean up the mess. Confident as ever, Zara strutted out towards the exit. I wanted to scream. This was not the day I was expecting to have. I opened up my desk drawer and pulled out my purse, slamming it back into place.

"Shall we get that champagne now?" Valentin asked without a care in the world.

"No, I don't think so. I'm going home." I tried to move by him, but he pulled me back.

"Home? Well, that's exactly where I'm going."

"No, I meant I'm going home to my apartment, and you'll be going home to yours."

He stood in shock for all of a second before catching up to me and hauling me over his shoulders and just for effect, slapping me hard on my ass.

"Ouch! Put me down right now!" I demanded.

"Oh, my beautiful dove, haven't you figured out by now that I always get what I want? And the home you will be returning to is ours."

I let out a frustrated sigh, and I know I heard him laugh under his breath. He only put me down to place me inside of his car. I slid over to the opposite side to avoid him, but he wasn't having it.

"Come here, Willow. Now."

His voice nearly made my insides clench with a desperate need to have him inside of me again. I hated the fact that he controlled me so easily that I wanted to be defiant and disobey, so I said the one word that I knew he would hate.

"No."

"No?" he repeated my answer, testing how it sounded. I knew he didn't like it. "Hmmm, have you forgotten already?"

"No, my memory is quite excellent."

"Then I'll ask again, something I never do. Come to me, Willow, so I can make you come." I shifted slightly, and then I was hauled up from my seat, with my body slamming into his. "Don't ever shut me out, Willow, not ever. Now, I see that you are angry, and I know I must be the cause of it. Once we are home, we will have a long overdue conversation about many things. I only ask that you listen and don't make any judgments until I am finished. Can you do that for me?"

"Yes," I answered breathily as he moved his hand under my skirt and inserted two fingers inside of me, making me cry out. "Fuck! Valentin, you make me crazy," I shouted louder, wanting to bite down and sink my teeth into his neck. The feeling was intense and overpowering. I was on the edge of my release, and suddenly he withdrew his hand, leaving me unsatisfied. "What the fuck, Valentin!" I pounded my small fists into his broad and muscled chest. "Please don't be cruel. I need you so much," I mewled with a voice I didn't recognize.

He held my face and kept me in place as he took my mouth in a savage kiss. "Look at me. What did I tell you about turning away?" I focused my eyes on him as he instructed me to do, and then his honesty broke me. "I would never be cruel, not to my beautiful dove. How do I make you believe how deep my feelings are for you?"

"Show me," I defiantly dared him.

With his hard erection pressing into me, he winked and then flipped me onto my back and held my two hands with his one.

"Challenge accepted, dove. I hope you know what you have just done. If you thought last night was rough, hold on and enjoy what I do now."

His promise of pleasure didn't scare me, because I knew deep down he was telling the truth when he said he wouldn't hurt me. Also, promises only worked with trust, and I did trust him.

"Don't move," he whispered as he released my hands and unfastened his belt and pants, pulling his briefs down just far enough as his dick sprung to life. He moved his body over mine and lined his dick up to my mouth. "Suck me, Willow. Take all of me."

Oh my god! How does he do this? I'm the one who has every right to be upset here, and yet, I'm about to willingly fuck him with my mouth.

"I'm waiting," he said, and then I opened my mouth wide for him.

He thrusted inside, pushing in and out until I was completely full. He gently rubbed the side of my jaw, continuing to be gentle and rough. I knew he was close, because I was too just by giving him pleasure. He came with such a force down my throat that I feared I might choke until his hand was at the nape of my neck, tilting me forward. I took all of him, and then his mouth was on my clit, teasing the hell out of it, giving me just enough to keep me where he wanted: on the edge.

"You taste amazing. I want you. Always," he said and then continued to roll his tongue over me and inside of me until my thighs clenched so tightly around his waist. I came and shouted his name until my voice was hoarse.

"Oh my god, that was indescribable," he said, kissing me so I could taste myself on his lips. After he put himself back together, he tugged me forward so I could sit on his lap. He held me, burying his face into my hair. "Just a taste, my dove. We will finish at home."

I sighed contently, knowing I had lost this round and probably a lot more in my future. I must have fallen asleep, having not gotten too much from the night before. *I may have to join a gym to keep up with him,* I thought, keeping that little fact to myself.

"Wake up, Willow. We're home."

"Okay, I'm up," I said, rubbing the sleepiness from my eyes.

He looked to his lap and said, "So am I," as he flashed me a sexy wink.

Oh my god, this man! And all his charm that just oozes from his pores. With just one look, he makes me want and believe in more, and because he says it's going to happen, it will.

Once inside his apartment, he called for Marta, the house manager. She emerged from a room down the hallway and greeted us both with polite pleasantries.

"Good evening, Mr. Vasiliev and Ms. Pierce," she smiled warmly.

"Marta, hello," he said a bit too frosty. "I would like dinner brought up to our bedroom in one hour."

"Yes, sir. Any requests for wine this evening?"

"We'd prefer champagne. The 2002 Dom Perignon."

"Excellent choice, sir. Shall I send that up to you now? Or with dinner?"

"In thirty minutes for the champagne, and I would like a bottle of chilled sparkling water as well."

While he rattled on about dinner choices and champagne, I stood there in silence, taking all of him in. *This is what it's like to be with a man like Valentin Vasiliev, and it's becoming easier to understand his need to dominate and make all around him submit, including me.*

He dismissed Marta and then grabbed hold of my arm, practically dragging me along at a rapid pace. He pushed me inside the bedroom and slammed the door behind him. I was frozen and not sure what was happening here. He removed his suit jacket and tie. With moves like a cougar, he had me lifted and placed on his bed with my hands tied above my head, using his tie to secure me in place.

"Valentin, what are you doing?"

"Patience, my dove. I need to remember how quickly your moods change. Shall I fuck you again? Maybe it's the stress from the day."

"No, it's more than that, and I believe you know exactly what I'm referring to."

"Possibly, but this is why we need to have a conversation."

"And securing me to your bed? What the hell does that have to do with talking?"

"It's my way of keeping you from running from me. No, Willow, you will no longer be doing that, and neither will I. If we have something to work out between us, it will be handled right here inside of *our* bedroom." He stressed the word *our* again. "Now, why don't you tell me why you are angry with me?"

I huffed, "As if you don't know?"

"I don't, hence the reason for why we are talking. Now, tell me."

"Okay, Valentin, we will play it your way, since it's becoming abundantly clear that's the way it works around here." *He didn't even attempt to hide his smile.* "I have several questions for you, and I might as well ask them all, since I'm in no position to go or do anything else."

"Smart girl, you're catching on." He kissed me and then pinched my nipple for effect, causing me to squirm on the bed.

"Ouch, Valentin, that hurts, and I'm sore."

"I'm sure you are, and for that I'm sorry. I promise to massage every inch of your body and lull you into a deep sleep. I'm very good with my hands."

"...and your mouth too," I wanted to say, but why bother when he already knows it?

He continued, "Ask me, Willow. It's the only way we are going to resolve this. The clock is ticking, and the champagne is due to arrive soon."

I squirmed back and forth on the bed, with Valentin enjoying too much at my expense. I was frustrated with pent-up energy and craved a release of any kind from him. I no longer wanted to talk about the reasons why I was angry in the first place and wanted to just go to bed and forget.

"I'm waiting. It's now or never."

"Fine! Zara Hill!" I shouted back at him.

He didn't react at all and simply asked me to go on. "What about Zara?"

"Oh, Valentin, please tell me you're not going to pretend you don't know what I'm about to say here. It's so obvious now as much as it was back at my office. You put her up to this, and when she didn't like my designs, you probably threatened her to like them and say just enough to stroke my ego, making me believe I was better than I actually am."

"So, we're back to that again. I had hoped after our last conversation about negative feelings you would have listened and taken my advice to do the opposite. The fact is, you are extremely talented. You can bring so much to the table with just a single idea and transform it into the next big trend. I've seen it happen to Zara, and I have no reason to doubt that you will be able to accomplish the same in your career."

"I want to make it on my own and not with help from my boyfriend or his connections. I don't feel as if I earned this, and whether you believe it or not, I do have excellent instincts, thanks to my tough as nails mother back home. This opportunity never felt right to me, and after watching you today with Zara, it didn't take me long to figure out why that is."

His expression had fallen from the cocky grin he usually sported to apologetic without saying the words.

I wanted out of these restraints and never wanted to flee from a place as much as I did right now. My need to go stemmed from all the years my mom drilled into my brain about always holding onto your independence and standing on your own two feet. *And, for the most part, I am doing all the things she has taught me but am I not allowed to lean on someone I love? Mom never had a Valentin in her life or anyone that came close to having what I have. Tears were threatening to fall, and this was not the image I wanted Valentin to see, especially when I'm tethered to his bed. Or, our bed.*

He kneeled closer and brushed the hair away from my eyes, asking me what was wrong. I shook my head from side to side. He asked again and then I said the words, not caring how desperate I sounded to him: "I need you, Valentin. Please undo these restraints and just hold me in your arms."

CHAPTER
Twenty-Two

Valentin

t would be my pleasure, I've got you," I whispered as I quickly loosened my tie that secured her to our bed.

As soon as she was free, she lunged into my arms, wrapping herself around me. If we were any closer, we would be one.

I said, "I'm sorry I hurt you today. I shouldn't have interfered in your career but I swear to you, I only opened a door for you. You are the one that had to walk through it and do the work. I am a man of many means, but I'm afraid I don't know a needle from a spool of thread. That's your area of brilliance."

"Your faith in me is just astonishing. Thank you, Valentin. I just want to prove her wrong, you know?"

"I do know, and you will. Don't allow Zara or anyone find an opening and make you doubt yourself into believing you are not up to the task, because they would be foolish to think that."

"I'll admit today did not go as well as I would have liked it to, but there's always tomorrow, and it will be better."

"You have a great attitude. Please forget about Zara. She was born with a silver spoon in her mouth and never had to struggle one day in her life. If anything, she should be honored to know you and take pride that someone admires her so much that she would want to pass down some wisdom to you."

"Thank you, but from here on out, I will take on Zara myself. May I ask what you two were talking about when I walked back into my office?"

"It was nothing to worry about. Just a squabble amongst old friends." *I lied and hoped this line of questioning was over.*

We were interrupted by Marta, who knocked once to let me know our champagne had arrived. I wasn't sure if Willow would be in the mood for it now, but I called out for Marta to come in and set it down on the table.

"Dinner should be ready soon. Can I get you anything else?" she inquired.

"No, that will be all. Thank you, Marta."

She smiled at Willow, which pleased me a great deal. I wanted Willow to be comfortable around our home and our staff. If something did not sit right with her, I would resolve it quickly.

"Will you allow me to pour you a glass?" I asked.

"Yes, thank you."

The releasing of the cork was loud without a drop being spilled. She looked happy and more at ease since we arrived earlier. Yes, our car fucking was again rough, but it was what we both needed, and it helped break the tension after leaving the office. My dove had a stubborn streak and temper that made me hard and gave me all sorts of ideas on how to tame her.

I exclaimed, "Cheers! You are amazing and talented. I love you so much and only want everything for you. I promise to do all that I can to make that happen for you."

"I love you too, Valentin. Another question if I may?"

"Anything for you. Ask me."

"Ollie…who is he to you? And what is he to me?"

I guess I couldn't avoid this forever, I knew it was coming. Okay, a moment of truth I knew I could not avoid any longer.

"Ollie is Oleg, but I believe he quite enjoys Ollie and wishes for you to continue to call him as such."

"That doesn't answer my question."

"No, it doesn't. I guess one of the reasons why I restrained you tonight was because I have a great deal to share with you, and I don't want to scare you off and have you leave me. It's a fear of mine, and if it becomes a reality, I'm not sure if and how I will handle it. I need you here with me. I am not going to settle for anything less. I want you to share my home with me and call it yours. Everything is yours, including this heart of mine. It's yours."

"I promise you that no matter what you tell me will not make me leave you. The only deal breaker I have is if you cheat on me. I know I would not be able to handle infidelity."

"You will never have to worry about me straying. You are all that I want and will ever need." I kissed her passionately, and she relaxed in my arms.

"Please tell me more about Ollie? Is he the one who has been following me?"

I tried to keep my reaction at bay, but it was hard to hide, especially knowing that Willow had known all along.

She said, "Okay, I guess one of my questions has been confirmed. Now I need to know why?"

How do I broach this delicate subject with Willow? I thought as my heart began to race with trepidation. *I could evade her questions by suggesting taking a bath together and then eating dinner. We both needed to relax, and I knew this was not going to be an easy conversation to have, knowing our relationship could be at risk. What will be her reaction? And how much is she willing to accept?* I took her hand and put an end to my incessant thoughts.

"Let's go take a soak in the tub. I promise to be the perfect gentleman. You need it more than you know, and so do I."

I got off the bed and reached for her hand. She accepted it immediately and followed me in through the bathroom. I grabbed the champagne and topped off our glasses.

Once settled with Willow nestled against my chest, I let out a relaxing breath enjoying the intimate moment between us. I massaged the tight knots from her shoulder and lower back, causing her to sigh in pleasure.

"This feels so good. Don't ever stop," she giggled.

"You sound better. Are you?"

"I am. I love being here with you." she placed her glass down and turned around to face me. Her body was covered with scented bubbles only revealing a small exposed area of her breasts.

"Careful, love, you are too tempting for your own good, and I am just a man in love."

"Yes, you are, and I love you too, maybe more than I should. You have become so important in my life, so soon that I've hardly had a chance to catch my breath. I know you are keeping something from me. I see it in your eyes. I want you to know that whatever you have to tell me will be okay, because I love you enough to handle anything. I didn't believe I could until I asked you to hold me, just like on the night I asked you to come for me at the deli. I trust you, Valentin, and I promise we're going to be okay."

I sat up and wrapped my arms around her body, breathing in her amazing scent as if it were my lifeline. "How do you know?"

"Because I know you, and I know this heart. You practically dared me to believe in it on the day we met back at the police station. And I ran from that heart and your kindness because I was afraid. I'm not afraid anymore, because you've made me stronger. That's what love does to a person, it changes them and makes them better. So, believe in me like you dared me to believe in you."

I had never felt more alive than when I was with Willow. Her honesty was not something I had ever experienced in my life. Most people I came in contact with were intimidated by my name alone, which had granted me a great deal of access to literally anything I ever wanted.

I knew I could easily forgo dinner and take her to bed, but there would be time for that. No, I wanted to just enjoy something as simple as dinner with her before I would have no choice than to share the harder and complicated parts of my life.

I left her with several kisses on her mouth and then led her to the outside terrace, my favorite place to dine, especially nights like tonight when it wasn't too humid. The view up here was like no other, but it didn't rival the beauty sitting across from me.

We switched over to wine as we enjoyed the perfectly prepared porterhouse steaks paired with green vegetables and red potatoes. When she was finished with her meal, she covered her plate with the silver dome and moved it over to the rolling cart.

"Have you had enough, darling? Have you saved room for dessert?" I asked.

"I'm full, and I'll take a raincheck on dessert…for now. Valentin, this has been a lovely evening. Thank you for dinner."

The way she said her words put me on edge a little bit. I knew this was me overreacting and looking for problems that didn't exist. *She has proven over and over how much she wants to be here, so I must give her the benefit of the doubt.*

"You sure I can't persuade you for anything else? Chocolate truffles, perhaps?"

"I'm sure you can persuade me into anything and I would let you, but I'm fine for now and would like to take a walk."

"A walk?" I balked.

"Don't sound too surprised by this. You know I like to take walks at night to clear my head."

I grumbled at the reminder. "Yes, and I don't like it one bit."

"You don't have to, but I do and would like to take a walk, and with you holding my hand. Will you?"

"I feel like an ass. I'm sorry for blowing up at you. I'm not my-self."

"All the more reason to walk and relax. I'm not avoiding our talk. I just think this is a better way to have it."

"Okay, but I will be holding your hand at all times, and you must not pull away from me if I say something you might not like. Agreed?"

CHAPTER
Twenty-Three

Willow

N ow that his true identity had been revealed, there was no reason to have Oleg hide in the shadows. He met us downstairs in the lobby and greeted me the moment I stepped off the elevator.

He smiled warmly, which I returned, but I knew that was as far as pleasantries would go unless he wanted to take on Valentin and his jealousy. Now, who was being ridiculous? The thought of even looking in another man's direction was just unfathomable to me, not when I was with Mr. Tall, Dark, and Sexy. I'd meant what I said about him ruining me for other men. No one could ever replace Valentin in my heart or my bed.

Oleg remained close but not so where it was becoming uncomfortable. With our hands linked, Valentin and I walked several blocks in conversation before spotting my favorite custard shop. The Big Scoop had rows and rows of frozen yogurt, custard, ice flavors, and gelato, which was why I wanted to come here.

True to his word, Valentin never released my hand even inside the shop. So when I moved, he moved. I smiled because it seemed like a game of chess and Valentin was about to claim checkmate and toss me over his shoulder like the dominating presence he was.

A young man came out from the back and was polite enough to ask what we would like. Valentin glared at him, and then I turned to tell him to behave. He smirked, and I knew that face all too well, and so did my backside.

"One moment please," I answered and faced my brooding man. Oh, he was so handsome even when he was cross. "What would you like?"

"It's not on this menu." He winked, and now I knew his jovial mood had returned. What a mercurial man he was.

"I can order for you. Is there anything you don't like before I do?"

"Be my guest," he replied.

"Yay!" I leaned up on my tiptoes to kiss him. "Excuse me! Hello, I'm ready." The young man came back over and opened the showcase. "I would like two cups of pistachio gelato, medium size, with an extra dollop of pistachio sauce."

"You know, I should punish you for your sly move back there in the shop," he said as we walked the city street, eating our dessert.

"For what?" I challenged him, knowing full well what he was referring to.

"By ordering a cup dessert that would require you to use both hands, hence breaking our agreement." He was teasing, I think.

"Well, I'm not sorry, because you have to admit this gelato is amazing, and you have just discovered a secret pleasure."

"Fair enough, you have me there, because it is good, but the minute you are finished, I'm taking back what's mine."

A few more bites and then I was finished and tossed my empty cup into the trash. He followed my gesture and then pulled me in for a hug.

I told him, "I know what you're doing, and I mostly understand the reasons behind your actions, but sooner or later, we're going to have to talk about it. What has you so troubled? And please don't try to evade my questions and use sex to silence me. Haven't you heard that communication is vital in a relationship?"

"No, because I've never had one before meeting you."

"Okay, neither have I, but I read and watch television. Please talk to me."

"I will, love, but not here. I would feel comfortable if we were back at home."

"Okay, you win," I said. "Let's walk home."

He crushed his mouth to mine and said, "I usually do in all things, Willow, and I'm done walking. Oleg will drive us."

I blinked in understanding, and he stepped out to open the door for me. Valentin looked still on edge even after my attempts to ease his burdens tonight. It was best not to say anything more and just comply with his wishes.

I left him on his own for a while so he could make some calls while I went upstairs to change. I didn't appreciate the full extent of what moving in meant until I took a closer glance at the closet. Valentin had filled it with everything I could possibly need, including items from my grandmother's apartment. *How did he do this? And without me knowing about it? Hadn't it only been a day since I was back there?*

"What are you thinking about?" he asked, standing behind me.

"All of this," I gestured with my hands pointing into the sprawling closet that contained thousands of dollars' worth of luxury clothing that I would never be able to afford in my wildest dreams. I sighed and tried to move away from the intensity of Valentin, but he was everywhere I was. He made sure there was no space between us.

I turned to face him and tried to explain how I felt but failed miserably when all my words came out wrong. "Valentin, I know you want me to accept this new way of life you have introduced me to, but it's a lot to get used to, especially for a girl like me who was not raised around wealthy people. My way of life was a lot simpler than yours."

The look of disappointment on his face made me feel sick. He stepped forward, and I stepped back. This dance of ours continued until I was now inside a room bigger than my grandmother's living room and kitchen combined. *And he wonders why I'm overwhelmed.* My back was against the wall, as his body caged me in the way I'd become oddly comfortable with.

"*A girl like you*?" he crossly repeated my words. "Do you really want to test me tonight? Because I believe we have already covered this topic more than once, and I will not discuss it again. You are my woman, and I will give you anything I want. This is just a small taste that doesn't even scratch the surface."

"And what about these things? How are they here when I know I didn't bring them?"

"Oleg," he answered.

Of course.

"And how does that make it okay? You've changed my entire life in the blink of an eye, and I've hardly had time to catch my breath."

"Willow, it's the same for me. I don't know how I will ever be able to explain the depths of my feelings for you. I just want to give you the world because I can, and why should you have to want these things when I am in a position to actually give them to you? Baby, it's just clothes. If you don't like them, I can send them back and you can choose anything you want, but they're also needed because of the life I lead. I'm a wealthy man, Willow, with an extravagant lifestyle that accompanies me wherever I go. I don't attend boring business dinners, more like state dinners at the White House. I'm not trying to boast here; it's just who I am. And now is the time I tell you the rest. Please, get into bed, and allow me to just hold you while we talk."

"No tying me to the bed?"

"Not unless you want me to." He smiled wickedly.

"Maybe later. Holding me sounds great."

I quickly changed into a satin robe, with Valentin wearing only bottoms, leaving his rock-hard torso beautifully exposed. He lifted me up into his bed and pulled me close to his side with my head on his chest and his back against the headboard. His skin was warm, and his chest hair was so soft. It was heaven.

He was quiet, and the only sounds coming from him were his deep sighs. Whatever he had to tell me had to be difficult, because I could feel his body tense with the obvious struggle emanating from him. I squeezed him tighter and assured him that I wasn't going anywhere.

"Tell me, Valentin. I promise I will listen to whatever you have to say."

"You'll leave me after I do, and that can't happen…not ever."

I tried to move so I could look into his eyes, which were always so telling. He kept me close to his body, holding on as if I were his lifeline, and in a way, I was. He had been mine since the day we met, and the more I spent time with him, the more that belief became true.

I said, "After everything we've said to one another and the physical connection we have shared, how can you still believe that I would so easily walk out of your door, never to be seen again? It's just preposterous. I know where this is coming from and thought we had settled it."

He was distracted, and then I was able to move before he pulled me back. I didn't leave his bed. I just sat up on my knees to face him.

"Valentin, I know I'm young and inexperienced, but that doesn't mean I'm so naïve that I don't recognize when my boyfriend has a problem and is finding it hard to talk to me about it. We keep telling each other things about ourselves. That is necessary for the both of us to be in this relationship. I get it and understand why. So here's another thing you need to know about me: I am a talker, a pretty big one. When you're raised by only one parent, they usually tend to take on the role of two, and that involves a lot of communication. When my mother wasn't there, my grandmother was, and she's twice as tough when it comes to life's lessons. I've heard them all, and it's made me a good listener, one that doesn't judge. You are ten years older than me and were raised very differently from how I was. Your past is your business, and I would never force you to share it with me if you weren't ready to do so. It feels to me that you want to, and you're allowing fear to stop you from doing so, no matter how many times I tell you different. It's late, and it's been a really long day. I'm going to go to sleep now with you holding me. When you're ready—and I mean really ready—to talk, I promise you that I will be here to listen. Okay?"

"Okay, thank you, Willow."

"You're welcome, Valentin. I love you."

He didn't say it back, but that was okay because I knew. I kissed him on his chest as he slowly began to fall asleep and come down from the mountain of stress he was feeling.

I continued, "When I was little and used to spend weekends with gram, she would tuck me in at night and always tell me to dream of good things. Now, those dreams could have been anything from ice cream sundaes to a new pair of sparkly shoes. I know we come from different worlds and whatever you want to tell me has to be pretty significant, but for tonight, can you forget about the hard stuff and just dream of good things? No matter where you come from or who you are, I'm sure you must have dreamt of something you wanted and hoped it would come true. I eventually got my sparkly shoes and wore them down to the soles and through a few repair jobs before I totally outgrew them. Valentin, dreams can be our escape when the harsh realities become too hard to bear. When you're young, it's easy. You dream of what makes you happy and bury the things that don't. For me, it was my dad and trying to reach some level of understanding why he didn't love my mom enough to stick around and love me too. I knew it wasn't going to do me any good dreaming about something I had no control over, so instead, I told myself each night and still to this day, to dream of good things. Why not? There's no harm in wanting that for yourself and others you love and who love you back."

His chest was rising and falling into a steady rhythm, and I knew he was asleep. *Good, he needs it.* I moved in closer to where I could kiss his lips. They were perfect, just like him. I knew I was so in love with this man and once again relied on my instincts to stay with him and give him the chance he was asking for.

"Pleasant dreams, baby. Dream of good things." I gave him one more kiss and then found my spot and joined him in sleep.

When I woke up, he was gone, and his side of the bed was cold. I looked around for a note and found one on his side table.

My beautiful dove,

You looked too tempting to wake, and I had an early morning meeting. I promise to make it up to you. Marta will prepare anything you wish to eat for breakfast, and I hope you do, because you are too thin. Breakfast bars are not substantial enough for the hours you work. Yes, I saw them in your purse. Call me when you get to the office. Oleg will drive you. I do hope you have a wonderful day and that it's better than yesterday.

One more thing...

All my dreams last night were of you. You gave me exactly what my heart and mind needed to hear. I love you.

Valentin

After reading his note, I hugged myself and then snuggled back to his pillow, breathing in his intoxicating scent. I loved everything he wore. And then I had an idea. I scanned my closet with all the selections he had chosen for me. I wanted to wear something that was bold and sexy, something to make me brave to face the day. I chose a pair of black and white pinstriped palazzo wide leg pants that fitted tightly around my waist. I paired it with a silk blouse and a big oversized tie, completing the look with a blazer.

Once my outfit was put together, I worked on my hair and makeup. I styled my hair in a slick ponytail tied at the nape of my neck. For makeup, I applied a smoky eyeshadow with eyeliner and a voluminous mascara that made my lashes extend and my eyes pop.

I almost didn't recognize myself when I stood in front of the floor length mirror. I remembered how Valentin dared me to open my eyes and believe in myself the same way he did. *It's getting easier. He makes it that way for me.*

I smiled, and all that was left was applying lipstick and a spritz of perfume. *I wanted to be bold, right?* I wore red, the brightest color I had in my collection and it screamed *Power, Confidence, and Sexiness,* all rolled up into one. I loved it and knew if Valentin could see me now, I probably wouldn't make it out of this apartment.

Visions of being bound to his bed came flooding back, sending titillating shockwaves throughout my entire body. *Fuck! What this man does to me.* I closed my eyes and sighed, holding my legs tightly together. I smiled and then had another idea. I walked over to his side of the long bathroom counter and picked up his cologne, my favorite one. Bringing the bottle to my nose, I inhaled the fresh woodsy masculine scent that was all Valentin. I sprayed my wrist and another to my neck. *Now, he's with me, and I am ready to take on the world with Valentin guiding me to be bold.*

Taking the extra time I needed this morning to get ready, I declined breakfast, but I think Marta was prepared for that and handed me a sack lunch as I stepped onto the elevator. *He's always taking care of me even when he's not here.* I accepted the bag and gave my thanks.

Oleg's eyes widened as he took in my appearance. Another win for me! Yeah, I'm sure it wouldn't take long for Valentin to hear about it, and that's what I was most looking forward to.

"Oleg, did you drive him in this morning?" I asked, seeing him flash me a smile in the rearview mirror.

"I did, and he's well."

I nodded and then felt relief. One more idea that would make this day perfect, and I hadn't even arrived to work yet: I snapped a selfie blowing him a kiss.

I beamed with happiness and then walked into work, ready for Madeline. Heads turned as I made my way through the showcase floor and up to my loft office. With no sign of Madeline, I made myself a latte and began sketching in my pad.

My phone beeped with an incoming message. I was hoping it would be from Valentin, and it was.

You're stunning and good enough to eat. I may just have to have you for lunch.

And I'll let you, I replied back.

I went back to my work and wondered where Madeline was. I tried her cell a few times, and it went straight to voicemail. I reached for my phone and dialed down to Peter.

"I'm not ready yet, Willow," he said without saying hello.

"Peter, I'm not calling about the patterns. Have you heard from Madeline this morning?"

"I have not, but she's probably sleeping over the bender she took last night."

"What? Why is she drinking so much?"

"Oh, the young. To be your age again! I'm sure she's fine, sweet thing. Don't worry."

"Well, I do, and I'm going to go check on her."

"Be my guest. Have fun with that."

And because he was being a little too sassy for my taste today, I gave a little back. "And when I do return, I'll have my patterns cut and ready to go?"

"Yes, you sexy diva!"

"Thank you," I giggled and then disconnected my call.

I grabbed my purse and made my way outside. I didn't think of calling Oleg and just hailed down a passing cab. It didn't take long to reach Madeline's apartment.

Using the hideaway key, I entered and called out her name. I looked around, and then I shrieked when I saw Madeline bound and gagged to a chair.

"Oh my god, Madeline! Who did this to you?" I asked as I removed the rag from her mouth and tried to untie her.

"Get out, kid, right now before they come back. Go get help and hurry!" Before she could say anything else, her eyes widened, and I was grabbed from behind, making me scream.

"What the hell is happening here? What do you want?" I shouted and kicked, trying to break free, which proved to be useless against my attacker.

"The perfect bait," he said. "Yes, you are exactly what I need to bring Valentin Vasiliev to his knees."

"No!" I kicked and struggled in his arms, while he maniacally laughed at my efforts.

He dropped me to the floor, and I hurried over to where Madeline was.

I said, "I'm so sorry, Madeline. I don't know what's happening right now, but we'll figure it out, okay?"

I was trying to catch my breath when he pulled me away from my friend, using my hair to do it. I screamed out in pain as he wrapped my ponytail around his wrist.

"I can see the allure and why he would be so drawn to you, any right man in their mind would. Yes, you are perfect. It will be a shame cutting you up and leaving all your pieces for Valentin to find," he threatened.

"Please don't do this," I cried.

Then a pack of armed men burst through Madeline's apartment, led by Oleg. I was frozen with fear keeping me still. I couldn't predict what would happen next, and I imagined the worse as Oleg aimed a flashing red bullseye onto my captor's forehead. We were surrounded by men all dressed in black and scary as hell with the guns they were holding. Although cornered and with nowhere to run, my captor did not flinch.

He spoke with a heavy Russian accent. "An eye for an eye, Oleg, or have you gone soft playing babysitter to this one? Hmmm?" He taunted Oleg as he yanked hard on my hair, pulling me close to himself.

Oleg said with confidence, "I haven't forgotten. And if you remember well, I never miss."

"Neither do I. It would take a second to snap her neck, and you know it."

"And it would take me less than that to put a bullet in your skull. Release her or that's exactly what I will do."

He squeezed my hair harder, and in a flash, the room erupted in silenced gunfire and chaos, sending me falling to the floor for cover. My captor laid bleeding out from a gunshot wound to his head. Madeline was screaming hysterically, and I was dragged up from under my armpits and carried out of her apartment and placed into a car.

I was so scared and couldn't stop shaking as I relived the horrific images that I just witnessed. I don't remember what happened next. I must have passed out, but when I woke up screaming, I saw two piercing brown eyes staring back at me.

"You're safe, dove. I've got you."

CHAPTER
Twenty-four

Valentin

Twelve hours earlier

I hated to leave our bed this morning, especially with Willow looking the way she did. I swear, she was exquisite in every way. I kissed her forehead and scribbled a note for her to find once she woke up.

I was caught up with all of my cases, and anything new could be transitioned to my staff, which freed up a lot of time for me for other matters that required my attention, namely my brother. I knew I could not hold off my father for much longer. Eventually he would return home to New York.

Once I left the apartment, I had Oleg drive me over to Zara's studio. I had some unfinished business with my so-called friend, and it would not wait. I was buzzed up and took the elevator to the top floor, where her studio, showroom, and small boutique was located. This was just one of several locations Zara used around the city.

Several assistants scurried behind me trying to stop me as I made my way into her office. Once I opened the door, she seemed surprised to see me and called off her staff. I closed the door behind me while glaring at her.

She looked guilty and gave me a remorseful glance. "I'm sorry. What more do you want me to say?"

"I want to know what in the hell you were thinking, speaking to Willow that way yesterday? Did I not make my wishes clear enough for you?"

"I told you this was not going to work, Valentin, and I was right. However, your *woman*," she said, using air quotes to make her point clear, "is not as fragile as you think. She didn't hold back when telling me how she felt about my opinions, so don't come down on me."

"I am well aware on how strong my Willow is, and it pleases me a great deal that she stood behind her convictions and didn't allow you to belittle her work."

"That's not true, Valentin. I gave her my honest opinion, and I did say the work was good. It just wasn't on the scale of great, and that's what I want for my line. She's no costume designer, even she knows that, so why don't you?"

"Because I recognize the true talent she is, and I will not allow you or anyone for that matter make her believe otherwise. Yesterday was about you and your bruised ego, because you believe I forced you into this working arrangement with Willow and Madeline."

"You did, Valentin. You didn't give me any choice to say no. I will admit I was angry with you, and I may have taken my cross mood out on her. You didn't tell me anything I didn't already know, because once I took a better perusal of her work, I knew it was very good and enough for what I expect out of a designer. I have no doubt the rest will be just as good."

"I'm happy we can come to an understanding. You're smart, Zara. Don't miss out on an opportunity just because I was the one that has given it to you. You are in a position to make a lot of money and showcase a rising star, for which I know you will take the credit for.

Take the stick out of your pampered ass, and work with Willow. It will make working together a lot easier for all parties involved."

"I know. You're right."

"Come again?" I said to Zara, knowing she was about to spit nails. I let her off the hook and lifted her chin with my two fingers so she could look at me. "Thank you," I softly said to my friend, and when her eyes glazed over with tears, she knew I meant my words. "I only want the best for Willow, and with your help and guidance, I know she can get there. Everyone needs help starting out. As you do well remember."

"I know, and I will do all that I can. You have my word."

"See that you do. I must run now. I'll be in touch."

"Oh, I'm sure. I can't wait." She responded by flashing me a sassy grin.

"Be careful, Zara. We just made up." I winked and took the elevator down to my waiting car.

I checked my phone for messages. One was from Willow. I slid my finger across the screen, and her beautiful face appeared. *Holy shit, she's gorgeous. What is she wearing?* As I stared at her plump lips covered in red, all I could imagine were those lips wrapped around my dick, sucking me off until I exploded down her throat. *Naughty girl.*

I quickly texted her back, which led to several more between us before my phone began to ring. I expected to see her name flash across my screen, but it was my father calling instead. I let out a breath before answering.

"Father, hello, it's so good to hear from you." I tried to make small talk, but all the hair was standing on the back of my neck, and I knew I was fucked.

"Come to the club. We have much to discuss." He didn't give me an opportunity to respond, because he hung up.

"Oleg, my father has returned and doesn't sound well. Take me to the club."

"Right away."

While we drove through the busy Manhattan traffic, I called Sergei to check on my brother.

"All is well, Valentin. He's doing so much better. No side effects with his new medication."

"Good, and he's eating and keeping up his strength?"

"Yes, he is. He even did a few miles on the treadmill. I didn't want him to overdo it, but he said he was fine."

"Yes, I'm sure that's what he believes, but we don't want him to get ahead of himself and rush his progress."

"Will you be visiting him today? As soon as he wakes, he always asks for you."

"I'm not sure. I may have a bigger problem to handle first. My father has returned, and I'm on my way to see him now. Sergei, please, has he been in contact with you?"

"Yes, but I've told him nothing. Let's hope all the care I've done for Sasha doesn't land a bullet in my head."

"It won't get that far, I promise you. All you need to do is protect my brother. Keep him safe, and I'll do the rest."

"Has something happened? You must tell me, or I will not be able to do what is asked of me."

"Shirmanov paid me a visit yesterday. We exchanged words, and I asked him to leave, but not before Pavlo issued me a warning in Russian."

"Do you think he suspects anything?"

"He was fishing, but that's all it was. I have to go. I'll be in touch soon." I hung up just as Oleg was pulling up to the club. "Oleg, stay here and keep eyes on the street. Have you checked on Willow? Is she where she's supposed to be?"

"Yes, I pinged her phone, and it shows her office."

"Yes, I see that as well, but I'd be happier knowing if I could see the proof with my own eyes. I want you to pull the camera footage you installed and send everything to my phone."

"Okay, I'll do it while you're inside with your father."

I fixed my suit and ran my fingers down my slacks as if I was smoothing out wrinkles that weren't there. I was nervous, and that's one emotion I never felt when it came to talking to my father. I stepped into the empty club, and Andrei was the first to greet me.

"He's upstairs in the office."

I nodded my thanks and made my way up the stairs, where my father was waiting for me. It was soundproofed and totally protected from surveillance of any kind. When we built this club, we only installed state of the art equipment to protect our business and keep the unwanted guests out. I rapped my knuckles a few times against the solid oak door before hearing him call me inside.

He was seated behind his desk, typing whatever on his phone. I stood there in silence, waiting for my father to say something. He was a bear of a man, taller than my 6'3" in height and had at least thirty pounds on me. He was not one I would win a fight with, and the physical damage he could inflict would be severe.

"Sit down, my son. We have much to discuss as I stated earlier."

"Welcome home, father," I greeted him, but he raised his hand to silence me.

"Is it? Because from where I'm sitting, it's not. Pavlo Shirmanov contacted me while I was in London. I was about to board the jet after our layover and had a very enlightening conversation with him. Shall I tell you what he shared with me?"

"Father..."

He cut me off again. "Avros is dead. A son of our rival is dead. Now, Pavlo believes it was one of my sons who murdered him. I denied any wrongdoing and told him that he was wrong. Is he, Valentin?"

"What do you think?"

"I'm asking the questions."

"Yes, questions you already know the answers to. I had to protect the family and step in your place and handle it the best way I knew how."

My father rubbed his hands over his face and sighed, already knowing what I would say next. He stood and walked over to the bar to pour himself a drink, downing it quickly and then pouring another for himself and one for me. I accepted and downed the shot. He remained quiet for a moment and then white-knuckled the granite countertop, not turning around.

He held his head down and said, "Where is Sasha?"

"He's safe," I answered. He turned and walked over to where I was standing and slapped both sides of my face before taking me in for a hug.

"But...? For how long, Valentin? How long will it be before my son suffers the same fate as Avros?"

"I will never allow that to happen. You must trust me as you always have. Father, this was a rogue power play created and sanctioned by Avros, and he used his girlfriend to lure Sasha. She pumped him up with drugs, and he was so high when Avros tried to take him out. But Avros didn't take into account how manic Sasha becomes when he stops his meds for recreational ones. He becomes absolutely unhinged. I wasn't there. It's Sasha's story to tell, but from what I gathered from the men, he had no choice but to take them both out."

"And leaving quite the mess for you to clean up. Fuck! I knew I stayed away too long. I'm sorry. This is on me, not you. Am I to assume the trail which led the FBI to Shirmanov is your doing?"

"Yes, amongst other maneuvers I had to put into play in the short amount of time I had."

"I will handle Pavlo. A request for a meeting has already been issued. As long as you take care of your brother, I will handle the rest. Understand?"

"Yes, but father, once this is finished, we're going to need to have a conversation."

"I know. It's been a long time coming, hasn't it?"

"I love you, father, you know that I do, but I cannot continue to lead my life on both sides of the law and have a semblance of a life. I've met someone who I am deeply in love with."

"I see, and does she love you back?"

"Yes,"

"Very well, then you must do everything in your power to hold onto that love and shield her from all of this," he said gesturing around the room. "I trust you haven't shared this part of your life with her yet?"

"No, I haven't and have tried very hard to avoid it altogether."

"We're not as lethal as our rivals but we do what is necessary to protect our family and safeguard our future. What others do are not our concern. You have legitimized our entire operation and secured our family's fortune for years to come. I can't say the same for Shirmanov. This is why his Avros took the risk. Word was circulating in St. Petersburg as well as in the Bratva. The dynasty he has built is crumbling at its foundation, and soon stronger forces will move in and dismantle what he has left, exiling him back to Russia."

"Father, do you think this makes Pavlo more dangerous, knowing he has nothing else to lose?"

"Yes, I do. You will need to continue to be careful and expect the unexpected until I have a chance to sit down and talk with him. Keep Sasha where he is, and I will go to him as soon as I am able to."

"What about mother?"

"She's in London with your aunt. I felt it was best to come back on my own. I don't want her to worry."

"Father, I'm sorry I didn't tell you sooner. I had no time to think, just act."

"I know, and you will never know how grateful I am for you. You are a good son, Valentin, and you were always meant for a life that did not include all of this. I hope to return you to it as soon as I can." He took me by my shoulders and whispered a Russian prayer. I knew what it meant for a man like my father to give this gift to me. It was his blessing. Then once again, he let me go.

My phone rang. "Excuse me, father. It's Oleg calling. Yes?"

"Valentin, we need to move," Oleg burst out. "Now! It's Willow, and she's in trouble! Shirmanov has taken her hostage."

"I need to go, father. He has her."

"Go! Save your girl. I will send everything you need behind you."

I never ran so fast in my life. I hardly felt the stairs underneath my feet as I sprinted for the exit and into my car.

Oleg drove and sped us through the city until the tracker led us to Madeline's apartment building. Within minutes, my father's mercenaries arrived and were led inside by Oleg. I took the back of the building using the other entrance. Our men stormed the doors and had Shirmanov surrounded, with Oleg's gun aimed directly at his head. He was holding my dove as she struggled to break free. *My brave girl. He would not be walking out of here alive if he hurts one hair on her head.*

This was a daring move for the head of the Bratva to do, but these are unusual circumstances, because Pavlo is grieving his son and wants our family to do the same. He knows I will never give up my brother, so he has chosen another way to seek his revenge, and that's on my woman. I don't want to hurt him, and my hand has never been forced where I had to. I'm praying today is not that day.

Oleg handed me a gun to use if necessary, cold hard steel in the palm of my hand with the ability to blow a hole through a man's chest. *This is not who I am, but I will if it means saving Willow.* I came to terms with it quickly as I made my presence known, bringing the room into complete chaos. Our men did not lower their weapons, nor did Oleg, who kept his weapon aimed right on Pavlo.

"Stand down," I commanded my men as I tried to reason with Pavlo without the need for violence. "What are you doing, Pavlo?"

He began shouting at me in Russian, which I understood fluently. He was enraged, and it was becoming clearer that I only had a small window to save my girl.

"You do know if you kill her, I will kill you," I threatened.

"It doesn't matter. I've lost everything anyway. You don't know the lengths I have had to go to in order to protect what's mine, and your father swoops in and takes it from me. First my business, and then you take my son."

"Pavlo, what are you talking about? What has my father taken from you?"

"Everything!!! Or haven't you been listening to me? Now, we finish this."

As Willow struggled in his grasp, Oleg, an expert marksman and one who never misses, took the shot that resulted in Pavlo falling to the floor with a bullet right between his eyes.

Willow was screaming and fell along with him. She had gone into shock, and I needed to get her out of here. I rushed to her side and lifted her up in my arms. Madeline had been secured, which we would deal with later. My only concern was Willow.

I brought her back to our apartment and removed her blood-covered clothing. She looked absolutely gorgeous today, and now she looked as if she's been through a war. She felt light in my arms as I washed her from head to toe and then placed her in our bed. The doctor would arrive at any moment to examine her. My jaw was clenched as I gnashed my molars together watching her be examined. I detested any hand that wasn't mine on her body, but it was necessary.

"Mr. Vasiliev, she's going to be fine. She needs rest."

"Thank you for coming out so quickly."

"No trouble at all. I'll see myself out."

I ran my fingers through my own hair and pulled the strands until I felt pain. *Fuck! Please don't leave me, Willow. Please wake up and give me a chance to explain,* I silently prayed as I watched her sleep.

I crept out of our room and dialed Oleg. "I need an update."

"It's been handled, and that's all you need to know," he responded, his way of talking in code just in case my phone was tapped.

"Stay close by, I may need you."

"I'm here when you're ready."

I pocketed my phone and then heard a bloodcurdling scream come from the bedroom. I was immediately by her side. Her eyes opened, and all I saw was fear behind them. I tried to calm her with my touch and was thankful she didn't recoil from me. I wiped her tears and then said, "I've got you." She closed her eyes and began to cry in my arms. "You're safe with me, I promise. I've got you, and you're going to be alright."

She buried her face in the crook of my neck and continued to cry until she fell asleep. I could do nothing but let her, while a little more of my heart broke. This was awful, sheer agony having to suffer in silence when powerless to do anything else.

I knew I missed important calls while tending to Willow and had to return them as soon as possible, or we would have another scene here right in the middle of our bedroom. I carefully slid out from our bed and checked my phone. Four missed calls from Oleg and seven more from my father. I called Oleg first from a burner and secured the line.

He called me back quickly and got right to his point. "Her girl Madeline needed to be restrained and sedated. She threatened to call the police, and I couldn't allow that to happen. I called up the doc and moved her to a safe house. Not with Sasha, but another one close by."

"I don't want her hurt, Oleg. She's scared and has a right to be. Do what you can to calm her once she wakes, and I'll call you. I have more than I can handle here with Willow."

"How is she doing?"

"She's resting but scared and hasn't been able to talk with me yet. I can't leave her, so it's up to you to handle my father and anything else that comes up."

"Speaking of Alaric, he's with Sasha, I couldn't stop him and neither could Sergei. Not that he really tried. Once word erupted on the street about Pavlo, he left with guards."

"I can't deal with this now. It's clear to me that he traveled home to Russia under false pretenses and used my mother as a cover. Don't call me again. I'll call you." I hung up and shouted, "Sonofabitch!" and then smashed the phone against the wall.

"Valentin," I heard from the doorway.

"Hey, I'm sorry you had to hear that. Come here, baby."

My heart stilled when she twisted her hands in the hem of my t-shirt, but then a new wave of tears erupted from her, and she practically lunged toward me. I wrapped my arms around her and breathed every sweet scent that was my Willow.

"Oh, my beautiful dove, I am so sorry you had to go through that today. I promise that you're safe, and no one will ever get that close to you again."

"Where's Madeline? Is she dead?" her voice cracked when she asked me.

"No, she's fine," I lied.

"I want to see her. Right now!" she screamed and broke free of my arms.

"Willow, it's not possible. Please let me take care of you, and then you will be able to see Madeline."

"No, Valentin, the only thing I need right now is to get the hell out of here and find my friend."

I tried to touch her, but she shouted at me to stay back. I had no choice but to comply.

She screamed, "You lied to me, something you promised you would never do."

"No, I didn't. I swear everything we have shared with one another has been true. I love you, Willow. You are my dove."

"Stop calling me that! I don't know if I can ever be your anything again until you tell me who the hell you are and what the fuck was that back there at Madeline's apartment? Are you like a Russian spy or something? Is that why I have a personal bodyguard and I'm under watch all the time? Yeah, I know about that too. I was angry at first, but then I think it may have saved my life with the tracker you put on my phone. Right, Valentin?"

"Yes, that's true," I whispered, feeling unapologetic for my actions.

"Of course it is! What the hell are you into? And how the hell do I get out?" Her words were like knives slicing me wide open with wounds that would never heal if I were to lose her.

No, I might as well be dead if that were to happen.

I stepped closer and said, "I love you, Willow, and there is not a chance in hell that you are leaving me." *Not while I still draw breath.*

CHAPTER
Twenty-five

Willow

"Oh, really? And just how do you intend to stop me?" I stood there defiantly with my hands balled at my hips.

He smirked and said, "Do you need a reminder? Because I'll have no problem showing you exactly how I will keep you here and with me. I know you're upset, that much is clear, but you need to calm down and listen to what I have to say. I promise you it will make the world of difference and, although it may change our relationship, I'm willing to take the risk because you are worth fighting for."

"Fine! I'll listen, but I will not make any promises that I will stay. If you don't agree to that condition, then please step aside and let me leave."

"Agreed, but I have a request of my own." I glared at him because it didn't surprise me at all that I would give him an inch and he would take a yard.

"What is it?"

"Believe me when I say that the conversation we are about to have, I've wanted to have since we met. I just didn't know how to share that part of my life with you. It's complicated, to say the least, and it may scare you a little. The minute I saw you that day at the station, I knew I was a man in love. You took my breath away, and I've been trying to catch it ever since. Please, I want you in our bed. No, that's not right. I *need* you in our bed. I have to hold you and feel your skin against mine when we talk."

"You're not restraining me."

"Not this time. I just want you close."

"Okay, agreed. I'm hungry. Would it be too much trouble for a sandwich?"

He laughed, and then so did I. It felt good to laugh. All I wanted to do was fall into his arms and have him hold me for the rest of my life, but I also knew we needed to talk first, so I had to remain strong no matter how much he continued to draw me in.

Marta had brought up a variety of deli sandwiches with a choice of salads to choose from. I thanked her for calling out for us, and then she flashed a knowing smile and left us on our own.

"What was that about?" I questioned Valentin, who wore the same expressive grin on his handsome face.

"I can imagine Marta's thoughts, and they're probably shouting, 'Over my dead body! I would never order anything I couldn't prepare in my own kitchen.' She smiled because she's already made you happy and knows she's that good of a cook to know you will eat every last bite. Nothing pleases Marta more than when her food is appreciated. I'm sure you two will be good friends."

I suddenly felt apprehensive and looked away from him.

"Hey, don't do that," he said, touching my cheek, bringing me closer to him.

"Don't do what?" I said, trying not to cry.

"Hide from me. Doubt your feelings. Think of every reason to run, which we already established would not be happening. I love you too much to ever let you go."

"I love you too." My voice sounded broken as I tried to fight my fear and be strong.

"Thank you, dove." I knew my words calmed him. "You need to eat, and we need to talk. Once we do, we can go to bed and put this awful day behind us."

"What makes you so sure? You talk as if I'm just going to fall at your feet and we are going to move on as if nothing has happened."

"I'm sure, because that's exactly the way it's going to be. Willow, you can't deny what you feel for me, no more than I can for you. Now, finish your dinner."

Bossy man! What made me think I could hold the upper hand? "I'm finished," I said and then covered my plate.

He wiped his mouth and dropped the napkin to the table. He stood with his open hand for me to take. I couldn't resist him and placed my hand in his. He brought it up to his lips and kissed it and then turned my arm and placed a kiss on the inside of my wrist, making me shiver with desire.

"Come, let's talk," he said.

I remained quiet and allowed Valentin to lead me back into his bedroom for the much-anticipated conversation. I was wearing under-wear and a t-shirt of his that he had dressed me in. I knew he wanted me naked, but I needed some covering on my body around him. He, on the other hand, put on a striptease right in front of me, leaving just his boxer briefs on. I swallowed hard and tried in vain to hide the physical attraction I felt for him.

I climbed into bed, with Valentin following. He sat up against the headboard, with me secured at his side. He crossed his heavy leg over mine, and even if I wanted to run, I knew I wouldn't get past the edge of the bed. Falling out of this beast of a bed probably would result in breaking a bone or two. It was that high from the floor.

"Let me ask you a question before we begin. Have you googled my name?"

"No, why would I need to do that?"

"I don't know, maybe out of curiosity perhaps."

"It never even crossed my mind. I guess that's stupid, right?"

"No, my love, it's not. It's one of the many qualities I love about you. You are trusting with a kind and generous heart. I know you wouldn't do anything to hurt me."

"No, I wouldn't. I trust because it's who I am and how I was raised. I don't have to question anything when it comes to you, because you promised you would never lie to me, well, up until today when your mislaid lies nearly got me killed."

"I never meant to keep anything from you, and after tonight you will know as much as I can tell you without ever putting you in jeopardy again. My family was born and raised in Russia, St. Petersburg to be accurate. My father is Alaric Vasiliev, and my mother is Irina. I have a brother, Sasha, seven years younger than me. He's bi-polar and suffers from extreme mood swings and depression. He uses drugs to mask his pain, and when the pain becomes too much, he becomes dangerous and very reckless. When he was born, my father appointed me his protector, and I've never stopped from the moment I held him in my arms."

"I'm sorry, Valentin. I can't imagine what that is like for you."

"It's manageable on most days but sometimes my baby brother tends to get himself into trouble, causing me to clean up his mess. I'll get back to that. Our name is known around the world because of its ties to the Russian Bratva, also known as the mafia or mob. The Bratva reigns from regions of the Soviet Union and all over Europe. They are not anyone you ever want to come in contact with. They deal with the underworld of sex, drugs, human trafficking, guns, and a hell of a lot more."

Goosebumps lined my skin and I began to tremble. He held me closer and kissed the top of my head, trying to calm me.

"Willow, although our family carries the stigma of what most Americans believe to be evil, I can assure you that we are not. Our businesses are all Russian-related sort of speak. We have business interest all around the world, primarily here in New York, where I can keep a watchful eye to ensure they remain legitimate."

"So, you are your family's lawyer?"

"Yes and no. I could never represent them in a court of law. I advise and keep them clean, far away from the American government, who monitors them closely."

"I saw you holding a gun today and ready to take a life if necessary. How can you be so calm and hold me like this, knowing what I witnessed today?"

He sighed deeply and kissed me gently before answering my question. "Willow, I had already rationalized and made peace with whatever would happen today to me if I had to pull that trigger to save you. Luckily, it never reached that far because Oleg did his job and protected you. I swear to you on my life that today was not part of the world I have invited you in to share with me. Today was about my brother and an old man's quest for unwarranted revenge."

"Are we still in danger?" *I can't believe I just asked that.*

"I'm working on it."

"And Madeline? Please tell me where she is."

"She's at a safe house, resting. I had no choice but to detain her until I could have the opportunity to speak with her. She became irrational, and my men had to subdue her until I get there. I swear to you she has not been harmed."

"What about your father? And the things that man said about him? What does it all mean?"

"I really don't know, and until I speak with my father, I can't answer anything more. Pavlo was on a mission that was only going to end one way, and that's with him dead. No one threatens the woman I love or anyone in my family. It's just a tacit rule that has always been in place, and he broke that by going after you."

"Valentin, let's just say I am able to live with all of this," I gestured around the room and back to him. "Where do we go from here? Does life just resume tomorrow morning? Or do I go in a witness protection program, never to be heard from again? I don't understand this at all, and you're right, I am frightened."

He flipped me onto my back, with his large body hovering over me. Usually, this was the part that excited me the most, but tonight he was gentle and careful. "I love you, Willow. That hasn't changed. Knowing you were in danger today and then having to witness another man's hands on you nearly made me go insane, and I did want to kill him. I will kill for you if it meant protecting you. Remember the café guy? Yes, he's only alive because I restrained myself that night because I thought of you, and that image of you saved his life. Tonight was different, and no matter how hard I tried to fight off the darkness, you needed me to save you, and that's all that mattered."

"But…" I interjected, as he placed his finger over my mouth to silence me.

"Please, let me finish. I love you, and despite your efforts tonight to be angry with me, I know you love me too. The thought of not having me in your life tomorrow would be way scarier than what you experienced tonight. Your heart, body, and soul are wrapped up in me as mine is in yours. You're wet right now just by the sound of my voice. Your appearance is flushed, and I can feel the intense heat radiating off your skin. You are so turned on right now, you are doing everything possible not to come and scream my name. Tell me I'm wrong," he said as he entered me with two fingers, causing my pelvis to react and push against his straining cock.

"Stop it, Valentin. You're being cruel,"

"No, I'm loving you and giving you what you need. So, tell me, Willow, what would you like for me to do next? Shall I fuck you with my tongue? Will that get you off?"

"You bastard! Fuck you, Valentin," I cried as he continued to rub his thumb over my clit, hitting the right spot every single time. I pushed my head into the pillow and screamed at the top of my lungs as I came, not shouting his name. *I have to hold on to some pride.*

"That's it, baby, come for me," he continued to seduce me with his velvety voice. He was just as desperate as I was. He just was better at controlling his feelings. "Open your eyes, and look at me," he demanded. I submitted easily under his tutelage which made him pleased. He leaned down to kiss me and then said, "You are mine, Willow Pierce, and soon you will be mine forever as my wife. I'm telling you this simply because you were made for me, and it's fates way of making my life complete. You will give me children, and we will love and protect them forever, I promise you. I'm never letting you go. You can protest all you want, but I know differently. You want to be here no matter what it costs you, so stop fighting me and say the words. Say it, Willow, and then I will fuck and love you so good, but I need to hear you say the words."

My eyes were filled with tears as the remnants of my orgasms were felt between my legs. This man is my choice, no matter what danger awaits for us. I can't say no because I know he would take a piece of me that I would never be able to find with anyone else, and I do not want that. I want Valentin Vasiliev forever. I've been his from the moment he invaded my dreams and sealed my heart to his with just one kiss. "I'm yours, Valentin," I said as tears streamed from my eyes.

He wiped them away quickly and asked me again. "And?"

"You're mine."

"Yes, I am and forever will be. You are my beautiful dove who brought this man to life. Your innocence and beauty beguile me in a way I have never felt before nor imagine ever having. I want to show you who I really am, and not just the dominating part that craves to possess every part of you. I can't stop myself from wanting all these things with you. I love you so much and cannot go on about my day without thinking of you every waking minute you're away from me. I give you my heart. It's yours, Willow. And with that heart comes promises of love, devotion, protection. I will never allow you or anyone you care about to ever suffer at the hands of my family's enemies again. Don't give up on me, Willow. Please trust me to care for you and keep you safe."

His love blanketed me as a shield, and I knew every word spoken was the truth. I had already given him the words, so now he needed for me to show him what those words represented for us. Although I was afraid of the unknown and those images of today would probably never be too far from my memory, I had to follow my heart. Fighting Valentin proved to be futile, not when it was so vividly clear how my body responded to him.

My eyes were opened to him, showing Valentin all of me. I didn't believe either one of us could say anything more that hadn't been said already. We didn't need to. He crushed his mouth to mine in a savage kiss, making me open for him, taking what was his. The shirt and underwear I was wearing were easily torn and ripped off my body. He positioned his cock against my entrance and plunged deep and hard inside of me. I was shattered into a million pieces, and then with every hard thrust, kiss, and mark left on my body, I was put back together, forever bound only to him.

I was hot with heavy limbs on top of my body. I rolled my neck to the right, and there he slept, finally at peace. We stripped ourselves bare and exposed every part of ourselves to the other, including Valentin revealing a secret and a past that was dark and very much a part of his life. *He promised to always keep me safe, and I believe him with everything I have, but what about his father? Will I be accepted into the same world Valentin has tried to separate himself from?*

My muscles ached, and I needed to give my body a good stretch. Maybe some yoga would help, but I needed to get out of this bed without waking him. His arm was across my chest, and his leg was entwined with mine. I had a lot of room on my side of the bed, so I carefully wiggled inch by inch until I was free.

Once I managed to get down from the bed, I practically sprinted to the bathroom. I knew the shower would wake him, so I quickly brushed my teeth and washed my face. *Ugh!* I looked dreadful. I had purplish bags under my eyes, and my hair was a tangled mess. After I got a comb through it, I brushed it until I smoothed out my long hair. I pulled it back into a twist and used a clip to hold it in place. His robe was hanging on the door. It carried all his scents. I put it on, and it was as if he was right here with me, reminding me of how I sprayed his cologne on my wrists yesterday before work.

That was yesterday? It feels like ages ago since I woke up so happy and played dress-up in my closet. And what about Madeline? God, I hope she's okay.

Valentin was still asleep right where I left him. I quietly crept out of our bedroom and made my way downstairs to his kitchen in search of coffee. I had no idea where anything was and didn't see Marta. I began opening and closing cabinets until I found a mug I could use. The machine was easy to figure out, and within a few minutes I was pouring my coffee and fixed it with creamer. I sat on one of the stools at the long kitchen counter and enjoyed the quiet.

About fifteen minutes later, the elevator door opened, and I turned to see Oleg with Madeline. She glanced over in my direction with her eyes widening and rushed toward me.

"Oh my god, Madeline, thank goodness you're okay," I said as she hugged me with such a force.

"I'm far from okay, kid. We need to get the hell out of here. You don't belong here with these people. They're dangerous."

From behind me, I heard Valentin clear his throat, alerting us both of his presence.

"Willow is exactly where she belongs, and it would be prudent of you to remember whose home you are standing in."

She practically shoved me out of her arms and then tucked me behind her back, as if she were protecting me.

"Oh, I know exactly who you are, Valentin Vasiliev, and you need to stay the hell away from Willow and get out of our lives."

I looked at Oleg telepathically for help. He nodded at my pleading eyes and remained where he was. I looked over Madeline's shoulder and saw the incensed look on Valentin's face. I finally moved out of her hold and immediately went over for Valentin to hold me. I expected him to kiss me hard as a show of dominance to my friend, but I think he was more relieved to know that I had chosen him over her. I whispered softly for only Valentin to hear, and I knew I was asking a lot of him, but he kissed me again and walked out of the room with Oleg following. I sighed and released the breath I was holding.

"Are you out of your mind? What the fuck is going on here? Is he holding you against your will?" Madeline screamed.

"No! And will you please stop shouting?" I gestured with my hands to calm her down, but that only made her scream louder.

"No, I will not calm down! And I think the more important question I should be asking here is why you appear so relaxed. Has your memory been wiped clean?" she mocked.

I sighed, "This is not a spy movie, and I am not here against my will. Please sit down, and we can talk. Would you like some coffee?"

"Coffee? Are you serious? Do you not remember at all what happened to the two of us yesterday? I sure as hell do. I was in my apartment, nursing a wonderful hangover, when armed men stormed my front door. They tied me up and spoke in a language I didn't understand. I thought I was going to die, and then you show up and they grab you too. Willow, you need to start talking. Make me understand why in the hell you are still here with this man?"

"Yesterday was a mistake, and I'm sorry you got caught up in something that had nothing to do with you. I can't go into details with you about it. All I could say is that you are safe, and it will never happen again."

"What? Who are you? Are you fucking programmed or something? What has he done to you?"

"Nothing you are imagining. I'm not a child, and I'm perfectly capable of knowing what I want. If forced to, Valentin would have taken a bullet for me. You have every right to be upset, but please don't direct it at Valentin. He had no idea that was going to happen to us, and he was placed in an impossible situation. What you do need to know and accept, Madeline, is that I love him, and we're going to get married."

"Oh my god, I can't believe I'm hearing this? What are you think-ing, kid?"

"I'm thinking I hate that nickname you have for me, and I would like you to stop using it. I have a name and would like to be addressed as such."

"Wow, he really has changed you. In a matter of weeks, I barely recognize you."

"Why? Because I have found a man who is completely devoted to me? A man who would do anything humanly possible just to see me smile? I. Love. Him. And I do not have to justify my feelings to you or anyone, for that matter."

"Fine! He's going to hurt you, Willow, and when he does, don't say I didn't warn you. I am your friend, and I love you. I'll ask you one more time: please leave with me now."

"A friend? Can you stand there and call yourself that? Do you not remember the fight we had when you told me off in your very colorful way?"

"I'm sorry for my behavior. That was a mistake, and I was still drunk from the night before. I can't explain it, alright? I felt jealous."

What? "Madeline, how are you jealous of me? What have I done to cause you to feel this way?"

"Nothing but be amazing and talented. And sadly remind me of what a failure I am. You had Zara wrapped around your finger, even after she tried to be snide and take you down. How does that happen? I have nothing left to offer you. It's just a matter of time before you break away from MW Designs and develop your own brand. Hell, you already are. I'm sorry for being a drama queen asshole, but not for this. I'm too old, and whether you choose to believe me or not, I do know a few things about your guy. You don't belong here. Not with him, or in his world. You're so innocent and naïve. Please tell me you're not that deluded into believing his lies? Good sex and a fancy lifestyle are not going to keep you safe. Willow, I'm begging you, please get away from this guy while you still can."

She was breaking my heart with every vile word she was saying about the man that I loved. I knew he must be listening and was probably going mad with anger boiling over, ready to explode. *She doesn't know him like I do. I know she's scared from what happened to her, but doesn't she see that he saved her life? And if she would just calm down and give him a chance, she would see what I see.* I glanced over my shoulder, and I didn't have to see him to know that he was there. I felt him all around me, and that's when I knew I had to do something to make this right with Madeline, or simply, let her go.

"Madeline, you know I love you and will always be thankful for all you did for me when you gave me a job. We built a friendship that was good for a while, but there's something inside of you that pushes away everyone who cares about you, and that's what's happening to us right now. You've changed too and not for the better. Between your drinking and your angry mood swings, I know I can't continue to be around that."

"Sorry, I'm not perfect like you, Willow. Some of us live in the real fucking world. You go right ahead and keep your head in the clouds, but if you stay with this guy, it will be just a matter of time before you do some afternoon drinking too. You want out? Fine! You were already there anyway. It was so obvious that day with Zara. I can't change your mind, because you're not going to listen to me anyway. I hope for your sake, you know what the hell you are doing. I have to get out of here."

She turned away from me, as I wiped away my tears. She hung her head low and then walked back over to me to bring me in for a hug. "I love you, kid, and I always will."

"Madeline, please don't go. We can work this out. Just give him a chance to explain." I implored her to reconsider but she was too obstinate for her own good. She ignored my pleas and made a quick retreat to the elevator. She continued to jab her finger on the button, but the doors wouldn't open. Valentin returned, holding a remote control in his hand.

"It won't open until I unlock it," he called out to her.

She turned around and glared. "Open this elevator right now!" she shouted, but he wasn't affected by her and walked closer to where she was standing.

"You're not going anywhere until you hear what I have to say." His tone was stern, but to someone who didn't know him as I did, he was scary. "Take a seat, Madeline." He gestured to the sofa.

When she didn't comply, he looked over to Oleg with a tilt of his chin. He grabbed hold of her arm and walked her over to where Valentin wanted her seated. She struggled in his arms and tried to slap him. I'd only known Oleg to be gentle and kind, but with Madeline, he looked as if he was losing his patience and forced her down. She huffed in anger, and when he was satisfied that she wouldn't attempt to hit him again, he released her.

I was in shock watching the scene unfold. Valentin called my name a couple of times before I responded, asking me to take his hand and join him on the opposite sofa to talk with Madeline. Once my hand was entwined with his, he brought it up to his lips and kissed it, whispering how much he loved me and not to worry.

"Now, Madeline," he said, "If your tantrum is over, maybe you would be so kind to allow me to explain a few things to you, and without interruption."

I closed my eyes and released a calming breath, while Madeline remained quiet and nodded in agreement.

CHAPTER
Twenty-Six

Valentin

"**Y**esterday was unfortunate and not expected. The threat has been neutralized, and no harm will ever come to you, and certainly never to Willow. It's clear you have a misconception of who I am and have drawn your own conclusions. I will not waste my valuable time trying to convince you I am not what you say I am. I already heard it once when Willow tried to reason with you. I certainly do not need to hear it for the second time and in my own home. Now, what I will say is this: contrary to what you believe, Willow does have a mind of her own and is free to act accordingly in what makes her happy. If she wishes to continue to work with you, and not for you, that will be up to her. If you are not willing to move forward and move past what occurred yesterday, then this is truly where you say goodbye to Willow. What I will not condone is you filling her head with lies that will only hurt her. No, Madeline, I will not have that. Do you understand me so far?"

"I'm not afraid of you, but Willow should be," she sat up straighter this time with no fear in her eyes.

I waited for a beat, and then my dove tried again to reason with her. "Madeline, will you please…" and then I had enough of this and stopped her from saying anything more. I was still holding Willow's hand and turned slightly so I could hold her and have her look into my eyes. I needed to show her that all would be okay and not to worry.

I asked, "Darling, will you please give me a few moments alone with your friend? Go with Oleg, and I will be along soon."

"But…" she sounded unsure as she looked over at Madeline and then back to me. "Please let me stay."

"No," I was firm. "Please do as I ask," I didn't need to hear her thoughts, because her expressive eyes showed me all I needed to know. "I love you. I'll be along soon." I placed a kiss to her lips, and then Oleg extended his hand out for her, and she accepted it without another word spoken.

I waited until she was far enough away before addressing Madeline. I got up and poured a drink and then took my seat directly in front of her. She would be a challenge but nothing I couldn't handle.

"Now, where were we?" I asked and sipped my bourbon. A little early for my liking, but it was necessary this morning.

"Did you enjoy that? The way you handled Willow and dismissed her as if she were nothing but a toy you could play with, and once you tire of her, you will simply cast her aside never to be heard from again. Isn't that right, Valentin?"

"Do not ever address me by my first name. It is a right you have not earned. You don't have a fucking clue on how deep my feelings are for Willow. She is my everything, and you will not turn her against me with your contemptibility for me and your unwillingness to support her decisions and our relationship."

She attempted to speak, but I quickly directed my hand to stop her.

"I wasn't finished. Now, back to yesterday. You can rant and rave to anyone who will listen to you and the claims you have threatened to make, but no one will believe the rantings of an alcoholic, down on her luck businesswoman. One who is so desperate for attention that she goes around and makes up outlandish stories about false kidnappings and scary men with guns. We are clearly at an impasse, which is regrettable because Willow cares so much for you."

"Do your worst. I don't care what happens to me, just don't hurt her."

"I will never hurt her, unlike you who claims to be her friend. Now, I've grown tired of your outbursts and need an answer from you. Are you willing to put yesterday behind you? Or are you going to be difficult? Think very carefully about what you say next. You've tried my patience enough, and you may not like what I do next. Take a minute. I'll be back."

Oleg returned, and I pulled him over to where I could still keep an eye on Madeline, but far enough where she couldn't hear us.

"How's Willow?" I asked.

"She's fine. I placed her back in your room, where she is resting. And before you ask, yes, she is secured until you return."

"Excellent, it's for her own good. She doesn't need to be around this twit."

"Has she complied yet?"

"No, but she will. Stay where she could see you."

I walked back over and took my seat. "So, have you decided to play nice?"

"I don't have a choice, now do I?"

"No, you don't. Here's what's going to happen. You are going to take the rest of the week off and take some respite care to regroup. Come Monday morning, you will be refreshed and ready to continue your working relationship with Willow. You have made a commitment, and I expect you to honor it. Once it has been fulfilled, I expect Willow to be moving on to bigger and better things on her own," I enunciated very slowly. "You have no contract with Willow, but I will make sure you are compensated and quietly fade out of her life. As for your friendship? It's run its course, and after how poorly you have be-haved in recent days and this morning, your toxic presence is not healthy for Willow."

I continued, "I will say that you were right about one thing. She is very talented. Once the fashion world takes notice on what she's ac-complished for Zara, it is only a matter of time before she's on Seventh Avenue with her own showroom and starring in Fashion Week with a line of her own. It will happen, you'll see. You just won't be by her side to enjoy it with her. I expect you'll be somewhere licking your wounds at the bottom of a bottle. You know with Jack, Johnnie, Cap-tain Morgan, and your favorite vodka of choice. Isn't that what you said?" I knew I was being cruel, but she had tried my patience, and I needed this complete waste of my time conversation to be over. "Now, have I made myself clear on all the issues that needed to be resolved?"

"You are so smug. Why are you doing this? You can probably have any woman of your choosing. Why does it have to be her? She's young and far too innocent for you to corrupt. She's intelligent and will see right through you once the façade of unrequited love fades. She's living in a fantasy world with you."

"So, I take that as a no?"

"Yeah, it's a no, because that's what I'm screaming inside, but I'll tell you yes only because I don't want to end up like that guy who bled out all over my wood floors."

"Wise decision, Madeline."

"Where's Willow? I need to see her," she demanded.

"No, you don't. Oleg will drive you to the spa and pick you up on Sunday to drive you home. Don't be difficult, and for your sake, do not do anything stupid to anger him, or me for that matter. We're done here."

I hit the button on my remote, and the elevator doors opened. Oleg escorted the wretched woman out of my home, and I was happy to be rid of her. There was no point explaining anything more, and I needed her to be gone. If she was left in anyone's hands besides mine, well, the outcome would have been swift and over in a heartbeat. I knew that by acting on those threats would have only hurt Willow, so her friend was spared.

I composed myself before returning upstairs to Willow. *What a morning! And not what I was expecting to have with my woman. She's probably so worried by now.* I unlocked the door and immediately found her. She was asleep on my side of our bed, curled around my pillows. *She takes my breath away with her beauty and the need she has for me.* Her hair was loose and flowing down her back, with some pieces covering her face. I gently brushed them away, securing them behind her ear. She smiled in her dreams, which brought me great comfort. I stripped out of my clothing and got in beside her.

As soon as she felt me near, she instinctively moved closer, making us connected with the other. I never wanted this feeling to end and hoped it never would. *She's been traumatized by my so-called life I've been trying to protect her from, and there's still the matter of my father. Pavlo said many things to me that I was not privy to, and a conversation is needed as soon as possible.*

Lost in all my thoughts, I didn't hear her wake until she leaned up and kissed my neck.

"You're here," she whispered.

"I am love, always."

"What happened with Madeline? Is she okay?"

"Yes, unharmed and sent to the spa for a few days. Did you believe otherwise?"

"No, of course not. You wouldn't have saved her if you intended on harming her. I believe you, Valentin, and I know that makes me foolish to her, but I trust my heart and yours too."

"Oh, Willow, you don't know what it means to hear you say those words to me. I know our time lately has been mixed signals, separation, and a heart-stopping moment yesterday, but I promise you that is over. I want you here in this home today. No more going back to separate places. It's hard on the both of us, and leaving the other just doesn't make sense."

She sighed and buried her face on the inside of my neck. I knew all of her tells, and this was one of them. She had something on her mind and was afraid to share it with me.

"Willow, please look at me, and tell me why you're hiding."

"My mom called and left me a voicemail. She's driving in on Sunday for our brunch date. It was a regular thing for a while, but since her work schedule changed, I'm seeing less and less of her. This weekend she's off and wants to visit."

"Okay, I don't see the issue here. May I meet her? After all, she will be my mother-in-law someday, and it would be nice to see the amazing person who brought you into the world."

She hesitated and snuggled back to my chest. My girl was a stubborn one, always making me work for information.

I remained quiet until I broke, which was under a minute, and then I asked the one question I was afraid to know the answer to. "Are you ashamed of me?"

"No, of course not. You are amazing, Valentin, and so loving toward me."

"So, what's the problem? Are you afraid because of yesterday? Or your mother knowing my family's last name?"

"I'm worried about me, and what my mother will say about our relationship. She's great, don't get me wrong, but it takes work on her part not to judge others. It stems from her relationship with my father. Yes, she raised me up to be so strong and independent, but the minute I told her that I met someone who I care about, she got quiet and advised me to proceed with caution. Men are like roadblocks to her."

"Well, I guess I have to be the one that breaks through her protective barriers and accept me as the man who loves her daughter more than life itself."

"Yeah? Then she will probably try to steal you away for herself. Yes, I'm kidding."

"Good to know. Anything else before I make love to you?"

"I need to go back to work. If Madeline is not there and with me gone too, it's not going to look good to our team. I also need to go home to my apartment. I have to get my mail and just…"

No! Keep talking baby. Don't shut down now.

"Just what? Willow, finish that sentence." It came out harder than I wanted it to. *She's incredibly frustrating when it comes to opening up to me.*

"I just need to think a little bit. Is that okay? I swear I'm not running. I just need a few hours to myself."

"Away from me?"

"Yes."

"I'll have Oleg drive you home." I flung the covers off the bed and was about to leave Willow alone, when she sat up and wrapped her arms around my back.

"Valentin, where are you going? Is that how it's going to be? I say something you don't like or agree with, and you flee our bed as if it were on fire. I was just being honest with you, and I think I'm holding up pretty well, considering what happened yesterday."

I took her in my arms and crushed my mouth to hers, taking all her kisses. When I came up for air, I said that I was sorry. "I'm an ass, and I'm sorry I behaved like one."

"You're forgiven. Will you drive me home? I want you to come into my home and kick your shoes off and see how I live. Let me show you my workspace and all my new designs. I even have some finished ones. Now, I'm not an expert, but I think this is how it works. I live in your life as your girlfriend, and you live in mine as my boyfriend. When you put the two together, voila! We have a relationship."

Oh, this girl! How I love her so much. I would do anything for her.

"Really now? That's how it works?" I said and continued to leave kisses under her ear, her favorite spot I found out early on. Lifting her chin with my two fingers, I wanted her to know I agreed with all she said and how much I loved hearing those words come from her mouth. "I love you, Willow. I need you to know that I am a man of my word who holds honor to the highest degree one can. I will never lie to you and will keep every single promise I make to you. If I get my way and my beautiful dove, and I usually do, you will only be my girlfriend for a short time, because I intend to make you my wife as soon as possible. And this body will be carrying my child." I placed my hands on her stomach, making her shudder beneath my touch.

"Valentin, the way you talk…" she hesitated.

"Yes? Oh, please love, I'm intrigued."

"Stop teasing, you know what I mean. I guess I'm just beginning to realize how true those words are."

"They are. I want a life with you and will do everything I possibly can to keep you with me always."

"I guess there is only one thing to do then." She smiled and kissed me on my lips.

"And? What might that be?"

"Help me pack?"

"I'll have your things packed, and we can spend the day together."

"No, I will pack my own things, and you will help."

"I'm not getting out of this, am I?"

"Nope, not a chance. It's going to take me a while to get used to your way of things, so give me a little room to adjust."

"I will give you all the time you need, and I hope it goes both ways because I'm not the easiest person that adapts well to change, so we will learn together."

"Thank you, Valentin. All this talking has made me hungry."

"Really? I was thinking the same thing. "I love you, Willow, and here's a perk to living with me. Sex will always be on the menu."

My body hovered over hers as I began to slowly make love to her. She smiled brightly and giggled a little while I kissed all her ticklish spots. We didn't make it to her apartment until hours later.

"Okay, I believe that's everything. Do you want to take one more look around before I have these boxes picked up?" I asked.

"No, I think we packed it all. It's not like I brought much with me from my mom's house. Most of my things are boxed up, collecting dust in her basement. All I needed for the city is in these boxes right here."

"I can always have them picked up and brought to our apartment."

"It can wait, and I'm not sure mom is ready to meet Oleg yet."

"Yeah? How about me? Do you think we can make that happen?"

"Soon, I promise. I need more time to get her used to the idea of you and what you mean to me."

I tried not to show Willow how disappointed I was with her hesitation about her family meeting me. If her mother and grandmother do not approve of me, I fear it may sway Willow and her feelings, and I can't risk that from happening.

"Don't do that," she said.

"Don't do what? Feel you pull away from me?"

"Never. I would never do that to you. I love you, and if anything, I want to be closer to you."

"I'm sorry, another overreaction on my part. Learning, right?"

We kissed and kissed until we were breathless. I wanted to make love to her right here, right now, but my phone interrupted our moment.

"I will get rid of whoever this is," I said. "Give me a minute?"

"No problem, I know you're not going anywhere. I'll be in the kitchen."

"Yes," I answered curtly as I picked up the call.

"Valentin, I need to see you. Now."

"Father, it's not a good time."

"Make the time. Your brother needs you."

Fuck!

"Father, you using my brother is not going to influence me anymore, and considering what you put me through yesterday, I should shun you forever."

"Yes, I know, my son, and you have a right to be angry. All I ask is you give me a chance to see and talk to you. And I wasn't using

Sasha. He needs you. He knows what has happened, and he blames himself. You need to reassure him that you're not angry with him."

"Father, he is the last person I am angry with, and you know it. It is you that started a war with your rival, and you didn't care who became collateral damage in your quest for power. You lied to me, and that will not be forgiven so easily."

"Yes, I understand. You have every right to feel the way you do, and I will respect your wishes, but today is about Sasha, and he needs to see you. Please come out to the house."

"Fine, but if you are playing with me, you will regret it. I'm done with this."

"I swear I'm not."

"I'll be there in an hour." I ended the call and held the phone to my chest.

"Everything okay?" she asked.

"Yes, it's fine. I need to see my brother and have to go now. I'll have you taken home and will join you as soon as I can."

"It's fine. You take care of your family."

I took her in my arms and crushed my mouth to hers. "You're my family. You will always come first in my life. Today, I will make that very clear to my father and brother. I no longer can condone my father's choices on how he runs his business. I've done all I can for him and my brother."

"Valentin, I'm not going to say I understand what you're going through, because it is not anything I know, but the way you talk about your brother? It's clear you love him and want the best for him. You walking out of his life will only hurt him."

"I would never do that, Willow. I just can't be there at every waking minute of every day. I have to find what makes me happy and live my life the way I choose. The way I see it, it all begins and ends with you."

"Okay, go before you make me cry. I'll be here waiting for you."

"I endeavor to never do that again to you. I love you, dove, and I'll be back as soon as I can."

Oleg met me downstairs as requested. I spent the entire day with Willow and locked the rest of the world out. I needed to know if anything was escalating that could bring harm to anyone I care about.

"Your father has been busy," he said.

"Yes, I know. What I don't know is how much."

"Pavlo wasn't lying. Your father was in Russia to secure new business here and bring Shirmanov's most loyal lieutenants to pledge their allegiance only to him."

"Why now? When my father has never made such a bold move like this before. He has to have a reason, some sort of angle he is using for his own advantage."

"Here's another thing I found out, and you are not going to like it."

"It can't be worse than nearly getting the woman I love killed."

"No, but it's the reason why he took the measures he did. Your father was responsible for Avros being in the club that night. He was behind the ruse to make Avros believe Sasha was messing around with his woman and the smash and grab you initially believed was, again, part of your father's plan."

"Fucking hell!" I shouted, making passersby look in my direction.

"Come, we are too exposed out here."

"I have to go, he's waiting for me to meet him at the house."

"I can't let you do that, Valentin, not until you know everything. Come with me now, please?"

The look in his eyes told me he was telling the truth, and I could trust him with my life. Whatever he needed to say had to be pretty important. Oleg had arranged security for Willow, pointing out the guards on all four points of the building. It was also monitored, so if anyone arrived and left the apartment, I would know about it.

"Why are we here back at the club?" I asked.

"You need to see something, and it's upstairs in Sasha's apartment. Please, follow me." We took the private entrance that led upstairs to where Sasha lived and spent most of his time when my father didn't have him on lockdown back at our family compound. Oleg led me inside to the bathroom and opened up the medicine cabinet. He took out the pill bottle and handed me one. "Take it. It won't hurt you, I promise."

I looked over at him and then back to the pill before placing it on my tongue. "It tastes like…"

"Exactly! It's a children's aspirin that looks exactly like his anti-psychotic medication."

"Are you telling me that my brother's medication was switched?"

"It's exactly what I'm saying, and I have the video proof to prove it. Here, have a look for yourself." He handed me an iPad, and when the screen came to life, I was horrified at what I was seeing.

The tall figure entered the bathroom wearing all black, including gloves. He opened the bottle, dumped the pills down the toilet, and then replaced it with pills he retrieved from his pocket in a plastic baggie.

"I don't see his face, who is it?"

"Wait for it. The big reveal is coming."

I was losing patience, and then he was right. The person in the video pulled off his mask, and I nearly dropped the device when I saw who it was.

"What the fuck? Sergei? No, this can't be happening. Please tell me this is not real, and it is the making of one of our enemies trying to hurt us?"

"I wish I could, but I can't. He is your father's most trusted soldier, and he will die before betraying Alaric. He lied to me too. The call he placed to me on the night I should have been with Willow was once again part of his plan. I was only acting on the orders I was given, but really, I was there covering his tracks for the crimes he committed. I feel so foolish that I didn't figure it out sooner. I'm so sorry, Val, but there's more you need to know. Your father has known about Willow since you ordered Sergei to bring the café owner to you."

"Are you saying that it was my father who orchestrated all of this? From my brother killing Avros to the abduction of Madeline Waters?"

"Yes, and it was Alaric who led Pavlo to her front door. He was on borrowed time with end-stage liver cancer. The story of Pavlo having Parkinson's was only made up to weed out the disloyal. He never had it. What he did have was cancer. The bullet I put into his head just sped up the inevitable. Hell, he probably welcomed it, knowing his suffering was about to end."

"And with Pavlo out of the picture and his family pledging their loyalty to my father, all that really needed to be changed was the name on the door. Fuck! How did I not see this sooner? He was in Europe for months traveling all over and then several months in Russia. He fucking did all of this and used my brother and my trust to do it. He needs to die. I cannot allow him to live and wreak further havoc on our lives."

"Valentin, I cannot agree with you more, but he needs to be handled carefully, and with everything he has in place, a bullet will not be enough. You are going to have to dismantle his business from the top and bring it down, brick by brick."

"And what of my brother? He used my brother to get what he wanted, and I will never forgive him for that. But fine. How do I do it?"

"Go see your father, and make sure your brother is safe."

"And how the hell do I do that without strangling him? The worst already happened when Sasha killed Avros. Sasha is fragile and vulnerable. He needs to be on his meds and under the constant care of his psychiatrist. And what about Sergei? Is he still feeding Sasha the fake meds?"

"No, I made sure of that. All Sergei is right now is a glorified bodyguard, nothing more. I have trusted professionals taking care of him. He will not be hurt again by anyone's hand, not even your father."

"Oleg, how the hell did you come about all this information?"

"It's been in motion for a while now, and with you meeting Willow, I had to expedite my plan in regards to your father and his duplicitous dealings. Sergei made some mistakes and although he tried to cover his tracks, I was already beginning to be suspicious and kept my reservations about him to myself. I installed the cameras in the private quarters to keep an eye on him when I couldn't physically be there. I was just in time doing so, because if I would have waited one more day, I wouldn't have known about the medication switch. From that point on, I worked in the shadows and never showed my hand to Sergei."

"Wait a minute. What about the night you were supposed to be on Willow? Are you telling me that was also a lie? Our argument at the club? It was all part of your plan?"

"Yes, it was. I had to come up with a way to show Sergei that I could be trusted. He knew that I was loyal to you, but he also believed that if your father asked anything of me, I would go and deal with the consequences later. Sergei never questioned your father. Why would he? When no one has ever done so before? He is completely blind to your father."

"Yes, I know. We all are. What happens now?"

"I have files on your father's business dealings that date back ten years up to present day. It is layered with everything that the FBI needs to lock him away for the rest of his life and destroy all that he built. You must always remember, Valentin, his empire was built on blood. You are not your father and never will be. His way of life will always be in existence. You can't put them all away. Gangs are networks. Networks are connected. What they all have in common are money, power, and greed. If it's not a bullet between his eyes, then this is the alternative."

How I was still standing was only driven by my thirst for revenge. *I have to stop my father, but how am I going to do that and keep Willow safe? I was a fool in thinking I was truly free from his world. He had already made me an accessory to the crime with Avros and who knows how many more that I was just too blind to see. I thought I had it all figured out. If I lived my life by my own convictions, then I would be spared the ugly side of his world. People get hurt when they cross my father, and the ones who are loyal suffer the same fate. They just don't know it.*

Sasha was innocent in all of this. My father used his own son to gain leverage over his enemies and didn't care what kind of hell that would declare on my brother's mind and sanity. *I know what I said to Willow earlier about allowing my brother to stand on his own, but it's clear he needs to be cared for. The further I get him away from my father, the better off he will be.*

I had papers in place for a while now which also stated that in the event of my father's death, I would become Sasha's advocate and hold proxy over his affairs. My father asked me a long time ago to oversee my brother's medical care and to make any decisions that needed to be made. That took precedence over any final wishes, despite what was stated in his will.

CHAPTER
Twenty-Seven

Willow

He only left a little while ago, and I already miss him. How is it possible that I have fallen so fast for this man in a short amount of time? I miss him and want to hear his voice.

"Come on, Willow, have some willpower." I gave myself a pep talk, knowing it was total bullshit. *I have this intense need to be with him. I'm in love, and it feels so good to know how much he loves me too.*

I doubled checked the apartment for anything I may have missed and looked through the boxes before taping them up. I guess I had more than I initially believed, but still, I felt kind of sad that I was looking at my entire life right here in grandma's living room. *I won't have a need or want for anything living in Valentin's tower of luxury. I'm still pinching myself that this is my new life.*

I miss Madeline and wish I could talk to her. I know I will see her soon and hoped our friendship could be salvaged after everything that happened between us. In the state she was in, she would never be able to understand my feelings for Valentin. Until she calmed down and pulled herself together, there was no point explaining it, not when she wasn't willing to listen.

I opened my laptop and answered my e-mails, both personal and professional. Peter had called and left me a couple of messages about the designs I had left with him and then asked about Madeline. I called back, and he said he was jealous that he wasn't at the spa with her and how I was working him to the bone with all my tasks. I laughed, and then he filled me in on work stuff. Everything was safe and sound and would be waiting for me in the morning.

When I didn't have anything left to do, I was thinking of calling my mom but hesitated. *Will she be happy for me? Or talk me out of living with Valentin.* It's not like she could stop him from making that happen. He was quite a force to be reckoned with.

I couldn't stop thinking about him, and just as I was about to send him a text, the doorbell rang. "Yes, he's back," I jumped happily off the couch and ran to the door. I opened the door and said, "I'm so happy you're here," and then was surprised to see someone else standing at my door.

"Aren't you happy to see me? Are you expecting someone else?"

"Mom! What are you doing here?" I asked. "Yes, I was expecting someone else, but I'm happy you're here. Come in." I stepped aside, and then my mom's eyes widened when she took in the boxes.

"Going somewhere?"

"As a matter of fact, I am."

"And? Were you going to inform your grandmother or me on your sudden need to move? How disrespectful of you to just pack your things and leave the home she has provided for you all of these months. I raised you better than this."

Wow! Rewind. What brought on this outburst?

"Mom, what's wrong? I have never heard you speak this way to me, and you are being completely hostile."

"I'm not trying to be. I'm just worried about you. I know we haven't seen one another for a while because of our crazy schedules, but you are never too far away from my mind. Are you mad at me?"

"No, why would you ask me that?"

"I guess I've been worried after the last time we talked. I know I went overboard with the advice and probably sounded like a man-hater, but I can assure you that I'm not. I thought long and hard after we hung up and realized you were right about me. For years now, I've been projecting my negativity about relationships onto you, and that wasn't fair of me to do. I never wanted you to get hurt in the way I did."

"Mom, I know you want to protect me, but when it comes to matters of the heart, it's impossible. It's part of life, and for me, I'm willing to take my chance on love."

"It's that serious? Are you really in love?"

I knew it drove Valentin crazy when I was not honest about my feelings and pulled away from him. I think it's worse when it came to my mom, so without another pause, I told her exactly how I felt about my future husband. "Yes, with all my heart and soul. And he's completely in love with me, so much that he intends to marry me and make us a family."

"Oh no, please don't tell me you're pregnant?"

Well? I don't know? Valentin made it known that he wouldn't care if he got me pregnant. In fact, he became excited about it and practically made it his mission to do so. His eyes glimmered when he discovered I wasn't using or was on birth control. What a caveman! My man.

"Willow, answer me. Are you pregnant?" mom repeated.

"Not that I'm aware of. Happy?"

"No, of course not. You are not ready for a husband, and certainly not a baby."

"I appreciate your candor, but it's not needed nor required when it comes to Valentin. I love him very much, and I will be moving into his apartment this evening."

"Okay, but what about your grandmother? Don't you think you

owe her something in return for all the kindness she has shown you? She's going to come home from her cruise and find her apartment empty. How do you think she's going to feel? I'll tell you: hurt. She will be hurt that you didn't talk to her first and share your news. And his name is Valentin? Like Valentine's Day?"

"Now you're being mean, and it's beneath you. His name is Valentin Vasiliev. He's a lawyer, a pretty big one who has lots of money and lives in a penthouse. Oh, and you'll love this; he's ten years older than me. He's made me into this sex-crazed lunatic who just craves orgasms all day long."

Oh, if I had a camera to capture the look on my mother's face right now. She's completely horrified. I know I said it in a joking matter, but it doesn't make it any less true.

"Very funny, and you've made your point. Are you really happy? And this man is worth the risk?"

"Yes, and yes. He's everything."

"When do I get to meet Mr. Everything?"

"How long are you in the city for?"

"I had some days off owed to me. I don't have to go home until Sunday night."

"Perfect. Are you hungry? How's pizza sound?"

"Starving. I would love that. Please tell me you have wine in the house?"

"Mom, grandma is my roommate, so what do you think?"

"Yeah, okay, I heard it. Speaking of the world traveler, when is she due to come home?"

"Not for a while. She sent another postcard. After her cruise ship docked in Miami, she was going to Boca to meet with some friends. I have a feeling she's met…someone."

"Bite your tongue, I can barely keep up with you."

"Mom, I know you're worried, but you don't have to be. I promise you that I'm okay and I know what I'm doing. He's a good man, and I know we are going to have this amazing life together."

"Oh, Willow, I wish I had your confidence."

"Mom, who do you think passed it along to me?"

She looked almost surprised by my question. "You really mean that?"

"Why are you surprised? Of course, I mean it. You are the strongest person I know. You are an amazing role model for me. Why do you think I was brave enough to leave home when I did and go to New York of all places for school? It was because of your belief in me. I could have never done this without your love and support, and grandma too. Mom, you need to let the past go and begin living again for you. Get out there and date. Have you seen you lately? Mom, you're just about to turn forty and easily look twenty-five. You can't tell me that a handsome doctor at your hospital hasn't turned his head in your direction? Because if you say no, I call bullshit."

"Okay, you're not the only one who has a man. I met someone too, but it's really new, and I'm taking the smallest baby steps I can manage. I'm not ready to talk about it yet, but when I do, you will be the first person I tell. Satisfied?"

"Much. Thank you for telling me."

"You're welcome. I only want the very best for you, and it seems you've met your prince, so this is me shutting up. However…" She paused and then pulled me down for a hug. "If he hurts you in any way, don't forget that I am a surgical nurse and know my way around sharp objects."

"I'll make sure to give him your message. Thanks, mom."

"You're my daughter. You know I would do anything for you. I may never be completely on board with the whole dating thing, but I promise to try for you."

"Do it for yourself, because it's long overdue, and just because it didn't work out the first time for you, doesn't mean love is lost, okay?"

"I guess all this confidence, faith, and wisdom is his influence?"

"Yeah, maybe. He makes me better."

"Well, I can't wait to meet him. Now, pour the wine, and let's order pizza!"

CHAPTER
Twenty-Eight

Valentin

The drive from the city to the country estate was maddening on my mind. The voices in my head would not quiet down and were literally playing on a continuous loop. I could not seem to grasp all that Oleg had revealed to me. I always believed my father was dangerous on some level. He had to be in order not to show weakness to our enemies. Families in power always seemed to have them, and we had them all around the world.

Family and honor always went hand in hand. Anyone of us would not hesitate to protect the other, so this was what I was mostly struggling with. My father made my brother collateral damage and tied him to a bloody secret that had the power to destroy him. This was Sasha, who for most of his life was treated as if he was made of glass. My mother and father doted on him and considered Sasha to be a unique individual despite his mental illness.

When he was properly on his medication, he was a walking library of facts. He only ever displayed cockiness when he needed to make a point, just like the night at the club. He was probably so high and lost in the many corridors of his mind that he probably didn't even remember how he got there. You see, he retreated to a place that was only known to him. You couldn't reach him when he went there, and it was excruciating on the ones who cared about him.

I've always been the one to pull him from any depth he's drowning in. I somehow believe he reserved a place for me to rescue and pull him back from the edge. I've saved him for years, and today is no different. He will be leaving with me, and I plan to get him away from our father. It will hurt my mother, this I know. It's clear she's in the dark and safely tucked away back in London. She is loyal to my father but loves her children more. I hope it will be a temporary separation, but if I am unable to trust her then she will be kept away from Sasha for as long as it takes, maybe forever.

I took the long winding driveway up to the house, totally protected by the forest that surrounded it. I parked my Jag right up to the front door, where I was met by Sergei. He greeted me as he always had. I played my part, giving him no reason not to trust me. He gave me his usual report on Sasha before I asked, which I always did. I thanked him for the update and asked where my brother was at the moment. He told me he was upstairs in his room.

I didn't need to look for my father, because he stepped out of the library and strode over, pulling me into a forced hug.

"Thank you for coming out here, son. Come, we have much to discuss."

I followed him back to the library, and he poured us two vodkas. He held his glass up for me to toast with him. I declined.

"I take it by your sullen mood, you have something on your mind? Let's not delay the inevitable. What do you know, Valentin?"

"Interesting you would go there right away, considering you were the one who requested my presence here. You're the one who owes me an explanation."

"I owe you nothing!" he roared.

"I disagree. Who do you think you're talking to? Sergei? Or some other fool under your command? I am your son. Sasha is your son. And you, Alaric Vasiliev, are going to explain to me why the fuck you hurt him in the way you did. Why did you do it?"

"Valentin," he said in a softer tone, which enraged me, wanting to hit something.

"Don't you dare say my name as if you care at all about me. You are responsible for my brother suffering a breakdown and making him believe that he went on a bloody rampage and took two lives."

"It never was supposed to get that far, I swear it. Pavlo was making moves in Russia to move his trafficking pipeline right to our front door. I could not allow that to happen. I knew that whore was after Sasha, and once Avros found out about it, I knew he would track down your brother. But Sasha was never in any danger. You must believe me, Valentin. I swear it."

"Yeah? Then who was the one that filled their bodies with bullets?"

"It wasn't Sasha?"

"Stop lying to me. I know it was."

"You know what I planted for you to believe, and Oleg too. Yes, I know he is displeased with how I have been handling things lately. I'm sure he's run to you like the good soldier he is. Was it very enlightening? Or did it paint me to look like the big bad wolf?"

"Stop it! I don't have the want nor time to play this game with you. Tell me the fucking truth right now," I demanded.

"I assure you, Valentin, I am not playing games with you. Have I ever? Do you honestly believe I would do that to Sasha? To hurt my own son? I swear to you that he was sedated just enough but awake at the same time. He has the memory that was told to him, and that's all he will ever remember about that night."

"What the fuck is happening here?" I shouted.

"Will you let me explain? Once Sasha went upstairs to the apartment with the girl, he had only a matter of minutes before he would pass out before coming to again. His drink was drugged at the bar, and he downed it all in one gulp. By the time Avros rushed inside, Sergei stepped out from where he was positioned and did the hit. When Sasha awakened, he was covered in enough blood to make it look as if he did it. You know what happened next, and life resumed until you played the martyr and brought him here."

"Another move orchestrated by you?"

"Yes."

"And Sergei? Has he been playing me the entire time? Giving me just enough information to keep me at a safe distance."

"Well, yes, and it was working too until Pavlo decided to kidnap the wrong woman."

I threw the glass I was still holding and hurled it at my father. He ducked, and it smashed against the wall behind him. "You are fucking lying to me! You led Pavlo to that apartment, because you knew Willow would eventually show up there, looking for her friend. You got sloppy father, and two women could have been killed because of it."

"No, you're wrong, Valentin."

"I don't think so. Let's just say that I believe you. What the hell happens now? Will you be including human and drug trafficking into your business?"

"No! I may be a lot of things, but I would never hurt innocent women and children. Drugs are easier to work with."

"Oh my god, I can't believe I am hearing this. Who are you? I have spent years working to legitimize your businesses and keep us far away from government agencies that would love nothing more than to see you rot in a supercell maximum prison for the rest of your life."

"Are you threatening me, son? Because that would not be wise for you to do."

"You can come at me with all that you have. Do your worst. I can take it, but my brother cannot. You will never hurt him again with your lies."

"And the woman you love? What of her? Do you think I won't be able to get to her again? She's at her apartment right now, probably waiting for you to return."

I charged him with all the force I had in my body. I didn't think he expected me to do that, but the days of playing nice were over. He was stunned as his body thudded against the wall, knocking down family photos. He matched me in height, but he wasn't as strong as I was, and I caught him by surprise.

"Listen to me, old man. You will never ever touch one beautiful strand of hair on my woman again. Willow is mine, and I protect what's mine, as you are well aware. I have loved you my entire life and have always respected you until the day you betrayed me and our family. You are no longer our father. I spit on you!" I shouted through clenched teeth and shoved him harder.

Sergei rushed through the door along with a few men. I shouted at them to stay the hell back, or I would choke the life out of my father. He glanced their way, and they quickly lowered their weapons and retreated. I released him as he began to cough to catch his breath. He stumbled only to his one knee with a hand to his chest.

I hovered over him and said, "I am not going to be your judge and jury. Your fate will lie in the hands of others. The only thing I want from you today is Sasha. You will release him to my care, and you will promise to stay the fuck out of our lives. This is not an idle threat. You chose greed and power over the ones you claim to love. I will not continue to take this path with you and will not permit my brother to be caught in the crosshairs of your ambition. Do you hear me?" I questioned him as he remained silent. He slowly slumped against the wall, and in all my rage, I grabbed him by his lapels and shook him.

"Answer me, you motherfucker!" I shouted again, only realizing now that his eyes were closed, and he was not responsive to me. I felt for a pulse, which was very weak. I released my hold on him, and he was in a state of unconsciousness. I blew out a huff of air and then bent down to pick his body up. I carried him over to the couch and placed him down. I checked his pulse again, and it barely registered against my fingers. He had all the signs of either having a stroke or massive heart attack. *A part of me wanted to watch him die but how could I look into the face of an angel knowing I carried that sin?*

I opened the door and called for Sergei. He rushed in with his gun raised, but not at me. "What happened?" he asked, winded.

"He's having a heart attack and needs to get to the hospital. This place is too far out in the country, so have your men drive him to the hospital."

He shouted for the two men who were outside when I arrived. I had never seen them before, so I wasn't aware of their names. "Take Mr. Vasiliev to the hospital, right away," he shouted in Russian. They carried him out to the SUV and sped away from the house.

He was barely breathing, and it would be a miracle if he made it to the hospital alive, but my father wasn't my main concern right now. The treacherous coward standing in front of me was.

"Valentin," he said as he looked down at the floor, not even brave enough to admit his treachery.

"Save it," I said, and then I punched him straight in the mouth. He stumbled and fell back to the desk. I charged him again, punching him over and over again until my knuckles bled. "You can go to hell along with my father, you spineless piece of shit! You pledged your loyalty to the wrong man. Did you honestly believe you could keep this from me? And all your sanctimonious crap that night with the café owner. What a joke? You advised me about secrets and keeping my father in the dark, but yet, you are the biggest liar of all. Isn't that right, Sergei?"

"Please, Valentin, I had no choice."

"You always had a choice, and you chose wrong. I don't give a fuck what you do for my father, but when it hurts the ones I love and care about, then we have a problem. My brother! You hurt my brother! No one does that and lives to tell about it."

"I'm begging you, please. I've always been loyal to this family, and I would never hurt Sasha. I love him like my own brother."

"He's *my* brother, and if you knew what love was, you would have never gone to great lengths to hurt him the way you did." I shoved him hard, and he cried like the spineless man I now regarded him as. I wouldn't kill him and risk having his blood on my hands, but I did leave him with a forever reminder never to cross me again. I grabbed the first thing I saw, and that was the gold letter opener on the desk. I brandished it like a knife and slashed his left cheek, causing him to cry out in pain.

I said, "Now, every time you look at yourself in the mirror, you will see the mark I left on you. It's your only warning, Sergei. You lie to me again, next time I will slice you from your throat all the way down to your dick. I'll do it slowly and watch you bleed out like the motherfucking coward you are. So, who are you loyal to?"

"You, Valentin, only you."

He made me sick. I had to get out of here and take my brother with me. I left him with a hard punch to his gut. "Clean yourself up. You are quite the messy bleeder."

I took the letter opener and wrapped it in my handkerchief. *Sergei has learned his lesson, I think, and as for his men, I'm sure they know to remain quiet if they want to see another day.* I called Oleg, who was positioned close by. I needed his cleaner here asap to wipe the house clean and remove all traces I was ever here tonight and with my brother. *I don't give a fuck about anything else.*

I took the stairs two at a time and reached the landing to find my brother swaying back and forth in the corner. My heart sank at the sight of him. I dropped to my knees and lifted his chin so he could look at me. His eyes were filled with tears.

"Talk to me, Sasha. What can I do?"

"I'm sorry, Valentin. I'm so sorry to make you worry. I was bad, very bad, and it's all my fault. You're mad at me and will leave. Please don't leave me here. I promise I'll be better." He continued to shake, reminding me just how fragile he was. He was smaller than me and weighed hardly anything. I lifted him into my arms and carried him down the stairs, meeting Oleg at the bottom.

"Is he alright?" Oleg asked, looking over my brother.

"No, but he will be once I get him away from here. Sergei is in the library. Take care of the house and report back to me when it's done."

"I will. Take care of Sasha, and I'll take care of everything else."

I said no more and left, knowing I would never lay eyes on the house of hell again. I always believed it was a place of solace where nothing bad would happen. Little did I know by bringing my brother here, I was actually causing him more damage, since Sergei was the one in charge of his care and was the one who ultimately hurt him the most. *Fuck! I should have killed him. He deserves no mercy for what he has done.*

I had no choice but to bring Sasha home to my apartment. The apartment was like a fortress, and he would be safe. I phoned his doctor and had her meet me at my place. I needed to fill her in and make arrangements for him. I had several messages from Willow with words that I needed to hear more than ever: "I love you. I miss you. Come home soon." *I want that more than anything, but I need to take care of my brother first.*

Sasha had fallen back to sleep, and it took me a minute to wake him. "Sasha, why are you so sleepy? What did you take?" I practically shook him to look at me, but his eyes were glazed over. *What the fuck!?*

Per my instructions, his doctor met me down in my private parking bay. Sasha kept mumbling words I couldn't understand, and his eyelids were fluttering on and off. She rushed over to my car and assessed his condition.

"I need to get him to the hospital. He's overdosing," she said in a panic.

"How could that be? I just was talking to him, and now he's barely awake."

"He may have taken too many of his pills and now his body is showing the signs of an overdose."

"Help him, please! I can't lose him."

"You won't, sir. I promise."

Her aides carried Sasha and loaded him into the back of her car, securing him with the seatbelt and keeping his head upright. "I'll call you later, but first we need to get his stomach pumped. He will be in a secure location and perfectly safe."

I leaned my head against the roof of my car when my phone buzzed in my pocket. Without checking who it was, I curtly answered and said, "What!?"

"I'm looking for Valentin Vasiliev," they said, speaking softly but right to the point.

"Yes, I'm Valentin Vasiliev. Who's this?"

"This is New York-Presbyterian Hospital calling."

"Yes, what's this about?"

"A man was found slumped over and unconscious in his car out in front of the ER entrance. He must have driven himself here and then passed out. His wallet says Alaric Vasiliev with your name listed as next of kin."

"He's my father. Is he alright?"

"I'm sorry sir, but I've been asked to call you and have you come in right away to speak with the attending physician who treated him."

"Spare me the privacy act bullshit, and just tell me. I'm a lawyer, and I promise I won't sue. Along with representing him as his medical advocate, I also have power of attorney. Speak freely. Now."

"Hold for Dr. Casey." I already knew, but I played along and waited to hear the words.

"This is Dr. Casey. I regret to tell you that your father suffered a massive coronary tonight. We used all our best medical capabilities but were not successful in restarting his heart. I'm very sorry for your loss."

"Thank you. I will arrange to have him picked up as soon as I can."

"Sir, don't you want to come in and see him first?"

"No, that won't be necessary. Have him sent to the morgue, and he will be picked up by the morning."

"Yes, sir, as you wish. Again, I'm sorry for your loss."

I ended the call and let out the breath I had been holding. There's only one person I needed right now, and that's Willow, but not like this. My knuckles were swollen and covered with Sergei's blood. I knew they would bruise, and my dove would be upset to see me hurt. She would make it better for me.

I made my way upstairs and stripped out of my clothes. I made sure to bag every last article of clothing. They would be dropped in the incinerator. I showered under the full blast of the hot sprays until I washed away all the blood that was on my hands, an ugly reminder of tonight's events. I breathed heavily as I relived it all in my mind.

He was my father first and foremost, and I loved him very much until he showed me a side to him that I never knew before. A version of himself who was motivated by greed and power, not caring who he hurt to attain those things. And now everything he worked for would be dismantled in a matter of a few days. I was the executor of his will, and I had it written for him very specifically so that it protects all of us. His rival was dead, and his men would scatter like traitors and join other families, renouncing one loyalty for another. This was how it worked. Word would spread like wildfire that two heads of powerful Russian families were dead, and the next in line would step up and take their rightful place.

I sent Willow a quick text letting her know that I would join her soon. Too much to explain in a message. The only words that mattered were the three back to her: I love you.

In a matter of a few seconds, she replied with a heart. It was all I needed to right my world back to where it belonged: with my dove.

"Is it done?" I asked as Oleg arrived back at the apartment.

"Yes, I did as you asked."

"Good, and Sergei?"

"He's back at home with half-assed stitches in his face. I guess he tried doing it himself. What about Sasha?"

"He's at Dr. Micah's clinic. I don't know how much he might have heard between my father and me. He must have taken something, and by the time I made it back here, he was in the process of overdosing. I've never seen anything like it and didn't know what to do. Thank god his doctor showed up when she did."

"Dammit, Sasha! I'm sorry, Val. I should have made sure he was protected better."

"No, don't do that. It's not your fault, and it's not mine either. If anyone is to blame for all of this havoc on our family, it's my father. But he won't be causing any more trouble."

"Valentin, you didn't…" he stumbled over his words.

"No. It was a heart attack, a fatal one. He's at New York-Pres in the morgue. Will you take care of the arrangements and have him picked up?"

"Of course, I will. What about your mother?"

"Say nothing. She's better off in London for the time being. It's late, and I'm exhausted. I need to pick up Willow and bring her home. Have her things picked up tomorrow and brought here. I take it all is well with her boss?"

"Yes, she's been more accepting of things since your talk."

"Good, she's a headache I do not need. As for Willow's work, Zara, etc. I take it you've handled all of that?"

"Absolutely. There's one thing left to discuss," he said and then pulled out the thick file wrapped up in a leather portfolio from his bag. He handed it over to me, and I just sighed, feeling all kinds of foolish not being privy to what was happening right in front of me. "Valentin, we can burn it just like the rest, if that's what you want."

"No, not yet. I can't deal with this right now. It will be in my safe, and once I'm ready, I will certainly read all the sins my father committed against all of us."

"Very well. Will Slavic's be sufficient?"

"Yes, he'll do. I'll call him in the morning. Just keep him on ice until I bring my mother home and situate Sasha. I can't do any more tonight."

"Shall I have Marta prepare some food for you? You're barely standing."

"Yeah, that would be great. I don't think the shower did much good."

"You'll be fine as soon as you see your girl. She's the best medicine for you right now."

Yes, she is. I closed my eyes, and all I envisioned was Willow's emerald green eyes staring back at me. The way they glazed over when she's about to come. I fucking love it. I love her. I want it all with my dove, and the sooner the better. I need her tied to me in every way possible, so she will never leave me.

For all I knew, she could be pregnant with my child right now. I fucked her so good, filling her body with so much of my cum. No apologies had to be said. She knew I was a beast and was accepting of all of me.

CHAPTER
Twenty-Nine

Willow

"Where is he?" I said aloud but not enough for my mom to hear. After our big talk, she was hovering to make sure I was okay. *Yes, I'm okay, and I'm tired of talking about my relationship with Valentin. Come on, Valentin, where are you?*

"Honey, staring at your phone will not make it magically ring," my mom said.

"I know that!" I snapped and then regretted the tone I used with her. She was only trying to help in her unique way without judging too much. "Sorry, I'm just cranky."

"It's fine. How about we get out of here and grab a bite to eat. It's New York. I'm sure we can find something that's open."

"I'd rather wait for Valentin. He'll be here."

"Okay, what do you have in the fridge? I'm sure I can whip up something."

"I can't believe you're still hungry after we finished off a large pizza, with you eating most of it. You can take a look and see what's in there. I haven't been home for a while, so anything I do have has probably gone bad by now."

"What can I say? I like to eat when I'm nervous."

I was about to go out of my mind if this tiresome conversation between us continued. *I need Valentin to show up. I can't believe he's been gone this long and without calling me. I loved his text, but even that was hours ago.*

Screw it! I'm just going to call him, I thought and hit call on his number. *This is stupid. What are you doing, Willow?* I was about to end the call, and then it connected.

"Hello," he answered, and I swear I felt it between my legs. My guy's voice was so sexy and irresistible.

"Hi, forgive me for how I'm about to sound, but...where are you?"

I heard him laugh. "I'm very close. Open your door."

"What!?" I happily shouted and unlocked all the locks, swinging the door open to see Valentin still with his cell to his ear, grinning back at me. I was so happy to see him that I lunged forward and jumped into his arms, not caring at all that my mom was watching.

He wrapped his arms around me and took my mouth just the way I'd grown accustomed to being kissed. Hard.

"I'm sorry I'm so late. I've missed you more than I can ever explain but how about I show you? I can't wait to be inside of you."

A voice from inside of my apartment cleared her throat, and he simply looked over my shoulder to see who it was from. You would think he might have been embarrassed, but not Valentin. He shrugged his shoulders, winked, kissed me again, and then placed me down and linked our hands together.

"Showtime. Let's meet your mom," he said and leaned in to kiss me behind my ear. "I promise, I'll be nice."

As for mom, she was hard to get a take on at the moment. Her hands were crossed over her chest, and she glared a bit having heard his intentions for her daughter. *I guess I can't blame her for being pro-*

tective, but I am an adult and I know what I want.

"Mom, I'd like to introduce you to Valentin Vasiliev, my boyfriend," I said proudly. "Valentin, this is my mom, Brooke Pierce."

She softened her stance a little and dropped her arms to her side, walking over with her hand extended to Valentin. "Hello, it's a pleasure to meet you. I've heard a lot about you in recent weeks."

"Mom," I enunciated slowly, "be nice."

Valentin gripped my hand, showing me that all would be fine. Then, as mom approached, he dropped my hand and returned her greeting in the form of a hug. I knew what he was doing, but this was my mom, also known as man-hater. She would not be easy to charm. He could try, but it would be easier getting blood from a stone.

"My daughter believes I'm about to go all mama bear on you and grill you with the many questions I have. You think you can handle a few?"

He chortled a bit and then flashed my mom a smile wide enough to bring the biggest man-hater to her knees. *Shall I say that I'm the one that wants to be on her knees? Oh my god, I have it bad.*

"I'd expect nothing less from a concerned mother, and if this tete-a-tete was happening on any other night, I would answer as much as you want me to."

"But? Not tonight? Even though my daughter has been here waiting hours for you to show up, and when you do, the only thing on your mind is sex."

"Mom! Oh my god, what has gotten into you speaking to Valentin that way?"

"I guess because you're not answering the right questions, honey, so it will have to be up to me."

As if he knew what I was going to do next, he let out a breath and gave a look to put me at ease. "Ms. Pierce..." he began to say.

"Please, call me Brooke."

"I'd rather not. You see, I understand why you feel the need to confront me so strongly. Willow is young, and I'm sure in your eyes, naïve and impressionable, but I can assure you that she's not. She can handle her own and certainly me with no problem whatsoever. However, I will not condone you or anyone else making her feel bad for choosing to be with me, because she does, Ms. Pierce. She's mine in every way possible, and I will be marrying her very soon."

"Wow, you are quite the player, aren't you?"

"No, not at all. I'm a man in love with your daughter. I'm also a man who lost his father tonight, and that is why I can't stay to have the conversation you want to have with me."

What? Valentin's father is dead? I put an end to this nonsense and rushed back into his arms. "I'm so sorry, baby. Why didn't you tell me this when you first arrived?" I asked him with tears in my eyes. I felt awful and ashamed of how my mom treated him.

"Please don't cry, not for me, and certainly not for my father," he whispered in my ear so my mom couldn't hear us. "I promise I will explain everything to you when I take you home. Can we get out of here?" he asked.

"Yes, anything you want. Let's go."

My mom picked that moment to interrupt our moment. "Willow, you're leaving?"

"Yes, I am. I need to be with Valentin, and since you were *so* kind to him tonight, I figure why test our luck?"

"Oh, honey, I'm sorry. You know I would have never behaved like that had I known about his father's passing. I'm just trying to be your mom and take care of you."

"Yes, I know that's what you believe you are doing, but all you've done is be rude to the man I love and basically tried and convicted him without ever giving him a chance to prove your suspicions wrong. I love you mom, I really do. But you need to get a life of your own and stop trying to control mine. You are an amazing mother, and you did your job. Now please allow me to stand on my own and live the life I want to lead. Stay here or go home to Jersey. Either way, I'll be with Valentin."

"Willow, please don't go, I'm sorry I hurt you," she cried out as I turned away and left with Valentin.

"Valentin, I am so sorry for my mother's behavior tonight. She's usually amazing, and I know once she has time to process it all, she is going to feel awful."

"Darling, it's fine, really. I can handle your mother, and I'm sure one day we will get along just fine, and if not, so be it. As long as I have you, nothing else matters."

I threw my arms around his neck in the back seat of his limo and kissed him. "You have me, Valentin…" I kissed him again. "For as long as you want me here."

"I want you with me forever, dove. You know that."

"I do, but I guess I was a little afraid my mom scared you off."

"Not a chance. I love you more than life itself."

"I believe you, Valentin, I always have. I don't understand why I questioned my feelings for you. I guess I was scared and blamed my insecurities on every negative reason I always believed to be true. Mom is not as bad as she appeared tonight."

"I know that, and I promise it's already forgotten. Don't be so hard on her, Willow. Parents need time to come to the understanding that children do grow up and eventually have to live their lives outside of their watchful eyes."

"Was that how it was for you? I mean, I know we have two very different backgrounds, but aren't most parents the same when it comes to their kids?"

"No, not in every family, but I'm happy you had such a loving mom to raise you into the woman I love."

I gave him the biggest hug I could manage, and that's when I noticed his bruised knuckles. I took his face in my hands and kissed him. He was hurting, and all I wanted to do was give him comfort and take care of him for once. He pulled me close, and then I lifted his injured hand to my lips and placed a gentle kiss on his knuckles.

"Does it hurt much?" I asked softly.

"It's nothing and not anything for you to worry about."

"Will you tell me about your father? What happened tonight?" I didn't want to push him for answers, but I needed him to know that I would be here for him and not leave no matter what he would tell me.

His arms were still around me as he buried his face in my chest. His body shook, and then I felt his tears as Valentin let go. He held on as tight as he could and just cried until he had nothing left inside of him. My strong man capable of everything was just a son mourning his lost father.

"How do I help you, Valentin?" I felt powerless.

"Oh, my dove, you're doing it just by being here with me. We're home. Let's go upstairs so I can lose myself in you and put this hellish day behind us. Will you do that for me?" His voice was broken, but underneath all the pain, he had hope, hope in our love and in me to get him through this. I would do anything for him.

We didn't need any words. All we needed was each other. I kissed him and placed my hand in his uninjured one, leading him upstairs. We locked the rest of the world out, at least for a little while.

CHAPTER
Thirty

Valentin

I was so happy to finally be home and with Willow beside me. I didn't release her hand until we were safely tucked away in our bedroom. I didn't give her a moment to catch her breath as I began to quickly remove her from her clothing.

Once she was naked, I asked her to take a few steps back so I could peruse her body, taking my time as she slowly turned for me. I was hard, so hard that I could drill nails into a board with my cock. *This is what she does to me and without even trying.* I pounced and carried her to our bed, dropping her clumsily in the middle of the bed. She giggled, which only made me more excited to take her.

My clothes were now gone, and I hovered over her small frame, staring into her green eyes. "I love you so much. I want to be rough with you, but I don't want to hurt you. We have no rules or safe words, so if it becomes too much for you, please just say stop, and I will. Do you understand me?"

"Yes, Valentin, love me and heal what's broken."

She was absolutely perfect, giving me everything I wanted and needed with her submission. I would spend no time getting her body ready for me. I could smell the arousal all over her skin and see the wetness between her legs. I wanted a taste but knew if I did, I would never stop and wreck her for the rest of the night. Her hands began to smooth over my ass, urging me on to fuck her. I knew my dove's body better than she did, and it was as if it was made just for me. Perfect.

"Are you ready?" I asked.

"Yes, please," she whispered.

I lined up my cock to the entrance of her pussy and pushed in with such a force, she lifted her head off the pillow. It was a cry I never heard before, and it worried me that I hurt her. "Are you okay?" I questioned as I stared at her expression.

"Yes, I'm fine. Don't stop."

I had her submission to do as I pleased. Holding her hands against the duvet, I pushed again and again until I was fully seated inside of my beautiful girl. Her soft hands smoothed over my ass, inciting me on. With her legs around my waist and sitting on my hips, I moved in a fast rhythm until I was so close of exploding. I knew what the driving force behind our fucking was tonight, and I hated that he occupied my thoughts. I shoved him out of my mind and concentrated on the woman underneath me.

She raked her fingernails into my back, shouting what she wanted. "Valentin, you need to move! I'm so close. Please, baby, stay with me."

The sound of her was all the focus I needed to bring us the pleasure we both needed. I crushed her mouth, making her open for me. My tongue swirled around with hers, and this was the best feeling in the world to be inside of Willow, my future wife. *God! I want her. I always want her. It is a feral need that burns only for her.*

"I'll never get enough of you, Willow. You're mine forever. I need to fill you up with so much of my cum. I need you tied to me." I pressed my hand to her flat stomach and told her exactly what I wanted. "If you're not pregnant already, you must know you will be soon. I want it all with you, Willow."

She screamed my name, "Valentin!!!"

I followed right behind her and did the same. We were both exhausted, as I remained connected with her body. I was holding my body up on my forearms, not wanting her to feel the heaviness of my weight. Even my arms were getting tired after the day and night I had and add a couple of hours of hot and rough sex with the woman I loved and, yeah, I was tired. I rolled over to the side, pulling Willow close. Her heavy lids were beginning to close as she let out soft sighs before falling into sleep.

For the first time since I left her this morning, I felt at peace, which was not easy to do for a guy like me. My mind was always running in a thousand directions, trying to make sure every piece of my life fit perfectly into the other. Willow made me feel that it was okay to mix it up and welcome the change, because that was exactly what she had done. She'd changed my life completely and made me want more, things that I thought would not be attainable until she flashed those green eyes at me and I was a goner.

My fingers combed through her long hair. It was always soft and smelled like flowers. I wanted to wake her just to hear her voice again. I whispered close to her ear, and her shoulder moved a little when my lips touched her bare skin. "Willow, I never knew how lost I was until you found me. I love you, beautiful dove." I placed a kiss to her cheek and then buried my face in her hair and allowed sleep to take me too.

"Willow!" I shouted, as my body sprang up from the bed. She wasn't in our bed, and her side of it felt cold under my hand. The only proof that last night happened was the smell of her perfume that still lingered all around the room and the indent on her pillow. *She's here. Relax, and pull yourself together.*

I rubbed the tiredness from my eyes and glanced over at the clock. Shit! *It's past eleven. When have I ever slept in? I'll tell you: never.*

When I went into the bathroom, it was clear Willow had taken a shower. Her cosmetics were strewn around the sink, and the smell of her perfume was strong in the air. I inhaled deeply, imagining my dove with me.

I stepped into the shower and let the hot water work the tension out of my mind and body. I had so much to take care of today and was avoiding my cell phone at all costs. What I needed now was my woman.

"Willow," I called out as my bare feet touched the tiled floor. "Willow," I called out again but didn't hear any response until Marta greeted me.

"Sir, is there something I can do for you?"

"Yes, can you tell me where the hell Willow is?" I shouted so loud it caused Marta to step back. "I'm sorry, Marta. I didn't mean to frighten you."

"No worries, Mr. Vasiliev. Ms. Pierce has not left. She's been in the kitchen, cooking. I think it was meant as a surprise for you."

"Marta, again, I'm sorry. It's been a rough couple of days."

"I'm very sorry to hear about your father's passing. If there is anything I can do, please let me know. Oleg was here earlier and dropped off an envelope for you. It's on your desk with today's and yesterday's mail."

"Thank you, I'll just take a peek in the kitchen and see what Ms. Pierce is up to."

She smiled warmly at me, not that I deserved her kindness when I was always biting her head off. Willow wouldn't like me behaving like this, and I knew I was a better man than how I'd been acting lately. It was from the nightmare with my father, Pavlo, and all the worrying I did over Sasha. I peered around the doorway, and that's when I saw Willow dancing around my kitchen in her bare feet, only wearing a simple summertime dress. She had her earbuds in and was reading a cookbook while stirring something in a large metal bowl. I said nothing and retreated to my office. I knew when she was ready, she would find me.

"Oleg, what do we know?" I asked and sipped my coffee, wishing it was scotch.

"Your father is with Slavic and will be ready by the end of the day. Sasha is good. I spoke to him on the phone and he sounded well."

"Really? He sounded better?"

"Yes. If it wasn't for your quick thinking. It may have gone the other way but thank god it didn't. He's going to be okay, Val. You have to believe that."

"I'm trying. And Sergei?"

"He's resumed his post back at the club and knows to be silent if he wants to see another day."

"What about the press? Word on the street about Pavlo and my father?"

"We really couldn't contain the news about Pavlo, considering the FBI was all over his family before he died. We know about his men and the new alliances formed with your father. Those remain still intact until we reveal that your father is dead as well. The medical examiner has been well compensated for his silence. To the outside world, your father is still abroad."

"Very well. Find Yuri. He's the only one next to Avros who could be trusted enough with all the secrets, including the buried ones. Call a meeting, and wait for my instructions. This needs to end today before I can lay my father to rest."

I worked for another half hour or so until there was a soft knock on my office door. "Come in," I called out. She practically danced her way inside and looked incredibly happy, with flour dabbing her cheek. "Come here," I invited her over to sit on my lap. She did more than that and began to unbutton my jeans.

In a flash, I had her back to my desk and my hard cock deep inside her. Willow's legs was wrapped so tightly around my waist, it was like she was a snake strangling her prey. She never looked away, not even once as I continued to fuck her. We kissed and breathed the other in as we both soared to our climax. I pulled her up, so we were pressed against each other, and she rode me perfectly until her head fell back and she came gloriously, with me right behind her.

After we caught our breaths, we broke out into laughter. My pants were down around my ankles, and her dress was pulled up, not disturbing anything else we were wearing.

"You sure do know how to make a grand entrance," I said and kissed her back.

"I missed you and figured since you didn't come looking for me, you would be working."

"I was giving us time I think we both needed. Are you okay?"

"I'm perfect. You?"

"Perfect," I answered back.

"Good, then I have a surprise for you, and it's waiting in the dining room. Put me down so I can freshen up, and then meet me out there in ten minutes, okay?"

I love this woman. "What are you up to?"

"You'll see. Ten minutes."

I placed her down, and she left my office, blowing me a kiss over her shoulder.

Just one more day to put my past to rest. To free me from all that is standing in my way of having a life with Willow.

I gave her a few extra minutes just to make sure she had everything ready for me. With all I had on my mind, I felt like a small child waiting to open the birthday or Christmas present that I waited for all year long. As I stepped into the dining room, there was Willow holding a cake with two candles lit on top of it.

"What is this?" I asked happily.

"Well, today is my birthday, and we have a tradition in my family that we also celebrate the next person's birthday too, and if memory serves, your birthday is at the end of August. So, happy birthday to me and you! You better get over here and make a wish before these candles burn my homemade frosting."

I forgot her birthday, and here she is celebrating mine?

"Come on, love. Make a wish. My arms are getting tired."

I quickly walked over and closed my eyes, knowing I already had everything I needed right here holding a cake and smiling back at me.

"You have it?"

"Yes, I do."

"Good, so do I. On the count of three, 1, 2, and 3, happy birthday, Valentin," she softly whispered and blew out her candle.

"Happy birthday, Willow. I love you," and I blew out my candle out too. "I don't need any more wishes because all my dreams became real on the day we met. You saved my life on that day and have continued to do so every moment spent with you. I never believed I would want and need someone as much as I do when it comes to you. I never thought I could love, not in the way it happens for most people. You are my life, Willow, and I would love nothing more than for you to become my wife. Please marry me, Willow, and make us a family."

She wiped away her layers of tears, and then more fell before she reached for my face and pulled me over the cake to kiss me.

"Yes, Valentin, I will marry you as soon as you want me to. Now, let's celebrate with cake." She cut a slice and placed some on a fork, bringing it up to my mouth to taste. It literally melted in my mouth.

"This is amazing. The flavor is out of this world."

"Thank you! It's a recipe from my grandma. I didn't remember the icing part, so Marta's cookbook helped. It's French Vanilla. Grandma says it's the easiest cake to make, and the one everyone loves."

"I couldn't agree more, but what makes it special is because you made it."

"I love that you think so, because you need more," she grinned and then smashed the rest of the piece all over my face before kissing me passionately.

The rest of the afternoon was spent making love and making new promises of forever sharing our hopes and dreams with each other. She gave me the best day of my life, one I will never forget until I take my last breath.

No one had ever made me a cake like that. Mother would have one of the cooks prepare one for me, and it wasn't as simple as the round cake Willow baked. No, it usually was a multi-layered tier cake you see at weddings. Mother never truly got the concept of birthday cakes, but it was what happened after that mattered the most. She would come into my room with another piece of cake and a candle. I always got to make another wish with my mom, and it would be our secret we would share until the next birthday. *After all these years, I'm not sure what made me think of that, maybe it's Willow's influence.*

She knew nothing about what happened to my father and what I still needed to deal with once I walked out of here and left her alone in this big apartment. She was curled up in bed, surrounded by sketch-books and a variety of pencils. I leaned down and kissed her softly on her cheek.

She stirred awake and smiled. "Hey, sorry I fell asleep. You kind of wore me out. I have to remember to bake often for you."

"I would love that. Happy Birthday, Willow. I promise to return with a proper gift for you."

"All I need is you."

"Well, that's easy, because you have me for life. I'll be back as soon as I can, and if I'm not, I don't want you to worry and just go to sleep. I promise you will wake up to me right beside you."

"You're scaring me, Valentin."

"I don't mean to. Please just stay here, and do not leave this room. Okay? Will you do that for me?"

"Yes, I promise."

I knew beyond a shadow of a doubt that she would keep her word.

"Are they all here?" I asked Oleg as I made my way into the grand hall of my father's home.

"Yes, and they are very eager to hear what the prince of the Vasi-liev family has to say."

"Correction, Oleg, I'm the fucking king." I had formed a plan on what I was going to say here today, and then once Oleg called me by my nickname, something just snapped inside of me, and I knew I would be going another way. *Let's see if they agree.*

When I walked through the double doors, all eyes were on me as they should be. I commanded a room and the people in it at all times, so today would be no different. I took my father's seat at the head of the table and called the meeting to order. Oleg was at my right, and Yuri Petrov at my left, now in command of the Shirmanov dynasty.

"Let's get down to why we're here, shall we? The patriarch of your family is dead, his son is dead, and that means his way of doing business is also dead. If you choose to fight today and go rogue to suit your thirst for a piece, all that ambition will get you is a bullet to your head and an unmarked shallow grave for all eternity." I paused for a moment to observe their reactions. These men were smart to show no emotion and to keep their mouths closed.

I turned to Yuri and addressed him personally. "Pavlo was dying and didn't have too many months left to put his affairs in order. With Avros dead, you saw your chance to seize control and take what was left, but you hit a snag when you discovered that my father had already staked his claim. Backroom deals in seedy bars all over St. Petersburg. Yes, back in the day he loved to hunt, and I guess he didn't lose that want after all these years. I guess he got bored and did it all behind my back, and that was my father's fatal mistake."

"Fatal?"

"Yes, Yuri, I don't believe I stuttered. Gentlemen, Alaric Vasiliev is dead, and after I leave here today, I will bring my mother home, and our family will put him to rest. What is not at rest is our business. Let me be clear, because it will only be said once. The Vasiliev family does not run drugs. We do not run trafficking of any kind. Most importantly, women and children are to be cherished, not used, abused, and sold off to the highest bidder. I will personally take a machete to your dicks if you ever forget these rules. Now, it didn't need to get that far with Pavlo. He made his choice, and it was the wrong one. My father took the easier way out by suffering a fatal heart attack right in front of me. Did he get what he deserved? What do you think, Yuri?"

"He wasn't my father."

"Yeah, but he was your boss, right? And for a quite a while, long before the demise of Pavlo's business. Don't bother lying. I know it all. Now that everything is out in the open, we can deal."

"And how exactly do you want to deal? It's clear to not only me but to all of us that you hold all the cards in play, and if one of us steps out of line and disagrees with you, we will be joining Pavlo and Alaric."

"I always knew you were a smart man, Yuri. I'm glad you see it my way. Each of you was asked to be here because you see the bigger picture for your future. Money is the name of the game, and if you play nice, you will all reap the benefits and more that will bypass your life and the future generations you create. However, in order to do that, you need to be smart. Never forget that big brother is always watching and will stop at nothing to bring the family down. You will all tow the line and run your piece of the business legitimately. You see, gentlemen, there is no other way but my way. I will give you the room to discuss amongst yourselves, and when I return, I expect unity at this table. A compliance that will serve us well." Oleg followed me out of the room and out into the garden, so I could catch my fucking breath.

"Are you alright?" he asked.

"I will be once this is over, and I can return home to Willow."

"Valentin, may I speak freely?"

"You may."

"How do you see this playing out? You just went up against twelve of the most powerful soldiers that have served by your father's and Pavlo's side. They are loyal to the highest degree. We know that, and we also know what happens when they feel they are cornered and have no other way out but to attack. Are you ready for that? Because if you're not, I advise you to leave here at once and go back to your law practice and leave this business to them to either run or destroy."

"No, Oleg, I will not run from who I am, nor this family. I am a Vasiliev, and I am what my father has made me. The only difference between us is that my heart is still beating, and I will never hurt or betray the ones I love. That's who I am, and I'll ask you kindly to never question me again. Clear?"

"I'm sorry, Valentin, I had to ask."

"Yes, I know and the reasons why. We will not speak of this again. Come, I believe our friends have had enough time to reach their decision." I would never hold ill will toward Oleg. He would always stand beside me and keep all my secrets until the end of time.

We entered the room with all twelve pairs of eyes solely focused on me. Yuri was the first to rise from his chair. He walked over to stand in front of me. I nodded, not sure what to expect next from him. I knew walking back in here could only end two ways. *The men had two choices to make here. They could stand united with me or against me.*

Yuri took a knee to the floor and reached for my hand. It was a show of respect for family and the honor that comes with it. He placed a kiss on my ring, the one my father gave me. One by one they followed his lead, and the house that my father tried to take down had now been restored.

The room was quiet after the men followed out. Oleg left to deliver the paperwork to my office, and then there was only one—me. I was still standing after the blood was spilled and promises were made for the new family I would lead. I looked around the house room by room trying to find one memory that I could take with me. I sighed knowing there weren't any to be found. The memories that shaped my life died at the moment my father hurt my brother. Those were sins that could never be washed away, and he would drown in them for all eternity. I would feel sorrow for my mother. She will mourn him as a wife should, and I would give her the time she needed in order to do that. As for Sasha, he would never know the monster Alaric became, and another secret would be buried.

I'll take tomorrow to tell Sasha, and then a press release will be issued to the public. I poured a drink and took in the family portrait that hung above the fireplace. *I believe this was taken on the day I graduated law school. Oh, he was proud and raised a glass in my honor in front of hundreds of people who gathered to celebrate alongside him. Isn't it funny that after all these years after this picture was taken, today I will do the same for him?* I looked up and centered on his eyes, I swear it felt as if he was staring back at me.

I said aloud, "Every life comes with a death sentence. I was happy to be with you at the end of yours. Goodbye, father."

CHAPTER
Thirty-One

Willow

Has it really only been six months since meeting Valentin? It *feels longer to me but I can't talk about time with the man I love because he's a little sensitive when it comes to our age difference.* He wanted to make every moment count with each other, and he didn't want to slap a time frame on how long those moments would last. He was so passionate when it came to our relationship. According to Valentin, our union was destiny getting it right, and as far as he was concerned, it would last forever.

It didn't take long to convince me how true that was. We had obstacles too that played a part in our relationship, and that was his family, a very complicated Russian mob family. *I still get the chills that run up and down my arm every time I think of it.*

The night he asked me to wait for him, I knew I would until the end of time. I loved him so much, and he made me open my eyes to see what we could have if we stayed together and trusted our feelings.

It was sometime in the middle of the night when he crawled into bed and pulled me close to his side. I asked him once how he slept before meeting me, and as I expected, he said that he didn't need much until meeting me, and then all he wanted to do was hold me and feel my skin on his. We were technically engaged, and he promised a ring would soon be on my finger and we would make it official. Well, he was right, and I didn't have to wait too long.

I woke up with my hand feeling heavier than it was when I fell asleep. I opened my eyes to see a sparkling three-carat emerald cut diamond on my left hand. I was shocked by its beauty, and then Valentin was there, on one knee, beside the bed.

"Will you marry me, Willow?"

"Yes, you amazing man. I will marry you!"

We made love and stayed in bed for the next two days, completely blocking the rest of the world out, including my skeptic mother and even my grandmother who had returned from her travels. She was thrilled and over the moon about my *love affair*, her words, not mine. She couldn't wait to meet my guy and wished me all the best, which was more than my mom initially offered.

After learning who Valentin was connected to and his family's background, it took a little longer for mom to accept him. We knew she was worried and feared for my safety, but Valentin promised her that he would lay his life down for me if necessary. And I knew that to be true because he already had with Pavlo, but she didn't need to know that. He shared as much as he could about his father, and the family he was born into. I never pushed him to reveal anything he wasn't comfortable telling, and I was okay with that. He said he never wanted me to know the ugly parts of his past, and the parts he did mention he feared they would cause me to be afraid and leave him. *Never. Not a chance. I knew where I belonged and who I belong to, and that was Valentin Vasiliev, my husband.*

Our happiness was put on hold until we got through the onslaught of the press following news of his father's death and funeral. His mother was beautiful, gracious, and welcoming toward me. I also got to spend some time with his brother, Sasha, and we talked for many hours one night, and I saw the bond they shared and the love they had for one another. I understood better why Valentin was protective of his brother and me. It was just who he was and what made him so incredible.

As if life would ever be the same, I tried to regain some level of normalcy by returning to what I loved to do, and that was to design and create beautiful things. It took nearly two weeks for me to return back to work, not knowing what to expect once I walked through the doors. My personal and professional relationship with Madeline had been strained, and it was a big question to whether it would continue. Valentin voiced his feelings about my friend, so much that I had to remind him of what caused her to say and do the things she did. She was suffering from PTSD, and what she went through was probably something she would carry with her for the rest of her life. I had Valentin to get me through it, but she had no one.

When I walked through the doors of MW Designs, it was like you could hear a pin drop. All work ceased, and all eyes were on me. I finally broke the ice and said, "Hey, what's everyone staring at? Do I have something in my teeth?" and with the laughter that followed, I was confident enough to keep walking through the showroom and up to my office, where I knew Madeline was waiting for me. I knew when she returned home from the spa and back to work, but with everything going on, there was no time to reconnect until today.

With Valentin's connections and my in with Zara, I probably could work anywhere of my choosing, but for now, my heart was here with Madeline.

The minute she saw me, she just shrugged her shoulders and said, "I'm too old to make new friends, kid. You're all I got. Can I get a hug?"

I placed my things down and rushed over and into her arms. We must have stood there for five minutes just hugging one another with Madeline apologizing over and over again. She said she would never be sorry for looking out for me, but she was sorry for hurting my feelings and promised she would never do that again if I gave her a second chance on our friendship.

Of course, I didn't leave her hanging, and I told her that she was forgiven, and yes, we could still be friends. How could I not forgive her after all I'd been through with Valentin, and what she and I suffered over because of my connection to the man I loved? I sat in a funeral home holding his hand as I watched him silently grieve, and his mother fell apart over the loss of her husband.

There is no love without forgiveness and no forgiveness without love. I've always believed in this and I wasn't about to withhold it from my friend. No one is perfect, and we all make mistakes. After Madeline left our apartment that night and boarded a flight to parts unknown, she said she had a life-affirming moment and vowed to change. I guess what I said had hit home with her, and although she didn't completely give up her favorite bourbon, she stopped drinking for all the negative reasons that made her feel less than who she truly was. I was proud of her, and she was proud of me. We worked together side-by-side and created one hell of a line for Zara Hill. Our designs debuted on Broadway in a hit show starring her talented niece.

Once the word was out, non-stop orders kept rolling in, and we soon expanded our operations and partnered with Zara. It was a dream come true, but nothing could top marrying Valentin. He didn't want to wait, as if I could stop him. He asked me to trust his plans for us, and all I had to do was show up in whatever I wanted to wear and say, "I do." The rest he would take care of.

Two months later, we married in an intimate setting on a private island in the Maldives. He had his brother, Sasha, as his best man, along with Oleg and his mother. I was joined by mom, grandma, and Madeline as my maid of honor. We were pronounced husband and wife just as the sun had set.

It was everything I could imagine, more like a fairytale. He was the tall, dark, and handsome prince who changed my entire life with just a small act of kindness.

Epilogue

Valentin

I won't say that I wasn't disappointed when the doctor confirmed my dove wasn't pregnant with our child. I wanted more than anything for her to be so then we could welcome a son or daughter into our lives.

For a brief moment, I feared I may have lost her after she learned the dark truth of my family, but no, she made it better by loving me and accepting my complicated past. She'd been wonderful with Sasha, a person he can speak freely with. My mother welcomed her with open arms and promised to visit as often as she could.

After we buried my father and dealt with the media storm that followed, life returned back to us, and we got married. *She's amazing, my wife, and I know she will make an amazing mother someday, I just wish that day was today.*

After the holidays passed, we saw a specialist. We hadn't been trying the normal length of time, but I had money at my disposal and would pursue every doctor until I believed we could get pregnant. They all said the same thing. Willow was young and in perfect health, and although I had ten years on my wife, I was not ancient and could easily get her pregnant.

We decided not to put so much pressure on ourselves and just enjoyed a healthy sex life. Yes, we had that, and it was mind-blowing. She never said no and always submitted perfectly to me. I loved her so much and would do anything for her.

She had been so busy with her work and preparing for her first fashion show. It was a preview for Fashion Week. The hours were long, which I hated, but she never complained when I did the same thing with a case I was the lead attorney on. We compromised and spent as much time as we could with each other. After all, we were newlyweds and hated to be apart from the other, even in the smallest measure of time.

In all the years I had been practicing law, this case by far had been my most difficult. There were days when I almost didn't believe we would win, but when the judge declared my client the victor, I nearly fell back into my chair but remained standing to hear it all.

After everything I had gone through with my father, I took a long look at my practice and what it represented. Sure, we were on top with clients from all around the country and some international. However, Willow made me see bigger things that I might have been missing when it was just me. I knew I was a damn good lawyer and could make a difference in the lives of clients that really needed my help. So, after I returned home from our honeymoon, I made many changes at my law practice. I offered a partner position to three of my best attorneys at my firm, with my name still on the door.

Until Willow, I never took a single vacation. I never just dipped my feet in the ocean and smelled the salty air. I didn't do or know a lot of things until my dove showed them to me. *Who I am now is who I always wanted to be.*

I took my reserved seat up in front along with Sasha, who was practically bouncing in his seat. He was doing great, and I couldn't be prouder. Through heaven and hell, he turned his life around, and for the first time ever, I truly believed he would be okay. He was out of the club scene and was a full-time student in college, working toward his degree to be a therapist. He wanted to continue the work that made him strong and healthy. He respected his doctors and made friends whom he could trust and would support him while he did the same.

With a smile on his face and, if I heard it right, a giggle to his voice, I finally nudged him and wanted to know why he was so happy. It was a great thing, but I swear this Sasha reminded me of the brother I knew so long ago, so carefree and relaxed.

"Hey, sunshine, what's with the grin?"

"What? I can't be happy?" He tried to look affronted but then broke out into laughter again.

"You can, and I love it. I just want to know the reason behind it."

"Okay, you remember that day when we met Willow at the park for lunch?

"I meet my wife a lot at the park. You need to be more specific."

"Smartass! I'm talking about when I was with you."

"I remember, and I'm just messing with you. So, what's up?"

"I'm dating one of the models who will be in the show today. It's new, but I'm telling you she's great and makes me so fucking happy. It's just crazy how two people can come together. She only does this for fun, and it pays the bills. I met her at school a few months back. We were in a study group together and went out for dinner that night, hitting it off immediately."

"I'm really happy for you, Sasha, but be careful. You have a lot on your plate with your recovery and school. Now a girlfriend may be too much."

"Stop worrying, Valentin. I know what I'm doing."

"Well, that may be a little hard for me to do but I will try."

"Thank you. I appreciate it. She's really great, and it feels right. Trust me, okay?"

"I trust you completely, and I'm happy for you."

I really did. We had come a long way with each other, and this was part of me letting go and trusting my brother. I had so many conversations with Willow about him, and each and every time I doubted, she would go over all the reasons why I shouldn't. He did look happy, and who I am to begrudge him of feeling that way? Not when I had so much in my life because of the woman I fell in love with.

Speaking of which, where is she? When I arrived, I wanted to go backstage to give her a kiss for good luck, but I was told I had to go directly to my seat, per the boss. I loved it and played along.

Over the loudspeakers, the announcer asked everyone to take their seats with the show about to begin. I scanned the crowd and spotted Zara, flanked by Madeline and Peter. Those three were never too far behind when it came to Willow. Their partnership was booming, and I knew it made my wife happy knowing she could share it with her friend. They all waved over at me, and then Madeline rose from her seat and went backstage. The music ended, and Madeline walked out on stage with a microphone in hand.

"New York City!" she shouted out with her hands in the air, getting the crowd excited. "Welcome to our afternoon showcase, featuring the work of Willow Pierce. I hope you are ready to be knocked out of your seats, because this line packs quite the punch. And now without further ado, let's start the show."

Applause rang out as the models began to walk down the runway in skyrocketing heels and flashy clothes, all from the brilliant hand of my dove. One after another, they strutted and did their thing, making the crowd erupt with applause and a few catcalls from my brother, who was definitely smitten by his girl who winked at him as she passed him.

"Are you amazed!? What a collection! But it's not over yet. Are you ready for the grand finale? I know I am. Put your hands together and welcome the amazing and brilliant talent behind all the wonderful designs you had the pleasure of viewing today. Willow Pierce!!!" she shouted loudly as the room was in standing attendance as I led the applause.

My god, she looked stunning and was in a very short dress.

"Thank you, thank you," Willow spoke with tears in her eyes. After the crowd settled, we all sat on the edge, quietly listening to her every word.

"Today is like a dream, and I'm standing right in the middle of all of it with love all around me." her eyes found mine, and I blew her a kiss. She caught it and put her hand over her heart.

"Now, I know you are all waiting for the showcase stunner, probably expecting one of my signature wedding gowns. Well, I decided to go another way for today's show, and it's intended for one person whom I love very much. This is for you, Valentin."

Sasha bumped my shoulder as the camera panned over to me. I was totally in awe of my wife and awaited what was about to be revealed behind the curtain.

The music began to play, and all eyes were on the stage as a parade of babies were carried out on stage, from infants to toddlers, wearing a range of outfits I'm assuming were designed by Willow. *But why? She never told me this was a line she was interested in doing.*

Willow returned to the stage surrounded by all the models in her show, along with the babies too and her team. Everyone was kissing and hugging her and giving her the credit she deserved. I wanted to just rush the stage and take her in my arms, but this was her moment, and I never loved her more. She was a star shining brightly.

"Thank you so much. You just don't know how much this means to me. So, I bet you're wondering why we have so many babies on stage right now? Well, let me tell you a little story behind the designs you've seen today. My biggest fan is my husband. His love and support have never faltered, not even for one day. I love you so much, Valentin, and that love is about to grow and make us a family."

She untied the belt at her waist and flung opened her jacket to reveal the biggest surprise I had ever received in my life. She was wearing a simple white tank top with sparkly words in pink and blue that said:

"Future Prince and Princess due to arrive in December, just in time for Santa."

Her hands moved lower to her small baby bump that I swear wasn't there a few days ago. She was smiling, and happy tears were streaming down her blushed colored cheeks. I was going to be a father and to not one but two babies! I was glued to my spot with tears of my own beginning to fall. She just happily shrugged and continued to smile as she walked over toward me. My brother hit me in the arm to get me to move and to bring me out of the shock about the gift my wife had just presented.

I climbed the steps and took Willow in my arms. The cameras flashed all around us as I crushed my mouth down to hers. "I love you, Willow, so much. I can't believe I didn't know."

"Well, it wasn't easy keeping it from you, but I wanted to make it special, and then I did by creating this line. All proceeds are going to go to Peaches Promises, a foundation started by fashion designer Freddy Mac. He's a visionary, along with his husband, who changed the face of fashion. Their story of how they became parents through adoption gave me the idea for the line and how to tell you that I was pregnant. I know you probably envisioned hearing this news in a more intimate setting, but you changed my life, Valentin. You always believed in me, and watching how you are changing other's lives with your work, how could I not do the same? It's okay, right?"

"It's perfect, just like you. Now, can we get out of here so we can celebrate in private?" I knew we still had to remain back so she could greet the press.

I gave Willow her moment, because I knew many more would follow with her, and soon with our children. We were a family, one I had been envisioning having with her and now all our dreams were about to come true.

Willow kept a journal in all the months that led to our babies being born. She never missed a day writing down her feelings, hopes, and dreams of looking forward to becoming a mother. Her mother and grandmother were a constant presence in her life, helping her plan and get ready for the arrival of the twins.

Some days, I sat back in wonderment and watched my wife just smile or laugh to herself when something happy crossed her mind. She was incredibly strong after many hours of labor, as she delivered our babies, making my world complete. Nothing would top the feeling when the nurses handed me my son and our daughter to Willow.

I was so in love with my wife and had fallen completely in love with our children. Our love made us a family here today, one that I would protect until I took my final breath in this life.

Before Willow, I was broken and burdened by a past that I never believed I could rise from, sins that would keep me in the dark and feel unable to have anything beautiful in my life.

And then my dove soared into my life and saved me. It was her love that healed me, and now she had given me more than a man like me could ever dream of having, our beautiful son and daughter.

As my wife slept soundly beside me with our twins between us, I looked down at my hands and had a thought: *Of all the things I've held, the best by far is my wife and our kids.*

The End

A NOTE
from the Author

Thank you, readers, for taking time to read *Broken Dove*. I hope you enjoyed it. Please go the retailer where you purchased this book and write a review. Even if it's just a line or two, it's the best gift you can give back to an author. They are always welcomed and appreciated.

Mary

Acknowledgments

Thank you, God, for giving me the ability to create my art.
Thank you, to my family who love me unconditionally.
Thank you, to my friends who never let me fall.

Thank you, to the talented professionals
that make my work come to life.

Thank you, Joe Marron. My editor.
You get me, and I love you for that.

Thank you, Julie Titus, @ JT Formatting.
Your creativity knows no bounds.

Thank you, Francessca, @ Francessca's PR & Design.
You are a cover goddess.

Thank you, Mindy Guerreiros for always reading my work first and giving me the feedback I need to make it great. The book world would not be what it is without your love and passion for books. Thank you for all that you do but most of all, our friendship and sisterhood. XO

Thank you, Ann Lister, I love our chats.
Thank you, for your support.
Your encouragement means the world to me.

And...

Thank you, to my readers.
You mean so much to me. I truly appreciate you reading and support-ing my work. Thank you, to my blogger friends. You work incredibly hard for authors in this community. Thank you, for always sharing the love. Writing has become an essential part of my soul, and without it, I would be lost. I am forever thankful for the gift I have been given.
Thank you, for sharing this incredible journey with me.

OTHER BOOKS BY MARY A. WASOWSKI

Forever Series:
Forever: Book One
Second Chance at Forever: Book Two
Our Forever Promise: Book Three
Happily Forever After: Book Four
Forever More: Book Five

Standalone novels:
A Changed Life
All Roads Lead Home
An Unfinished Life
Return to Kildare
Revive
You Belong to Me
Run

ABOUT the Author

Mary A. Wasowski is a best-selling author who writes adult contemporary romance. Best known for her *Forever* Series, Mary loves creating sexy alpha book boyfriends for you to swoon over. When she is not writing her happily ever after love stories, she is an avid reader of all romance.

A romantic at heart, she shares her zest for life with her husband, Henry, and their three sons. Proud to be an indie author, she lives in North Carolina and works as a full-time writer.

Stay in Touch
I would love to hear from you.
Please stay connected wherever you are.

EMAIL:
AuthorMaryAWasowski@gmail.com

FACEBOOK:
https://www.facebook.com/Author-Mary-A-Wasowski-
332971356804341

MARY A. WASOWSKI

TWITTER:
https://twitter.com/wasow6

INSTAGRAM:
https://instagram.com/authormaryawasowski/

GOOGLE +:
https://plus.google.com/+MaryWasowski